MILI HALF-ORC

Escape from Bondage

BOOK ONE
OF THE HALF-ORC SERIES

By

J. R. Marshall

Copyright © J. R. Marshall 2018
This book is sold subject to the condition that it shall not, by way of trade or otherwise, be lent, resold, hired out, or otherwise circulated without the publisher's prior consent in any form of binding or cover other than that in which it is published and without a similar condition including this condition being imposed on the subsequent publisher.
The moral right of J. R. Marshall has been asserted.
Front cover illustration by NJ.
ISBN: 9781728610344

DEDICATION

To *my* wife, Susan, whose patience, sometimes during antisocial hours, allowed the completion of this story, without hope of monetary gain.

To Mark Young, sitting on a beach sipping beer, reading yet another so-called 'final' version. He must have read the book ten times.

To Phil Knight, playing chess, sat in my yard, papers flapping in the wind, rereading my introductions.

This is a work of fiction. Names, characters, businesses, organizations, places, events and incidents either are the product of the author's imagination or are used fictitiously. Any resemblance to actual persons, living or dead, events, or locales is entirely coincidental.

CONTENTS

PRELUDE 1
CHAPTER 1 3
CHAPTER 2 18
CHAPTER 3 49
CHAPTER 4 76
CHAPTER 5 93
CHAPTER 6 115
CHAPTER 7 136
CHAPTER 8 168
CHAPTER 9 183
CHAPTER 10 188
CHAPTER 11 221
CHAPTER 12 250
EPILOGUE 263

ACKNOWLEDGMENTS

Anglophenia "How to swear like the British" (Youtube)

Rollforfantasy.com/tools/map-creator.php (Map Creation).

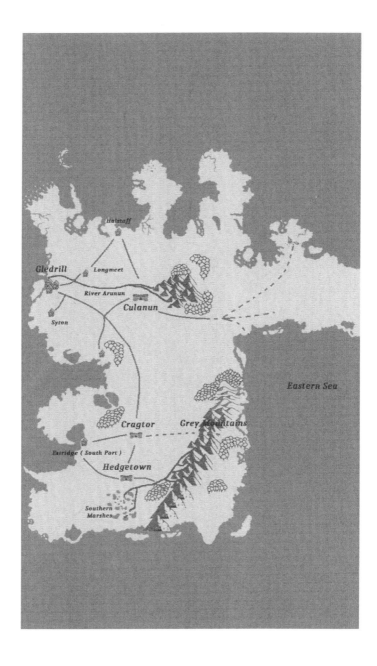

PRELUDE

Miller's Story

Have you heard of 'Good, Evil and Impartial' as ways to describe humanoid philosophical society? Stupid, brutal, and normal could easily be substituted. I have enormous sympathy for any man who on occasion struggles with the piously self-righteous moralistic morons who claim light and blessing only originate from their deity.

During the years of my captivity from the age of eight when bound and chained to work on a farm to the completion of my arcane apprenticeship, I had the gross misfortune to attract every stupid priest within a week's walk, it was as though I was on the curriculum with points awarded for effort.

Patience and self-control, which the stupid extol as worthy of contemplation and thus virtuous, are by a peculiar quirk of my miserable youth, inexorably bound to haunt and guide me throughout my life. This was not due to the divinely inspired ramblings of a spittle-spewing cleric, but rather the inexorable application of my intelligence and a weakness inherent from my mother's blood combined with a youth filled with servitude.

For the pleasure and benefit of my childhood I was repeatedly bound and beaten thus patience was a natural by-product that through little choice the mind cogitated on, chewing the cud, seeking a grim delight in the act of revenge. My application of justice would forever be slow and a veritable joy where possible.

Strength came through the blood of my father and with every drop of sweat my body produced, with every callus on my hand revenge was sworn. My body grew in both stature and might; there was a brooding presence, a dark malevolence forever haunting the depths of my master's troubled sleep.

So it was that as with all nights, half an hour after Tam had left and an hour before midnight, Joe, my master, came to chain me, bidding me sit with my hands behind my back and with a practised skill secured me, chains fastened to a stake, a little movement, enough to sit down, scarcely to lie, but enough.

CHAPTER 1

Tam Bluebottle was curious, being of a race that none knew of in those parts, a halfling, that is to say not half anything, but half in size to humans. Each night I longed for her visit, loving her company, respecting her, learning skills that had my master known, would have filled his heart with terror.

Joe had known better than to deny her access, for she was rich, with considerable influence and powerful friends. All the more curious indeed, that she would spend time with a dirty uncouth slave. Thus on one occasion Joe had tried to eavesdrop but intuitively Tam had known and rebuking Joe, he had been dismissed.

He never questioned me, nor tried again to listen, always we were left alone. What words may have been said in private outside of my hearing I knew not. Five years elapsed, and each night she visited.

Disused sacks made from hemp acted as a pillow or as feeble warmth during winter. Now propped against the stake, I was careful to place the most threadbare and ruined sacks on top, for given a chance my master would confiscate any that might with darning be repairable. All to save a copper penny, tight-fisted bastard, he thought nothing for my comfort. Too many nights had passed whilst chained in squalor, working all day, slaving without gratitude for a mean and ungracious master.

No hope, no future, only misery and despair, knowing all along that there was a world outside; a world where others throve.

Sat there bereft of boots, scarcely a rag on my body, oblivious to the night's chill my mind dwelt on the hours ahead. The brutality of orcs is well known, violence is perhaps hereditary, but my intelligence allowed for reason and control of temper, my human side cautioned against haste.

Crouching down, my feet planted in the dust, my right hand instinctively touched the ground, momentarily connecting with the earth, listening to the secret song that few knew. My mind was keenly attuned to the other sounds that are so familiar, the rhythmic clicking of a late Nightjar, well past dusk, an Owl, the wind drifting gently through the lattice walls of the barn, my home, my imprisonment, all that I'd known since the age of eight when Joe, my master, had bought me from an orphanage.

Promising to raise me fairly with good pay and conditions, and train me as an apprentice miller, the keepers had known I would be treated like shit, whipped, starved and worked till I either died or fled, they had heard it all before. Nonetheless five years ago a small silver coin had been sufficient for the deal, and I had become indentured. After all, who wanted a half-orc mixing with humans, even the scum and waifs of the street?

Tonight it was all coming to an end. Knowledge is power, knowledge everything, I was feral.

With neither thoughts nor senses alarmed, nor mind dimmed by fear, words were uttered that are immutable, indelibly impressed upon my mind, even now remembered. Tumbling across my consciousness, I can still smell the air, hear the sounds, feel the dirt beneath my feet, thus began the application of a spell, so well-rehearsed that at least in this, there was accomplishment, a simple incantation.

Click! An abrasive grinding of metal followed by two more snaps.

Two shackles raising and twisting as though guided by an unseen hand, vibrating gently as though an excess of force sought further application.

Watching, chains loosened, the padlocks in betrayal of their creator lay fallen upon the floor, the rusty chains that bound me to my stake were falling away. Such a simple thing, two locks undone.

The farm, which grew hops, wheat, barley and milled grains for the production of beer, was positioned about three miles south west of Gledrill, a large town of some wealth as it lay at the mouth of the River Arunun which was itself navigable, lying adjacent to the great sea, and thus the docks throve.

Trade came from distant lands and onwards into the interior of the kingdom.

In any farm or mill, for Joe's farm was both, there were tools, knives, hammers, and such-forth, yet my master had always sought to limit my access, a vain attempt, indeed futile, but he had essayed nonetheless. Perhaps he slept better, for I have noticed how easily people deceive themselves.

Hidden and buried behind a plinth, lay a rusty twisted knife, scarcely more than the shards of a scythe bound with a wooden decaying handle that I had reinforced some days before, such that now the haft better fit my grip. This along with a reaping hook would be my weapons for I knew my master always carried a knife, maybe not whilst he slept, I knew not.

Gently opening a side door and stepping outside, the air was fragranced with the pollens borne on the winds of a harvest, the grass seeds and the scent of spring. I stopped and listened. Ned, one of my master's three dogs, looked up, espied me, cocked his head. "Quiet, get down," I whispered. Ned settled; I was familiar, thus no alarm necessary.

Not so geese, for these most base of creatures since ancient times have been used as wardens against trespass. Geese would not shriek at me, for like Ned there was a familiarity, but neither would they be silent, thus in the gentle night I circled around the back of two buildings, an indirect route between two sties – the pigs grunted, but no more than that.

Hesitant and wary, I listened, but no sound forewarned or disturbed my purpose. The house fashioned of timber and wattle, thatched with straw instead of rush, for it was cheaper, was lit under a waning moon standing like some colossus, the beginnings of a climb, a crag, a portent of hard labour to come. Knowing that when I entered there would be no retreat other than to flee, a fugitive in the countryside, hiding in hedgerows, stealing from farmsteads, and likely destined for the gallows.

Armed with my reaping hook and rusty bent knife, I stood in front of the door bolted and barred from within, indeed all the ground floor windows were equally secure, shuttered internally for added protection. There was but one glimmer left, an incantation, needed for later.

Nonetheless this was not my route for I knew of a grate, inconspicuous to any would-be intruder, but providing disused access to the cellar, itself adjoining the larder which led in turn to the house kitchen, that would be my ingress, my access to my master's seemingly impregnable fortress.

Chaos was descending upon the world, tonight this oasis of peace where all slept according to their dreams would be rent asunder.

Never again would Joe, his wife, and ignorant daughter treat me like shit.

Violence was stalking the farmstead, and I was death personified. Apprentice Miller, the half-orc bastard, slave and servant, was about to shed blood and commit murder. *Too many times have you whipped me, too many times have I bled.*

Walking some fifteen feet along the south-west facing wall and with caution sliding between a narrow gully, the disused grate appeared, or rather it showed as a rough indent of something below. Grass and dirt had long ago concealed the true outline, but having worked cleaning my master's cellar, its existence was known to me.

Bending down, it took longer than expected to remove the earth and soil that had built up over time; each piece was carefully removed, placed aside, the intent to replicate its former condition upon departure.

Eventually the rusty iron grate was revealed, approximately four feet by three feet, lying flat within an outer cast-iron surround.

Taking hold and with considerable care the grate was prised aloft, making barely a sound for the soil cushioned the edges whence metal met metal, perhaps a slight grinding, not more than sand rubbing against stone. Nothing to infract upon the peace of the night.

The upper sides of the passageway appeared matted with fungus, like some undisturbed crypt, violated by the moonlight it thought never to see again. Slowly dropping beneath the house I crawled, descending lower until coming upon ancient lime-clad walls which years before had been whitewashed. Now many years later my sides scraped against the edge, leaving a white decaying residue on my body and clothes.

Eventually after what was probably only fifteen feet at most, the passageway came to an end, a short drop to the cellar floor.

Lowering myself down, silently and with care, my orc heritage gave me the ability to see in the dark, albeit only in shades of grey, for there was absolutely no colour perception. Nonetheless this ability to see in greyscale was enough to gather the reaping hook, and familiarise myself with my surroundings. The room smelt damp, it was indeed useless for storing foods, grains and the like, even iron left long enough would rust away. Only a couple of barrels with rusting hoops lay decomposing on the floor.

Slowly ascending the stone stairs my thoughts focused on each and every step; silently, without a sound I would seek revenge, my master would pay, his wife murdered and as for his daughter, well, we shall see. Having been subject to every depravation, humiliation and torment, there was a debt to repay.

Knowing the brutality of my father's blood, the furious rage, the bloodlust heaving war within, my heart laboured, my limbs shook, but caution ruled, there would be no impatience, care and stealth resisted the urge to rush in and destroy. There would be no warning, each step would take an age.

Entering from the adjoining larder, the kitchen served as the main room of the house, its hearth set back in the wall formed an alcove whereupon during cold winters the family could sit either side of the fireplace, the hearth glowing with the failing embers of the previous day's fire, a small cauldron hung atop, probably containing a stew of mutton that would still be warm the coming morning.

With my mind focussed, my bare feet felt the undulation of the cold flagstone floor, each step taken gently and with great care, not a sound, they would be asleep upstairs. The house contained perhaps three main rooms downstairs excluding the larder and cellar, but as to upstairs, master had never allowed me to see. Why would he, not the least mistress kept complaining of my filthy, and how much I smelt.

Walking down the passageway I smelt oil in the air, and turning a corner and seeing a faint glow, stopped. Standing at the foot of the stairs I cursed my lack of insight. *Shit, I'll have to charge, damn!* I cursed my incompetence, my mind considering the options.

In front lay the stairs, made of wood. Each run of this stairway ready to creak and groan under my considerable weight, in the stillness of the night, to place a foot on those most ancient of timbers would have been as a trumpet blast from some city herald announcing my arrival.

Atop the stairway hung an oil lamp; the smell of oil had been unexpected, now I knew the origin, the flame was turned low, almost guttering and in jeopardy of being extinguished by anything other than a gentle draught, but this night Joe had set the flame correctly, 'saving a penny'. My mind considered the options.

Joe and his wife, but probably not the daughter, would be asleep in the main room, first left atop the stairs, probably, for whilst I had considered their likely location, my lack of knowledge of the first floor was a concern. With downstairs windows and doors barred the chances of the family escaping at least swiftly were slim, that's what I wanted, it was crucial the daughter or wife were trapped.

Grasping my reaping hook in my right hand, and my makeshift dagger in my left and steeling myself for this, the most dangerous and perilous of moments, I charged.

Storming up the stairs and upon the landing within

three mighty strides, I kicked open the wood-panelled door. So violent was my assault that the door whilst ajar hung now on one hinge, like some cantilevering bridge, swaying for a moment.

The room was dark, the feeble light from the lantern hung on the landing ceiling was insufficient to illuminate the room. *Tight-fisted shit, should have turned the flame up, his undoing.* As for me, I'd got it right, there lay my master and his plump, ugly, nasty wife. The lack of light was ideal, all to my advantage.

Hell, like some contiguous nightmare was loosed, Joe was sitting upright, hand outstretched desperately trying to orientate himself, reaching for something with his right hand, no doubt a weapon, whilst his eyes tried to adjust to the grey image he could scarcely make out in the doorway, so dim was the shadow.

Mistress trying to get out of bed caught my reaping hook as I wielded it with fury but not much skill. It swung across her face, like a small sickle at the end of a pole, and rent a three-inch gash to her cheek just below the left eye. She fell back, both hands clutching her head, screaming.

Lunging forward and thrusting down my left hand stabbed wildly at Joe, missing. I stepping back and swang the reaping hook, but succeeded only in clubbing my master on the side, such was my ineptitude.

Joe with little to guide his aim but much in the way of motivation leapt in my direction, guessing at where I stood, indeed with some modicum of success, for half grasping my hip he tried to pull me to the floor. My knife swung sideways and downwards, striking his shoulder; the blade scraped on bone, as the ragged blade naturally serrated, tore flesh. The wound was grievous.

Joe, releasing his grip fell crashing to the floor in writhing agony. I stabbed each leg, *He's not walking anywhere*, then moved to the far side of the room and grabbed my mistress by the hair. She screamed hysterically, franticly wriggling as I, lifting her head and forcing her neck forward, dragged my blade slowly across her throat; she was making too much noise. Blood pumped from her severed arteries – she coughed, choking, trying to draw rasping breaths. In shock she lay twitching and convulsing for perhaps a minute, but she died too quickly.

My master begged for mercy, first threatening then pleading; he offered gold and silver, all a lie, for I knew it was hidden and a deceit. If his life was spared, mine in turn would be forfeit. Besides, the daughter would tell. Of that there was little doubt, she did.

Joe died slowly, my dagger initially stabbing lightly in his throat, not intending to kill too swiftly, then thrust below the ribs, flesh pierced, tissue and sinew forced aside, blood spilling onto the external blade, cutting and slicing into cartilage and thrust upwards towards his ribs. He looked into my eyes as I sought to hurt, five years of misery being revenged.

Joe died, in the end, ruined by my hand.

An hour of slaughter and cruelty, and my hatred and bloodlust was slaked. Each of the dead were returned to their beds, and gathering a small purse containing a lot of silver and some gold, the building was put to the torch. There would be no evidence, only ash and bone.

Leaving the house via the cellar passage, the grate was replaced and the dirt and grass covering were reinstated. I rolled in geese shit, masking the blood and lime rendering that was discernible on my rags. Hands, feet and face were smeared with mud; finally I rolled in hay to age the dirt. I stank. The purse, an unexpected bonus, was placed beneath the roots of a large sweet-chestnut tree some fifty yards from the main house. These coins would be useful, but firstly, I needed to be found innocent, there is no liberty without freedom.

Deep in thought, I stared at the splendour of my crime; the house lit the night sky as a flaming beacon. This would be seen from ten miles or more. In the morning I would do obeisance to the guards, for they would find me in chains and a supplicant; ignorant of the night's events.

As I sat waiting, chained once more to my stake, I cogitated on the night's events, anxious as to the future. Had I left clues? No! I knew there were none, I had been careful.

Two hours passed. Krun, a militia guardsman from the local town of Gledrill, had just walked into the barn. They had been searching the ruins for some twenty minutes, for the geese had announced their arrival, and my hearing was keen. Now he walked in accompanied by a couple of other townsfolk, whose names I didn't know.

They looked around, wondering what they might steal. "There are tools, grains and…"

"Oh look, the ugly bastard's alive!"

Krun was a thug, thick in stature and no cleverer than a pig. It's true that I was certainly a bastard, being half human and half orc. Krun probably had marginality better looks, but it was close.

My bonds tight and locks refastened by magic, were perhaps too tight, for my torn skin shed drops of blood that glistened upon the rusty iron.

"So what do we do with him?" Krun referring to me as he studied the chains, checking that I was bound and secure. The comment was for his companions.. "Do we kill him? No one will want him!"

"Aye, perhaps not," said one, "but he rightly belongs to Joe's family, what's left of them; he has a cousin in Longmeet, a slave is still worth something." He looked doubtful.

"Has master sold me?" I asked, wanting to appear stupid. I needed to look stupid, for there was no reason I should know of the night's events.

"He's dead, burned to cinders and I bet you had some part in it."

"I smelt smoke," I confessed, "but my mistress and daughter, they will look after me, I will work for them." I kept my head low in feigned submission.

"All dead, died in their beds by the look of it, smoke must have done them in before the fire." Krun wanted to believe I was responsible, but the chains were tight, and my ignorance played to his simple mind.

"It'll be light soon," said Krun, turning to the others. "I'll get this orc working in the morning."

"I'm human." But it was a mistake that was

instantly regretted. *What's the point of arguing with this peasant?* I should've kept quiet, being only thirteen years old, mature for an orc, but not for my mixed blood. And discourse wasn't wise either. *Shut up,* I told myself. I didn't – idiot that I was.

"Oh, I forgot," said Krun. "Your stinking bastard father must've raped some human whore, either that or she was blind." He kicked me, but half missed.

"Can you imagine the joy of whelping that?" Krun pointed at me whilst looking at the others. "His mother must have cried tears of happiness as she gazed upon that face." He turned to me. "She should've drowned you rather than face her shame, or did she die when you were born?"

"No? I don't know, but I think your brother was not yet born." Krun didn't understand but after a minute the penny dropped... when I finally came around I was looking up at a blacksmith.

Of course I had a bloody lip, my head throbbed, bruises and welts replete across my body. I swore Krun would die, not yet, but he would, I knew I'd kill him. I smiled, it hurt.

There had been no keys to release my bonds so they had hacked at the stake, all the while Krun had stamped and kicked. Eventually I was carried or dragged to a cart. I guess I was kicked and dragged to the cart, perhaps I was conscious for I cannot understand how else they managed.

So here I was staring at the blacksmith who had already removed half my chains and shackles.

"You are to be transferred to the Lady Tam Bluebottle," he said gruffly. "She will be here shortly."

But she wasn't, and after an hour or so a servant arrived with a small jar and a tiny scroll.

During my captivity I had been visited by many, many travellers, clerics in particular; they were fascinated by my intelligence. My master being devout had suffered their visits, whilst Mistress had complained continuously of the cost in ale, bread and board.

Nonetheless the visits had continued, and I had learnt languages, reading and writing along with history and a lot that was crap. Knowledge is power, the fact that half of it was bollocks was irrelevant. Some believed in it, therefore I had listened, needing to know everything!!

Now I've said I respected Tam, and I did, but here is a point that readers need to understand; my admiration for Tam was without desire. If there was any person who would tether me to my human mother's nature, it was her.

Tam was a halfling, neither of mixed race nor elf nor dwarf, neither human nor orc, just a little person of a breed that is rarely seen in the world. She was what clerics call 'good' but without being obnoxious. Her appearance was fair and she was wise and fabulously clever. Some say she ruled a kingdom, although in the months that followed I found that she ruled but a small land, an impregnable keep under a cliff with a town no bigger than Gledrill, protected by perhaps a hundred men at arms. She was a lady of lands, but not a queen.

In the future, when I walked into an inn, people would look into their tankards and say, "Oh shit," but when Tam walked in, people were blown away, people whispered and stared. When she was with me I was always ignored which was an improvement on most of my experiences. Sometimes she would walk in with me, I would be proud.

Most thought Tam as simply a wealthy learned person with the ability to heal grievous wounds, yet I knew she was a sorceress of immense power. She was 'my Tam', 'my tutor', not a bully like myself; not blunt, not brutal, not ugly, not poor, all the things I was… She inspired me, I guess I used that last insight to keep myself in check.

Now in my old age as I recount this story I understand it's pure vanity. Who wants to read the story of an educated orc? But there's no denying her. Whenever I was good, it was because of her.

She had appeared one night, looking up at me whilst I lifted grain into a hopper. I never saw her appear nor heard the door open. So it was, that hope was given me that night, five years ago. It was Tam that through many evening visits had taught me simple spell-craft.

CHAPTER 2

It was perhaps midday and Gledrill was bustling with the daily activities of any normal town. Sitting outside the smiddy I had been told to sit and wait but, "Don't touch anything or talk to my customers." This, the admonition given by the blacksmith.

The hammer would strike the anvil, the hiss of steam, a cry from some merchant across the courtyard, a pony and cart creaking as its wheels fell in and out of ruts along the pathways that crisscrossed Gledrill. The blacksmith was working but passing glances in my direction.

So many shoes. I knew that people wore shoes or boots, but everyone? Every observation was bewildering to me, it felt uncomfortable. I wasn't working, it was strange and what was my immediate fate? Recover the purse as originally planned? Seek

Tam? But she knew of my location.

A little after midday, a smartly dressed, important-looking man was walking towards me, hand outstretched, smiling, looking at me? I looked behind to see if it was some other party that attracted his gaze, but no! Was this a jest? Should I thump him?

"Ah, 'Miller', I was told I would find you here, my name is Thrandar and I serve Lady Bluebottle. I've brought some salve for your injuries and a message by way of a scroll, I was told you could read, quite remarkable. Oh, err, sorry, that was terribly rude of me. Your pardon, sir." He appeared confident, albeit slightly effeminate.

Sir. *Sir?* A sudden urge to throttle him flit across my consciousness. I had not the grace to reciprocate the proffered hand, and after a hesitant pause the stranger's arm lowered.

"The salve I understand you have seen the like before?" I nodded and snatching the small pot from his hand proceeded to peel off the vellum cover and apply the cure to the worst of my injuries.

"And your message, sir," as he handed me the tiny rolled and sealed parchment scroll. Finally on familiar ground, I broke the seal, sat down once more, angled my backside and farted, for this was a hope beyond hope. I read, re-read and read again, staring at the tiny words that spelt out my liberty and succour.

"If you're stuck on any words, sir, I could, errr…" Thrandar faltered as I stared at him with a darkness, and natural menace that I so easily projected. He was chilled in his heart, for he took a step back.

Miller,

You are released from indentured servitude, time served under your late master Joe has been acknowledged as fulfilment of obligations both in apprenticeship and financial dues. Records have been lodged with the guild and you are now a free party as to future activities.

Notwithstanding your freedom you have no realistic means of gaining an honest living and I didn't visit you these last five years for you to fall into despair.

With that in mind, your studies with me are incomplete, your skills with a weapon are non-existent, your manners and hygiene are desperate; you need clothing, food and a place to study.

I will pay you a one half silver piece a day, plus lodging – obligation is for six months obedience and due diligence in mastering ALL that I command.

If you are agreeable you will accompany Thrandar.

I do hope you agree Miller, you are so close to success.

Tam.

ps I'm furious with your behaviour... I was about to secure your release!

pps Don't hit Thrandar, he doesn't deserve it!

A part of me that sat there, the weak human side, was almost emotional. "Bollocks," I said to myself. Sentiment is crap, but I knew I was lying. I was overcome with relief, with joy. My stinking rags, my bare feet, the matt of my hair and the lice that scurried through the filth that was caked upon my limbs, now these were an irrelevance. Tam had come to my support. By the gods, how I felt saved.

After what must have been half an hour I proffered the scroll to Thrandar. "Do you read Elvish?" There was embarrassed astonishment on his face. "No? Ah, no matter, I do, and several other languages besides."

"I am to follow you."

As we approached Tam's lodgings I marvelled at the size of her property; truly the existence of great halls and lodgings were known to me through many years of study and storytelling, but the reality infracts upon the senses in a way that is hard to describe. Tam's dwelling was positioned on the outskirts of Gledrill, bordered on three sides by farmland, there numbered perhaps three main structures along with a further seven outbuildings. These buildings whilst thatched seemed beautifully maintained, not at all like the farm mill I had only this morning left.

Passing stables and outhouses I wondered which location would prove to be my quarter; a carpenter's workshop, brewing sheds, buildings of unknown purpose, so much industry as I saw it.

Thrandar seemed nervous, increasingly so as we approached a large, thatched, open-sided barn. He fidgeted, glancing at me. He stepped back and gestured to a line of servants that were hurrying to position.

"The Lady Bluebottle wishes you to bathe and be clothed with new attire. These, your fellow companions, are tasked with assisting you." His voice was terribly nervous, almost becoming lost as he struggled to compose himself.

Now the strange thing was that I had read of

washing, of people who immerse themselves in water. I for my part had never participated, but my former mistress allegedly had, although I was unsure of the procedure. And as for being naked, well, the girls looked okay, but the male on the end could bugger off.

In the end I was washed, brushed down with lotions derived from plants that kill lice, I was clothed with linen and wool, given boots that I couldn't stop staring at. I suspect I was hard work, for although I co-operated with the girls, the water in three separate pools needed replenishing several times. The experience was fascinating – nails cut, hair brushed and tied back, teeth scrubbed with coarse linen and powder, but under no circumstances did they succeed in splashing scented oils on me.

Looking back, I was truly filthy, I just didn't know it at the time, and whilst I admired my boots and the clean cloth, I smelt of lye.

Some days pass slowly, clouds pass overhead in a nonchalant manner and the day drags. Today a hurricane had blown, it was already late afternoon, and I was bidden to wait outside the main hall.

In the early evening perhaps two hours from sunset I spotted Thrandar hurrying between two buildings. "Trandoor!" I bellowed. "When am I to see Tam?"

He hesitated but turning towards me, strode over, smiling. It was a conceit; he carried several scrolls and looked flustered, tired and somewhat apprehensive. "The Lady Bluebottle is still in Cragtor but should be with us shortly." Having seen my cleansing/washing, and perhaps in his eyes a modicum of subjection and conformity, he was marginally less nervous than an hour or so earlier.

No, I must have misheard. "Cragtor?" I said. "The only Cragtor I know of is fifty leagues away." And with my non-existent grace and total lack of tact I told him he was talking shit.

"If you say so, Miller, I know not how far away the place is." Thrandar was quick and eager to retreat, an expression of consigned misery upon his face for despite my more wholesome appearance, and the fact that I smelt better there was, as was obvious to Thrandar, far more to improving my social skills than water and cloth, also with hindsight I wondered whether he knew of extending duties in my regard.

At least the 'sir' had been dropped. "Lying git," I muttered under my breath. Sitting there observing the cleanliness and the all too beautiful nature of this place, doubt momentously crossed my thoughts. Is this what I want? But looking down at my boots, fabulous… if a little tight, besides, I liked Tam.

Pondering awhile in the darkness of my thoughts, I was strangely annoyed that the black clouds of my dreams were being inexorably pushed back by lighter skies.

*

After a while…

"Hello Miller," said a soft, keen and clear voice.

I turned round to see Tam sitting down beside me on the step. She was wearing a light grey fine woollen cloak covering a supple leather jerkin between the clasp at her neck and the belt at her waist. She smiled gently and for the first time I really noticed how beautiful she was. Never had I seen, even in this failing twilight, her beauty; she had always visited the farm at night by the light of a guttering candle, or a hooded lantern.

I leapt to my feet and then fell to my knee, head bowed low. "My lady…" But I was lost for words.

"Please get up, Miller, you need not kneel before me, nor call me 'Lady', for you have never done so before and I don't want you to start now. Please sit next to me, perhaps a step lower, so I can see you." Tam smiled and beckoned for me to sit.

"I understand that life has been hard and a torment, but if you stay with me, there will be no repeat of Joe, or of your solution, neither will you be idle, not that you were ever so. But if you agree to a little more apprenticeship, as I suspect you will, you must work harder than ever, for I know how much needs to be accomplished before your patience is exhausted." She paused, looking closely at me, judging my expressions. "Do you so agree?" Tam held up her hand. "But before you say anything, you must understand what is expected of you.

"You will eat at dawn, study, memorise and practise every lesson in arcane spell-craft that will have been taught the night before. At midday you will work for three hours in any matter that requires your strength or skill, to any person in my service that needs your help. You will neither threaten nor bully nor intimidate anyone who serves me, in any way, in any shape or in any form, neither for any reason. In the afternoon you will learn the art of combat, becoming skilled and proficient with the sword and battle axe; you will learn defence and all martial awareness. You will obey your instructors, you will hold your temper. Two hours before dusk, you will wash; one hour before dusk you will learn how to conduct yourself in civilised company, and you will learn, properly. When the sun has fallen you will eat with your fellow workers...

"Afterwards you will study with me."

Tam looked closely at me, studying the fine lines of my face, looking for any sign of deceit. "Now you can answer."

That evening I was given quarters; a thickly padded straw mattress lay in one corner covered with four fleeces, each stitched to form a larger area. A bench and chair made up the other side, and clean thresh was on the floor. Aside the bench there was a plank of wood, with books, ink, quills, scrolls, and a hook for a lantern, a small phial of oil and next to it a tinderbox, with separate flint and steel. On pegs at the end of the mattress side was a long vest, spare belt and leather purse, with one small silver coin inside.

The following day, deep in the shadow of my own thoughts I had chosen to lie down on dry grass not far from my quarters. I had taken a book from the single shelf above my study area, and was proceeding to read a subject on spell stealth and concealment. "Shit," I cursed as a drop of beer fell on the page which I quickly made worse by smudging lamb and gravy, part of the previous evening's supper given late and not consumed in full.

Shit, this book's expensive. I knew from my studies that written works were rare and over many years I had frequently been admonished how to turn pages gently and respect the weeks of patient labour in their creation.

As I lay aside my food and book, trying to recall the incantations of a spell that undid damage to an inert object, a skill I was taught but had despised as less important than destructive spells, Tam and Thrandar came and sat next to me. I was oblivious to their approach and also the dwarf that stood some eight feet from the three of us, smiling whilst gently scraping a thumb across a giant axe. Clad in mail, with a sword hung at his side, he looked both formidable and wealthy for his helm was ringed with gold and the shield slung on his back although mostly hidden was bound with iron and silver.

"Try," said Tam, "but stealthily as per the passage in the book." She looked at me and knew exactly what I was thinking. "You're not practised, but try."

Looking at the three of them, I hesitated for despite having no virtue, was strangely ashamed and very much troubled by the prospect of failure.

Spells need to be prepared in advance so that when required they can be recalled quickly as the need arises, but to cast an unprepared spell requires meditation and patience.

Gently I placed my hand on the ground, and with a deepness of thought that is beyond the ability of most, gradually became aware of the earth's song. The quickening of new life, the grass growing, a tree absorbing water, the intense energy that dwells deep in the bowels of the earth, they whispered to me, or perhaps I eavesdropped.

Tam had told stories of sorcerers seeking to fabricate the most powerful of spells being drawn so deep in thought that they became immersed in the rhapsody, not realising until days had passed and their physical bodies had suffered injury.

My mind drifted without thought of time and space, seeking, searching in sensual awareness for the parts of a song, the snippets and connections needed to fashion my simple transmutation.

After a while or perhaps an age I brought my mind back, travelling across an ocean of altered perception. Coming out of the meditation, pausing but for a moment, I then invoked the fabricated spell, gently uttering words that were like waypoints of a journey. As gossamer blown on the wind I saw the dweomer covering the page.

Power trickled through my body, and looking at Tam, I asked, "Was I a long time?"

"No, not really, perhaps five minutes." Tam pointed at the book. "Very good, well done, that was excellent."

I stared at the damaged page, and yes, it did look better, but not perfect. Secretly, in the presence of strangers there was no embarrassment, nor was my confidence undermined, indeed the page was much improved. Tam, I suspected, would privately complete the task when I wasn't around.

"Excellent," repeated Tam, as she stared at the book for a minute, before turning once more in my direction.

"This, Miller, is Grimnir, an old friend of mine; and you will never best him in combat, but you will learn to best one of his men." Tam looked up at Grimnir, and smiled. "What do you think, Grimnir?"

"And you're teaching him your skills as well? You bloody fool, he'll be lethal if he survives long enough." Grimnir laughed and looked teasingly at Tam. "Why are you doing this, Tam?"

"You agreed to help, thank you." Tam ignored the last remark.

Grimnir suddenly turned and looking around bellowed at a girl entering a stable; he had caught sight of her in the corner of his eye. She stopped and turning to face Grimnir, curtsied. "Lord, er, me?"

"Yes indeed, you! Bring me a chair and some ale, oh, and a decent pie, or something better and, er, oh, please," as he caught sight of Tam scowling at him.

"What!" he exclaimed, looking at Tam. "You should have brought me a servant girl, you don't expect me to get the bloody things myself?"

"I did appoint a servant and he's in your lodgings," said Tam, marginally amused. "He's preparing to bathe you."

"Sod that! I had a wash last month, don't you go bullying me, Mistress Tam." Grimnir, laughing, presented a feigned expression of dismay. He laughed some more and after a minute threw off his shield, helm and axe, looking around for a chair. "Bloody hell, where is it?"

All the while I, Miller, was absorbing every subtlety of nuance. What was Tam doing? What didn't I understand? Who was Grimnir, that he spoke so equally with Tam? How did Tam know I'd never beat him in combat and why did Grimnir have a servant? And if Grimnir was a Lord, why was he associating with Tam and offering to help me, an ignorant, for I knew I was, half-orc?

"Now, young Miller." Tam looked at me, then gestured to Thrandar. "Please, Thrandar, stand in front of us." Thrandar rose and stepping in front looked thoroughly miserable. Grimnir shuffled around, keen to observe the proceedings yet periodically casting glances for a chair that was eluding him.

"Miller, pay attention… Thrandar will be teaching you manners…" Suddenly there was a roar of laughter.

Laugh, did Grimnir laugh. He bent over, coughing and wheezing and eventually after what seemed an age but probably only two minutes said, "Oh, you poor bastard," looking at Thrandar who seemed wholly overthrown and in abject misery.

"Miller looks like a pig's rear," said Grimnir, "eats like the front end and smells like the sty! You poor, poor sod, Thrandar." Grimnir looked at each in turn and finally once more at Thrandar and laughed again, just as two servants brought him a chair, bread, ale and half a cold pie.

I sat there, incredulous. *What the bloody hell do I need to learn manners for?* I liked the idea of pulverising Grimnir's henchmen, but the idea of being taught anything by some effeminate fop was beyond a bad joke.

But Tam sat there quietly and after a moment or two, calmly and with gentle firmness carried on, "Miller you will learn, and you will obey, and if you do not co-operate then all other studies will be suspended until Thrandar reports that the lessons are learned. Do you understand?" I just stared, and there was silence.

Over the next six months I learnt to proficiently and reliably cast seven out of fifteen spells that were my potential to cast; I kept myself strong seeking out the heavy manual jobs that needed doing, and to Thrandar's delight, learned amongst other things how to fart quietly.

My skills as a warrior were impressive, somewhat an improvement on the first day of combat training whence I had been left bruised, battered and wrathfully embarrassed. Roderick, one of Grimnir's men, had made me look foolish, for every clumsy attack had ended with my sprawling on the floor, or a dagger at my neck, or worse a kick in the groin.

Eventually after a month Roderick was being bested too often, and other more skilful tutors were found, including Glamdrun, allegedly a guards' captain; he would fight like the devil, determined that an 'orc', for he kept on insulting me, would never gain the advantage.

Five months later, Glamdrun was getting hammered, bruised, bloodied, and demoralised until one morning I strode out, confident in my ability to kick the shit out of any man that Grimnir deigned to pit against me.

My attire consisted of a padded leather jerkin, leather helm and wood shield plus a sword made of Hornbeam. Autumn was upon us, but whilst clouds scurried across the sky, it was still a beautiful day, and I was enjoying my time in Tam and Grimnir's company.

Grimnir stood in front of me, smiling. "Now then, Miller, you've done bloody well, but you've gotten far too big and cocky." He laughed, though looked slightly more serious than normal.

"Lord Grimnir, where's that witless oaf Glamdrun? Or have you found someone more competent?" There was no doubt I appreciated Grimnir's tutors, but matters had gone off-the boil.

"I need to be challenged, for I reckon myself much improved... indeed thank you... it is appreciated, your guidance that is, but just of late it seems you have allowed too many weak opponents to test me."

I did like Grimnir, he wasn't intimidated by me, and I could imagine after some hard-fought fight, the two of us getting drunk and recalling the day's valour. Farting, belching, swearing, and being totally crass, an enjoyable prospect, as the two of us drank the inn dry.

"It's great that you've bested my captain, he hasn't forgiven you yet," Grimnir laughed, but a dryer laugh than usual, almost forced.

Tam sat down to watch, a gentle smile on her face; she pulled her cloak tight, fastened it and shivered for it was indeed getting colder. She had a pot of salve cradled in her hands.

But, Grimnir went on, "Tam has told me that me that I'm getting fat, too old, that you could beat me. Tam and I have fallen out over you, I only agreed to help but always had my doubts."

"I don't think so, Lord." I turned around and looked at Tam. What the hell, I liked these two, I didn't want the people I respect falling out over me. Tam seemed disinterested.

Grimnir went on, "Never liked the idea of teaching one of your breed, but you did learn some manners, that I'll admit entertained me."

Shit, this wasn't good, I had liked the way my studies had gone, and was looking forward to keeping these two as my friends; the gods knew I had slender pickings in that regard.

"Miller! Your mother was a whore, and you were abandoned quicker than a turd leaves the backside, not surprising really," bellowed Grimnir. "You do know? The only reason you were allowed to beat such weak opposition was a private arrangement between Tam and myself, to build up your confidence, you had such a shit start in life it seemed only fair that we gave you a little charity."

Grimnir issued many more nasty, blunt insults, with a sincerity to dispel any thought that this was play acting.

I was gutted; never had I thought to be so easily deceived, the world was a cruel place, and I was falling into a pit of despair.

Nasty half-truths were hurled at me, but the laughter issuing from Grimnir's sneering face, all an act? By the gods I hoped so.

A small crowd assembled, and a milk maid sniggered and offered her tits if I wasn't mature enough. Others laughed.

"You're a boy, stop pretending!" she cried.

I was angry now, for I'd liked that girl.

"One of the servants swears he saw you shagging a goat," said Grimnir. "If you're up for it, she'll be in the side field in the event you win," Grimnir laughed again, but a despising, nasty laugh. "I've brought her along to cheer for you."

A bleating goat appeared in the corner of my vision, being led by a rope tether. I didn't like Grimnir's behaviour, this wasn't funny anymore.

However whilst not entirely convinced that Grimnir genuinely despised me, perhaps I was still hoping that this was deliberate provocation and for an unknown purpose. Nonetheless act or no, I had had my fill of insults, of being belittled. Six months ago my heart had soared, hoping this had all ended.

"Bastard!"

He'd learn the fury of my ancestry, the wrath of an orcish heart. I'd show him what manners were.

Grimnir, was good, tough as old boots; he was nigh on impossible to hit, every stroke swung at him was finding empty air. If I got close he parried with alacrity each and every thrust. I sought to anticipate the position, not where he was, but that to which he would be. Essaying to smite the dwarf, he laughed, goading me with yet more insults; he seemed almost casual whilst I swung with violent ferocity, sweat dripped from my brow, and having been pommelled and bruised, for the swords were wood and designed not to cut, I finally struck him a magnificent blow. Grimnir staggered dropped momentarily to a knee, the crowd gasped, then the cheering fell silent for Grimnir stood up with blood dripping from his mouth, and I knew I was buggered.

"There will be no spells," a voice crystal clear uttered in the temporary silence. Tam had spoken, for I was indeed murderous in my intent, and would have fired an explosion at him given the chance. I always had this spell prepared, always.

"Oh, let the goat lover do as he pleases. Go on, Miller, cast your spell at me." Tam winced as I stood back and loosed a jet of flame; it fled from my hand, hurtling straight at Grimnir who as it exploded rolled away with surprising agility. Screams rang out as the crowd staggered quickly backwards. Tam looked anxious but sat back down.

After a moment the smoke dissipated, and Grimnir strode forward. I swung dozens of blows against him, each parried with grim professionalism. Eventually Grimnir kicked me in the groin, and smote a devastating blow against the side of my temple. I was felled, a roaring wind filled my mind as blackness enveloped.

I awoke in a bed with the milk maid gently tending my bruised and battered body. She smiled and pled for my forgiveness. "I was told to say the things I said, I didn't mean them, you know?" She kissed me, held my hand and said her name was Miriam.

"Leave her alone, you ugly brute," came a laughing and cheerful Grimnir. "Not bad, you ignorant peasant." Grimnir was walking into the room, a grin on his face. I could see salve residue on the side of his jaw.

"Never believe anything you hear in battle. You did bloody well, and will put the fear of God in all that face you. I admire how you've come on." He laughed some more. "Apparently the goat says it wasn't you after all.

"Oh, by the way, your spell was pathetic, couldn't have lit a candle."

I was still reeling from this counter revelation; had it all been a lie?

"You haven't fallen out over me, you and Tam?"

"Don't be stupid, you ugly bugger, it was all an act, a lesson if you like? My idea, Tam thought it unnecessary, but agreed to my superior wisdom." He laughed again.

"Not a bloody nice lesson," I told the dwarf. "I'm not sure how I feel." Indeed I was pissed off but deep within, my heart sang. Friendships were precious to me, for I'd never had any.

"Oh come now, stop being pathetic, you sound like an old maid. You needed to learn. The lesson had to seem real." Grimnir strode over and thrust his hand forward in friendship. "Grow up, young Miller, welcome to adulthood, even though all the world's a shit, but by the gods I like you, I really do... Does it hurt here?" he said, as he poked me in the side.

Tam stood in the doorway. "Let's get pissed," said Grimnir, glancing at Tam, "but not here."

Tam sighed, and after a moment's contemplative thought, said, "Okay, give me an hour."

As Tam turned to leave, she wavered. Turning around, looking at me, a moment's hesitation, she approached and grasped my hand.

"Always for you," she said, "I'm so proud." Her fingers barely wrapped around three of mine. I knew this was without crudeness or perversion, neither deceit nor machinations. By the gods how these words would haunt me in the future.

Grimnir hesitated, looking at Tam. "Show him what real magic can do somewhere special, 'Castle Quay'. I can also replenish my funds. Not the least it's a good beginning for Miller, if that's your mind? My work is done, he's as good and ready as only practice can make."

"Miller, we're moving, get yourself packed, you can leave the wooden weapons and combat equipment behind, you won't be needing them." Grimnir looked positively cheerful. "Just like old times, eh Tam?"

I looked at Grimnir. "Moving? Why? Where? Getting pissed isn't moving, I've things to do. How about in three days?"

But Grimnir, ignoring my comments strode out into the late afternoon air. "Ah, this is splendid!"

Hobbling out towards my quarters, Miriam was looking anxious, and whilst trying to offer support was proving more of an impediment.

"I'll be back in a month or two," I said, studying the outline of her breasts, imagining them naked. Even though I had no idea whether I would be back or when, certainly I had unfinished business in Gledrill, rolling Miriam around on some straw, or behind a hedge was fairly high on the agenda, but Krun needed to visit the undertakers. I hadn't forgotten.

It took a few minutes to stagger to my quarters, gather a few mementos and combine my purse with that stolen from Joe's farm, when Grimnir arrived pressing me to hurry.

Given a new idea he was like a petulant child, impatient beyond belief. It was early evening; my gait was impaired and every breath was a labour. *Shit, it hurts. Sod him.* I tried not to wince.

He followed me around like a shadow, no, not a shadow, like some bloody lost dog that I had had the misfortune to stroke, and was now glued to my heel!

With each step my muscles ached, much to Grimnir's amusement. "Couldn't hit a dead squirrel, could you? Useless, incompetent, wasted my efforts on you. What would Glamdrun have sai—"

"Look, Grimnir, fuck off, if you don't mind the Orcish! I need some time on my own." I was still cross with the dwarf, so the words were easy.

Grimnir, looked surprised, but not terribly offended, then with a modicum of empathy said, "Miller, you have nothing, but that will change. What's there to do here? It's just a place."

I turned to face him. "Unlike you I may well not have the privilege of coming back. For you this is easy, but for me, well, it's like a bereavement, this is the best my life has ever been, now sod off and give me some space. Twenty minutes, and I'll be reconciled in my thoughts."

Grimnir left me alone for an hour, before returning with Tam, who gently offered to postpone our departure for a couple of days.

I looked at the two of them. "No, let's get on with it, but thank you." I was glad for their company, besides, *What the hell's wrong with me? I need to wallow in some mud and sleep rough for a week or two, I've become sentimental. Shit!*

Tam and Thrandar spoke for a few moments. Thrandar had run up momentarily before, receiving instructions on a couple of incidental matters, along with apologies for a cancelled appointment with someone I'd never heard of, and confirmation that all three of us would be departing for Cragtor, and no, we didn't need any provisions and yes, Miller would be coming with us.

Thrandar brightened upon the news, asking when I might be expected back, and should he keep my quarters ready? Learning that it wouldn't be necessary, he lowered his head in an attempt to hide a smile; he wished us all a safe journey.

Git, I thought. *Don't hit Thrandar, he doesn't deserve it,* quoting Tam's admonition in my head. *Yes he bloody well does.* Grimnir also laughed, seeing me glare at Thrandar; he'd seen the smile too.

"We'll need to head towards the docks," said Grimnir, "but we won't be boarding a boat, it's really for show. Can you walk that far?"

"Of course I can bloody well walk, you weren't that good." But I was without doubt in considerable pain; Tam's salves were incredibly powerful but usually took a day to work and whilst some two hours had passed since Grimnir's lesson, my muscles were only now tightening. I quickened my pace. *Bastard.*

Grimnir chuckled. "Stretcher! Make way for the invalid," he said, loud enough that a servant, hearing Grimnir, looked in our direction.

We walked about three quarters of a mile through the winding paths and street of Gledrill, unencumbered by provision, for these I was sure would be waiting for us upon arrival at the dockside. *What did Grimnir mean about not boarding a boat?* I didn't understand.

As we passed through the crowded thoroughfares of Gledrill I noticed that Tam had thrown back her hood so that her countenance shone; she was easily recognisable, and as for Grimnir, there strode a Lord of War – he was resplendent; replete in full battle dress, his sword sheathed in a leather scabbard threaded with silver, his helm of iron and gold, his shield made of ebony bound in iron and silver, and emblazoned on the front was a large golden battle hammer. He carried a great two-handed axe, the haft embedded with a gem atop the shaft, and I sensed a dweomer upon the axe, shield and upon the fingers of his right hand. The setting sun drenched his freshly scrubbed mail so that it shone with a golden glow. He looked like a Dwarf Lord from the days of legend.

Walking in the company of the most powerful people I could ever imagine, I basked in the shadow of their glory, these two, walking with me, unassailable, imperishable. People stared at us, and wondered how it could be that I secured such company or perhaps how they suffered such.

I did notice Tam tuck herself slightly behind Grimnir, as a child might shelter from a storm behind a parent. It felt wonderful as merchants and tradesmen, peasants and the scrum of the street made way for us. I wanted to be like Grimnir, one day I vowed I would. *Oh, if only someone would insult the dwarf, or knock Tam over,* how I would have revelled in the consequences. Now I knew why Grimnir laughed so much.

Eventually we joined a larger cobbled road, which

had been maintained to higher standards; there were so many people of different sizes carrying on trades, rushing about their business, trying to turn an honest penny into two, or not, as the case might be. The smell, sights and sounds were fascinating, I really hadn't explored the place properly having had such limited free time, it had been all I could do securing leave to visit the charred remains of my old farm and retrieve the purse hidden some six months prior. Towns and cities were fascinating. But you needed silver, and whilst I had more than people thought, it was clear wealth was useful.

As we approached the docks, Grimnir seemed to know the way to go; he purposely headed for an inn that was close to the water's edge but of a more wholesome appearance than most of the hostelries we passed.

Along the way I marvelled at the merchant vessels. The sails, halyards and sheets, the men working with skill and thrift. The efficiency and sometimes tardiness of individuals moving cargo. Barrels and hessian sacks, stacked along the edge of wharfs, each known to some as to location and destination. Enthralled by all, I looked out over the sea. Yes, I knew of the sea through study but this, the reality, the great massive grey expanse of ocean, for this I needed to stop and stare, yet there was a strange disquiet.

The sun was dipping below the farthest point of my vision. Would I see the green flash told of in stories? Were all adventures this good? I waited and watched, beautiful, yes, even a half-orc is not without appreciation.

Nothing happened – no green flash, the sun

vanished. *Just a bollocks story told by an idiot.* Still, the sun setting over the ocean was worth seeing. Worth seeing, not worth going to see. I excelled in ignorance, always would?

"No green flash tonight," said Tam. She stood some thirty yards ahead, also watching the horizon.

"So it's true?" I asked as I approached her.

She smiled and said she had heard of it from reliable sources, so, "Yes, probably, though I've yet to see it myself."

The cry of gulls wheeling overhead would forever remind me of that moment, my first sight of this alien landscape, the great ocean.

"That," said Grimnir, pointing to a large merchant vessel, "belongs to Tam, myself and two other former companions who I haven't seen in many years. One I think is dead, the other cares not for it, I don't know." Grimnir looked closely at the vessel. "Looks a bit shabby, Tam! Is it nearing the end of its days?" Tam didn't hear or was deep in thought. "It's been useful for Tam and I, saves us silver."

"You own a boat, Lord?" I asked, looking more closely at the ship.

"Yes, but don't ask me how they work, bloody dangerous things, they don't go where you want them to, leak water, and you need others to help you, and stop calling me 'Lord'." He marched onwards, just a little farther and stopped outside a fine-looking inn. Tam not needing to stoop, entered through an arch. Raising her hood as though instinctively, she walked down a short passage and into the common area of the hostelry.

The place was busy, but not crowded. There were alcoves, tables and chairs also a fire, but with three men bent huddled around, talking over beer, and 'bloody stealing most of the heat', there was little spare for the rest of the room. I wondered whether I should get them to move.

Whilst there were private places to sit and some of the alcoves remaindered empty, Tam sought an area visible to all near the middle of the room. Casting back her hood once more, she sat down; either the chair was too short or the table too high for she looked diminutive and vulnerable.

Where's Grimnir? My thoughts were somewhat protective of Tam, but Grimnir had marched to a far corner, and was beckoning to someone.

I sat down opposite Tam. "Are you okay here? I can find us a better place by the fire."

She looked at me. "I think someone's already sat there, Miller, but thank you, this is a good spot."

It wasn't a good spot, Grimnir needed to find somewhere better, a little privacy would be good. Scarcely a moment later a voice echoed across the room, "Ah, Lady Bluebottle, you must be sailing tomorrow, I'll be with you shortly."

A plump bald man perhaps five foot one inch, apron fastened too tightly for his overhanging belly protruded out concealing a belt, rushed up, Grimnir walking slowly behind.

"Lady Bluebottle, err, are you wanting your usual lodgings before sailing?" He wasn't quietly spoken. *Too bloody loud,* I thought. He needed lessons in discretion, the Lady Bluebottle's business ought to be treated with privacy.

"Yes please, is it available?" asked Tam.

Of course it bloody is, or soon will be. She's far too polite. I scowled and brooded in thought. *Grimnir and I could sort out any guests in the wrong place at the wrong time.* Grimnir looked at me, said nothing but imperceptibly shook his head. He held his gaze a moment longer than normal.

Oh! I was missing something, some subtlety, a deception, what eluded me. No, no I wasn't, this was all an act. Tam wanted to be seen, people were meant to hear us.

"Ah! You must be leaving on tomorrow's neap tide. Do please follow me, we have your accommodation ready, three adjoining rooms."

Rising rather noisily, chairs scraping, the innkeeper helped Tam to her feet. We were led down a scrubbed corridor, flags on the floor, clean walls with paintings of boats, sea-storms and other irrelevances.

Tam, Grimnir and I, were each in turn ushered into adjoining rooms, Tam the nearest, then Grimnir, and finally myself at the end of the corridor.

As I stepped inside I wondered at the cleanliness of the place, the luxury, a bed raised off the floor – I'd never seen the like – a chair made of cloth and padded with something, perhaps horse hair or straw, a window, with shutters, and two, not one but two oil lamps.

The walls were adorned with tapestries, finely crafted furniture made from oak and yew provided storage for provisions and cloth drapes fastened back on either side of internally shuttered windows allowed for privacy from the outside. Next to a desk complete with writing utensils, there stood a pitcher with, oh, only water!

"Don't get comfortable," said a voice.

Turning, I saw a door in the middle of the wall stood ajar. Only moments before the middle of the wall had seemed hung with fleeces, but apparently they simply concealed a party door between the connecting rooms.

I peered around the door frame, and could see through Grimnir's room and right into Tam's, another door connecting the final room.

"Please come and join us, Miller, when you're ready." Tam's voice, slightly distant, drifted across the rooms.

Please! The obvious difference between Grimnir and Tam. Perhaps Thrandar could have a word with Grimnir, now that would be worth laughing at... I'll mention it to Grimnir. I knew I wouldn't, but it made me smile, as I walked from my room into Grimnir's near identical chamber before stopping and knocking at Tam's door.

"Bloody hell, who is it?" said Grimnir, looking around, deliberately ignoring the blindingly obvious. Me! For I stood waiting in the party wall doorway.

Grimnir with a grin walked to the main entrance and looked both up and down the corridor. "No! No one here, Tam!"

"Do come in, Miller," said Tam. Turning very slightly, but not fully to Grimnir, she said, "Miller exercises a kindness and grace to me that you once had, perhaps you should observe and learn from him!"

"Bollocks," said Grimnir as he belched, "he just got lucky. I've got impeccable manners, at least when I need them!"

*

"I'll be ready shortly, please give me a moment." Tam was searching for something in her waistcoat pocket. "Do you know how far Cragtor is, Miller?"

Staring down at her, a moment's doubt crossed my mind, remembering Thrandar saying 'he knew not the distance'.

"The only town I know by that name is some one hundred and fifty miles away, the far side of Culanun, in the foothills of the Grey Mountains, above Hedgetown and the Southern Marshes."

"Not bad," said Grimnir, before Tam interrupted.

"Yes, you are correct, but before we travel, there are some matters you need to know of." She paused, considering her words. I noticed the level of control she exerted, as though reconciling or stealing herself to duties not altogether relished. The pitch of Tam's voice lowered and a sternness of words came forth.

"When Grimnir and I return to Cragtor, it will be to responsibilities, duties and obligations; there will be sycophants, fools, traitors, and people who cannot be trusted. There will be false friends, and hidden enemies.

"When we arrive you must be cautious, exercising discernment of every person's motive. Never trust anyone until they have had their trust proven worthy, remember that!

"You, Miller, have an intelligence and understanding of both good and wickedness, please use it. You will be flattered and fawned over, conned, cheated and deceived." Tam hesitated, looking at Grimnir.

But before she continued, I interrupted. "What is this place that it should be so different from Gledrill?" I gently asked, being somewhat worried. "And surely we have time to discuss this during the weeks of travel?"

"There is no time like the present." Grimnir appeared stern and there was a gravelly rumble in his voice, a return to maturity and formidable presence; suddenly he projected an aura of authority, but with a severity and purpose not seen before.

"When we arrive in Cragtor there are duties involving the control of people's lives, responsibilities affecting the management of others. Discipline must prevail."

Grimnir asked, "Miller! What is your most powerful spell, if you can forgive me asking?"

Hesitantly, I answered, but looking firstly at Tam, seeking her wisdom, her permission, for the revealing of skill is counselled against, and Tam had laboured the value of secrecy, that 'no one should ever know the limits of your power'. Her words had chimed with my natural caution, and I had remembered that lesson well.

Knowledge is power, knowledge is everything. Don't forewarn your enemy, never reveal your skill in craft. My thoughts recalled to mind wise counsel.

And now Tam nodded approval, so as I looked

Grimnir in the eye, I explained that without certainty, I could 'usually' travel many yards between two points, a portal spell, but I was not yet proficient.

Grimnir smiled. "I know that spell well. No, no, I cannot cast it," he saw the surprise upon my face, "but that is a remarkable accomplishment, well done Miller," and he looked sincerely at me. Thrusting out his hand, he shook mine with a firmness and genuine warmth of friendship. I smiled, pleased with the goodwill shown.

Grimnir looked at Tam. "Bloody lethal!"

Grimnir, turning around, explained about the area of Cragtor, the 'secret' of Hedgetown. Much I knew, the lands were wilder than Gledrill's farmland, famous for outlaws and being on the edge of the wild the lands were frequently under attack. It was frontier territory, a difficult place to defend and as such farms were concentrated close to the town walls, nonetheless trade flourished and the town had under good governorship thriven these last thirty years.

That didn't account for Tam and Grimnir's cryptic warnings. What was the difference!

Hedgetown's hedge was not much of a secret, I was looking forward to seeing it with my own eyes.

"Grimnir, tell me."

"The difference," Grimnir glanced at Tam before grimly staring at me once more, "is that I am the Lord of Hedgetown and Tam's steward during her absence from Cragtor. And you, dear Miller, will be used by every worm, scoundrel and chancer, because of knowing us, we must protect you and…"

I suddenly felt sick. No, it wasn't the beating from Grimnir, nor a reaction to the news of Lordship.

The room seemed chill, a sudden realisation gripped my heart, and my blood ran cold, with shock and doubt.

"NO! It's not possible," I spoke out loud, but I'd heard of it in fairy tales, the same ones from whence bedtime stories were told to small children.

The blood drained from my face, and Tam, smiling, took my hand and sat me down.

"Yes," she said.

"How long?" I asked, barely able to speak, my throat tight. I shook.

"Two minutes."

CHAPTER 3

Offering to become a supplicant, to be brought in chains, so as to appear without favour or friendship, indeed there was value; I could spy, be of use, no one finding advantage in deceiving me. Grimnir and Tam's enemies might be more visible, I might learn matters not so easily gained, I was after all unknown, it would be wise, better.

There was merit to my argument, but Tam, looking at me almost with a tear, point-blank refused to allow another chain to ever bind me, even for the sake of friendship.

"I forbid it, Miller." She was most earnest, having the greatest empathy of all to my former misery. "Never, never shall you go chained, especially so undeservedly. No! Absolutely not."

Grimnir didn't want to disregard the suggestion,

and between us, both he and I, persuaded Tam to a partial feint.

We would transport together, to a permanently locked apartment deep within Cragtor's citadel, whereupon armour and weaponry would be supplied; only one person would know me for certain, Glamdrun, and he would not be advised. It was a protection, in case of emergency, he at least knew me though there was no great friendship, and in the event of desperate need he could be summoned. His duty would prevail regardless of any private animosity.

On my arrival I would be prepared, that is to say, given weapons, suitable attire, and coin. And finding myself transported outside the town, a spell I could almost perform myself, I would gain entrance as with other travellers seeking lodging, and enquiring about work.

Grimnir himself would travel down to Hedgetown with a routine caravan train, normal activities, I would join with that caravan.

And so it was, I still ached. The salve hadn't been applied generously enough.

It was late afternoon, and Grimnir was looking seriously at me, as I sat upon the edge of my cot, painful muscles contractions rippling across my midriff. I was smothered in salve. Tam had wanted to call a professional healer but I was hard to explain, and besides, her salves were extremely effective, when applied properly and not walking around within twelve hours.

Lying in a luxurious cot, I stared at the tapestries adorning the walls of this, a locked private chamber deep within the mighty fortress of Cragtor.

The journey had been nigh instantaneous. Grimnir had undoubtedly been transported via Tam's craft before, perhaps many times, but as Grimnir stared at me, deep in thought, I myself pondered, had he any understanding, any comprehension of the magnitude of the power Tam wielded?

For whilst Tam had prepared herself, Grimnir had paced up and down the inn rooms, apparently totally devoid of any appreciation as to the task in hand, only when Tam had said she was ready did Grimnir show any comprehension, any recognition, a forced smile as he took hold of Tam's left hand and bid me grab-fast the other.

I, Miller, no longer an apprentice in crushing grain, was without doubt merely a new born infant, a novice in the craft of magic. Learned in languages, reading and writing, and having the ability to listen to the earth's song I was quite simply an ignorant peasant, and in awe of Tam.

Was this the limit of her power? I knew never to ask, but limits there must be. No longer certain of anything, I looked up at Grimnir.

"I'll leave you now, Miller, I have work to do, but will speak to you in the morning. The door will be locked and there are standing orders in place, no one is allowed inside this part of the castle without Tam's leave."

He looked at me and was about to say something but changed his mind. "I'm sure you could escape if there was a fire." A faint smile, as he stood up and walked to the door. "Try and rest."

The door opened and closed followed by the scrape of an internal bolt being thrown; I was alone.

The sun had set, and I lay listening to the sounds of the town, the shouts and exclamations of multitudes of people, trying to single out conversations only half heard.

*

The sun had risen some hours before. Stirring slowly, coming in and out of consciousness, I looked up at the ceiling, reflecting upon my circumstances.

All through my long years of servitude I had sought freedom knowing that captivity is onerous and thus less than ideal, but my previous understandings had been a conceit. Freedom was far more than the release from bondage, it was 'choice', the freedom to choose devoid of coercion, to make decisions based on your understanding of events, to enjoy life and to pursue any route that made oneself ultimately happier, right or wrong.

During my captivity, clerics had tried to influence my thinking, to teach me morals, to make me an image of themselves. They had extolled virtues such as kindness, mercy and meekness.

Now in old age, looking back at my life I have been kind, sometimes stupid. Some people even, much to their own surprise, thought me good! It was never thus. But it's true, I have occasionally made a mistake and exercised too much kindness, for as the priests said, kindness is a 'virtue' and it is one I actually agreed with. How else was I to motivate profit from a stranger or new acquaintance? The gods knew I was disadvantaged by birth, but I have noted with some certainty that kindness has its uses and with careful application of intelligence, I have become quite skilled in the selective use of kindness.

Mercy, bollocks! The thought makes me vomit. It is nothing but a statement of weakness for worms, for cowards, for those who refuse to challenge the malefactors that infract.

Meekness? Well this is contentious, for having studied many a long cold night I submit that the priests don't know the meaning of the word. I was meek, for five years of arcane apprenticeship; I sought knowledge, was teachable. Undoubtedly I was in the true sense meek, this is the real definition of meekness, not the gut-wrenching humility that erroneous clerics frequently claimed.

But as in all matters there is conflict in thought, none of these human social norms allow for one virtue, the one that influenced me the most. I think I have it, perhaps the only one? Loyalty!

Tam visited about midday, only briefly, checking up on me. Outrageous really, that the Lady of this town big enough to be classed as a city by some should in stealth call upon a guest in her own keep. Nonetheless, I was glad of her sight and for the company.

"Miller, you slept late this morning, how are your injuries? For there are no residues of salve and you seem comfortable."

I raised myself into a sitting position. "Excellent, cured, not an aching muscle in sight." Almost truthful, for there was actually a slight remembrance of the previous day's pain, but only a shadowy twinge. "I have been wandering around, within the confines of the door, and believe these to be your own chambers. Where have you been resting? I have no right to expect such treatment and am undeserving of such, it's not right, my lady."

"Not right?" she mused, and I got the point. *Bollocks!*

"The bed gave me back ache, it's far too soft and smells of perfume," I scowled. "It's making me say stupid things." I shut up.

"Tam! You call me Tam, although perhaps in the short-term. Lady, only in the company of strangers, but yes, they are indeed. I'm not shy of options, and no doubt there will be gossip. The chambermaids will think I've had company, they are already perplexed as to my habits."

"I should not be here, cast me out, I have silver, enough to keep myself watered and fed, I'll lodge in an inn, I should never have deprived you…"

"Tomorrow, is time enough," she cut me off. "Tonight, we will practise reciting craft and discuss your future – your future, not mine or Grimnir's, **your** choice." She looked at me, and knew my mind. I wasn't surprised, suspecting it was only through her incredible perception and intuition that she spoke, not the application of craft, for Tam would have asked permission, and besides I probably would have known if she had.

"Grimnir is ferreting around in my armoury, half the equipment's his anyway, he'll be along shortly."

Tam left, for it was only a fleeting visit.

'How could I ever repay such kindness?" Oh, by

the gods, what was wrong with me? I arrested my thoughts, blinking. This is shit, incredulity, to even think of debt was anathema. Had I changed that much? No! Then what the hell was wrong with me?

After an hour, I heard the door mechanism unlock; slowly the door opened, and Grimnir entered, barging the door wider as he carried a sack over his shoulder.

"Now then, Miller, a bag of presents for you." He kicked the door closed, and I heard the lock fastening on its own.

Grimnir stood in fine clothes, a sword hung at his side, a broad finely fashioned belt with small pouch but no armour; he had clearly been attended to, for his beard was combed and his boots were different, softer. Around his neck hung a scarab on a gold chain, and he looked clean.

"Try these on." He emptied the sack, heaving it up so that all could fall cleanly on the floor. The room vibrated as the metal fell with considerable force, such that those below would have looked up at the ceiling, for the floor was part spanned by giant rafters, albeit half the room was not, being stone bound.

In front of me lay clean clothes, including a cloth vest, belt, full-length chainmail, two leather jerkins – one for under the chainmail and one studded as lighter protection, a sword, battle axe, and beautiful new boots shod with iron, small metal plates had been sewn internally as greaves. A helm of good craftsmanship, but still of base metal. A fine dagger, rope and what appeared to be a half-full backpack, with bullseye lantern hanging off a rear strap.

Under no circumstances did all that come from Grimnir's sack, but I'd seen it with my own eyes.

"If you want to put them on, I'm pretty sure I've got your size, let's look at you."

Incredulous, I stared, for the cost of these items was far beyond my means of payment, and looking at Grimnir I shook my head. "These items will get damaged, I can't." And for the second time that day, said, "It's not right."

"What's the matter with them? They'll fit."

"Here is a wealth beyond measure, and I will not try on equipment that I could never afford," at least not from Grimnir, and I wouldn't steal from him, not unless my life was in jeopardy and perhaps not even then.

Grimnir was examining the mound of items, carelessly sifting them with his foot, and reaching down, moved the chainmail to one side, spreading the equipment more evenly on the floor.

Looking up, "The cost? No you bloody well cannot afford them, that's why Tam and I aren't expecting you to, but if it makes you feel any better they're too big for anyone else, there's no charge. Put them on, you miserable bugger."

Grimnir went off and sprawled on the couch, touched his belt, and looked away. "I've seen some ugly sights in my time, but your being naked isn't going to be one of them, I'm not adding that to my list of nightmares."

I didn't rush, it was all too much to absorb, scarcely six months prior I had had nothing, even the rags that clung to my wretched body were begged from my late master, and now this. And as for being too large for others, I suspected that wasn't true, I'd seen some pretty large humans in my time.

After about ten minutes, for dressing in armour is neither quick nor straightforward, I hitched the axe over my shoulder, sword hanging without a scabbard, but secured through a loop of metal chain fashioned for just such a purpose yet separately attached to the belt. The boots felt heavy, the helm needed more padding to fit correctly, but it was easy to adjust and was close enough.

"You should wear it as often as possible, the weight will become irrelevant after a few days for whilst your strength is greater than most men the unfamiliarity will impede any combat in the first week or so, indeed significantly slowing you down, though you won't think so. After a week you will remove the armour and it'll feel like you're floating, you'll walk funny and look ridiculous, but that'll pass."

I stood there listening, for only a fool would disregard or ignore Grimnir's counsel.

"Sleep in it, at least for the first few days. Yes, you'll smell, the bane of being a warrior. I suggest you lay on the floor tonight, otherwise Tam's mattress will be ruined."

Warrior? I'd never thought myself thus. "I thought I'd be in an inn tonight, that I'd be coming through the main gates, and finding lodgings?"

"Maybe, I don't know." Grimnir looked thoughtful. "The gates shut at sundown but are always manned, they'll let you in. I might even discreetly watch to make sure they question you correctly, but you don't know the town, perhaps tomorrow morning would be best. Towns and cities aren't always safe at night and you have little experience of Cragtor, not to be unfair Miller, not of any town, day or night."

"Tell me where to lodge, that's recommended by you, but not too salubrious, but safe enough. I'd rather get out and stretch my legs."

Grimnir thought about it for a moment. "Okay, if you insist, I'll inform Tam." He seemed to be privately considering other matters, but after a brief pause continued with the immediate matter in hand.

Grimnir spoke of many aspects of warfare in mail, much I already knew, for whilst I was trained with padded clothes and fought with wooden swords the art of warfare and martial skills had been taught alongside the practical side of combat.

We sat and talked about Hedgetown, the caravan and what hopes I had for the future, but in the end it was the final conversation that Grimnir had that was hardest of all to forget. But that was for an hour's time, Grimnir needed to go.

After Grimnir departed, I examined everything in the back pack. Tinder box, thirty-five feet of coiled rope attached to a small hook, oil in a tight leather bladder, an empty water skin, two torches. *Not really necessary,* I thought. Chalk, a small jar of Tam's salve, ink and parchment, and numerous tiny items such as a lodestone, spikes and spare purse. There was also a small hidden seam concealed in the side of the fabric, the use of which I knew not.

I folded my studded jerkin and placed it inside, not

much space left. Even though the pack was large, the jerkin was equally so.

Grimnir returned an hour later, perhaps a little longer for light was failing, and I was looking forward to Tam's visit; we had much to discuss, not the least plans for tomorrow and timescales for joining the caravan.

Grimnir stayed a while, he was just returning because he said he would. Nonetheless, I wished he hadn't.

"Miller, I'll be seeing you tomorrow, about noon. There's a statue besides the east gate, a representation of four strange characters, the caravan will depart from there, or at least half of it will. I'll be joining and ignoring you as we agreed, eh?"

A moment's pause and he continued, "And you will be walking with the main section." He scratched his arse. "No one can stop you walking out with us, these transits contain an eclectic mix of merchants, travellers and family groups, all travelling together for added protection. There will also be men-at-arms, some militia, though mostly inexperienced.

"Oh! And this caravan will be large, several hundred, probably too many families, not the least because I'm travelling down with them, they'll feel more secure in my company." He thought for a moment, and added, with a slight wistfulness, "I'll be glad of your company, Miller!"

"And I of yours, why should it be otherwise?" I asked, not expecting a reply.

Grimnir looked squarely at me. "The stragglers will be attacked at the rear, we all know it will happen!

Not a matter of if, but when, and it'll happen five miles either side of the halfway mark."

Grimnir jumped to his feet, swearing as a wasp tried landing on his arm. "Bloody wasps! I hate them, they're always reversing into me."

Having swiped the insect away, he continued.

"The caravan will string out, the slowest falling behind, whilst the main body will urge haste. They won't give a damn about their fellow travellers, have my ears bashed from protesting groups, my work will be keeping the caravan moving forwards whilst protecting as much as I can. There are insufficient fighters to protect everyone."

Excellent, I was looking forward to being an arse, and an inadequately guarded caravan seemed perfect.

"We could never have enough, for the greater the security the larger the caravan grows. One half-orc, will become much loved."

Much loved? I thought he exaggerated.

"Accordingly," carried on Grimnir, "there will be opportunity enough for you and I to drink and eat together whilst appearing for all intents and purposes, totally formal."

Grimnir seemed so sure, which I assumed came from years of experience.

"I want you to understand very clearly that whilst one day we may be enemies," he held up a hand, for I had baulked at this comment, "At this point in time I am only your friend and ally."

He took an item out of his pouch that hung aside of his belt, looking for something else near the bottom.

"I have never met a man of your ancestry that didn't let me down, didn't turn to treachery, didn't leave the company of friends, and wasn't seduced by power and mistaken fealties."

"Bloody cheerful company you are, Grimnir, what the hell's the matter with you?" I said looking at him. "Are you pissed or simply in a bad mood?"

"You'll never be good, never be charitable, never be merciful, but by the gods I hope you remember my friendship and that of Tam's. If you can remember these days, you may make something of yourself."

He's pissed? I looked hard at Grimnir.

"I say this because, I sincerely hope you will be different. Tam feels the same, I guess that's why she invested in you, it's a foolish game for old champions to play, but it's reality."

Rummaging in his pouch, he handed me a scroll. "You can read that, I can't, I cannot even action the glimmer that's contained therein, but you can. I kept it as a remembrance of battles gone before, where such a scroll is priceless, at least when you have no silver to pay for a healer."

Grimnir got up and left the room.

Sitting there staring at the scroll, a healing scroll, and yes, actionable with my skills, Grimnir's words troubled me; was he right? Would I forget this friendship? Could a half-orc never be trusted? Did my blood condemn me? Would I be different? Did I want to be?

Grimnir had had many years' experience; was my character bereft of salvation, or was that a thought for the weak? Did it matter? Do friends count? Is one merciful to friends, or is that simply gratitude?

I was conflicted in thought.

Grimnir's pissed! But I remained troubled.

The thought of my independence and the lack of access to friends, plus the comments of Grimnir spun around my mind, like some repetitive dream that refuses to change in theme.

Logically I sought to distract myself, and touching the stone wall, I tried to feel the song, to hear the music of life; but being so high off the ground, and insulated by dressed stone walls, the song whilst present was diminished, like listening to conversations whilst immersed in water.

Still for a while I tried, but feeling neither distracted enough nor fulfilled my hand moved from the wall and I allowed my mind to drift back. How it must be miserable for older people who gradually lose their hearing, an isolation, an unwelcomed exclusion from the world they knew.

The sun fell below the horizon, and I counted my silver, studying the hammered seal on each coin, observing the clipped edges. Some coins were smaller than others, halves, some cut in half, and thus quartered. But silver is silver, and merchants weigh each piece in any given transaction.

Time marched slowly forward, and I practised drawing my dagger, whipping my sword from its retaining hoop, and releasing my axe.

I need to escape this room, I need to get out. My thoughts coalescing, I was reverting to the Miller that sat outside the blacksmith's shop listening to the activities of life, yet through goodwill, thanks to unexpected friends being far better prepared for the future that lay ahead.

"Good evening, Miller." Tam, knocking, had entered the chamber. I'd heard the door opening, but because she was expected I had shown little initial attention, for my thoughts were somewhat depressed, indeed I was melancholic, the realisation of being without friends.

"You look splendid" said Tam, and she paused for a moment, contemplative, observing me for I was sat on one of her padded chairs distractedly twisting a stray thread. "I'll be back in a moment." She rose and walked away.

Looking up, Tam was already disappearing through an archway and out of sight into the adjoining room, all within the confines of the locked main door.

"Sorry!" I spoke rather belatedly. "Thank you for the armour and equipment," I called after her.

"That's okay, I hope Grimnir found everything you needed," came Tam's slightly muted voice. I heard a large scraping sound and the floor shook slightly. "I'll just be a minute."

Yes, I was curious, but not too intrigued, and after all, whatever Tam was doing was none of my business.

Staring at my boots, and angling my heel slightly, I was unaware of Tam's return, and after what may have been five minutes I looked up and noticed her sat ten feet away, observing me.

"So tomorrow, I'm travelling down in a caravan, and I'll find lodging in town this evening." I looked at Tam, half wanting her to initiate the conversation.

"Is that what you want?" Tam was still studying me.

Tam always had the answers, but this freedom was difficult, I didn't know what I wanted, never having had to choose before, and to be honest, not really knowing my options. Trying to correlate my thoughts, I explained…

"I'm conflicted between friendship and liberty, knowing that I'll let you down, that you'll hear reports of me that may be partly true." I was unsure of my words. "Now that I'm faced with the reality of my existence I don't want to be close and not able to associate. Your friendship and that of Grimnir's is precious. When Grimnir challenged me to combat and with all the insults… well… I was gutted."

Tam encouraged me to continue, listening attentively.

"I do not know what you had in mind for me, nor perhaps if I'd like it, but I just feel confined, and it's not the last two days, it's probably the reality of what I always wanted to be, fay, able to make my own mistakes, without you and Grimnir being ashamed."

This was too much, for feelings were not my strong suit.

"If I stay as previously planned, and I concede it was forthrightly argued, my idea, then I would be remote, yet close and still subject… if only in my heart.

"Look, I've said it, these feelings aren't me, it's not in my nature to express myself, to be circumscribed by duty."

Tam, for once didn't smile, but neither did she show any inflexion of thought. I studied her face, but either by chance or skill, she gave away no hint or suggestion of what she was thinking.

"You are under no obligation to follow either mine or Grimnir's counsel. Miller, you have silver and a great deal of intelligence, the wisdom will come with experience, but..." And she, for the slightest of moments, hesitated. "If you need at this late hour one last point of guidance, at least in this matter..." She slowed, choosing her words. "If you would like me to say it straight, I will for friendship's sake give advice. You must be free to take any course you desire..."

Tam looked straight into my eyes; the ten feet apart seemed as inches. "Go with Grimnir tomorrow. Hedgetown is unlike any other experience you will have had, not at all like Gledrill, yet only thirty-eight miles or so from Cragtor, totally different from the two towns."

"You know..." I hesitated. There was finally a resolution of the conflict in my mind, the tumult of trying to empathise. Empathy for me was intuitive, rather than considered, as a wild animal instinctively knows, for I was akin to them. If any human was so closely aligned to chaos, I was that creature, partly domesticated yet with wits and comprehension, and a feral heart.

But at the last I knew the problem, comprehending finally. I understood my internal conflict.

"...I value your advice, appreciate your opinion, look forward to your company, but, my oldest friend, what I really need is *your* permission to ignore you!"

Said with a heavy heart, yet there was exhilaration, a surge of adrenaline, as stepping over the River Styx, into the shadow of night, the sword of Damocles, no longer threatening.

Tam finally smiled broadly, and laughed. I confess she cleared the air, with that most wonderful of sounds, Tam's laughter.

"My dear Miller, oh, you most wonderful of souls. May the gods bless you, for I have trod carefully, anxious not to direct too much." She spoke with genuine sincerity. "You are free from reproach, do as you will, the six months' apprenticeship, your contract with me ended. But the contract of friendship may bind you yet... but look at me... please look at me." Hesitating, I caught her gaze.

She looked deep into my eyes, and I was embarrassed, finding it hard to maintain the connection, until with a firmer voice her courage reinforced mine, so that I dove into her mind. I looked, and there was no flaw. Only power, perhaps wisdom, but I saw the power, and surprisingly, the song, as though bound, maybe I was drawn to it, but it was there. Why had she given me this insight?

"You are free, released!" came a small voice as on the wings of the earth song, distant through the castle walls. I heard it and was strangely not surprised.

So, the fleeting connection was broken.

Sat finally comfortable on the padded chair, I said, "Will you inform Grimnir, or shall I tomorrow? I'd rather you do it, for, for me it's hard."

"Well, he already knows, I told him so! He will be pleased to see you tomorrow, but he has steeled himself for your non-appearance, in case I was wrong. Will you travel with the company, tomorrow?" Tam asked.

She already knew I would.

It was perhaps ten o'clock in the evening, and I had everything on my person, the armour, backpack and a small rusty nail.

Tam had passed this tiny, rusty, worthless nail to me, saying that if I was in peril, devoid of friends, and desperate to find sanctuary, the nail would facilitate my return to these chambers, once only, and regardless of distance, but and she had warned me carefully.

"It's restricted to the prime material plane or suffer potential mishap. Plane travel is possible, but ill advised."

Preparing to depart, I stood beside Tam.

"Shall I, or do you want to try yourself?"

"You do it, I need to practise." So I held her hand and she said no words, and her craft, her spell, brought us both outside one mile from the front gates next to an old ruined sentry post; it was raining.

Tam gave me a hug. I half reciprocated, but without skill. Tam started walk towards the town, her silk clothes scarcely protected by a fine cloth cloak.

"Tam, you're not dressed, you'll get soaked." She turned briefly and said she needed to think.

"The rain won't upset me, I'll be fine."

I waited, giving Tam a few hundred yards head start, watching and guarding her, but as we advanced, there was nothing to disturb the night's peace and as the northern main gates came into view. I held back and watched as the guards allowed her access, the gates banged shut behind, a scraping of wood on metal as a bar was drawn to seal and secure.

I waited ten minutes and started walking. The gates as a wall of wood stood like some foreboding malevolence barring my entrance. Approaching, I wondered whether I was observed, for no one appeared between the crenellations, yet the moon shed a little light.

Nothing, no activity. I stood beneath the gate, some twenty paces back, and other than the muffled noise from within the town there was silence.

The rain trickled down my neck between the helm and my mail, slowly absorbed by my cloth vest and jerkin.

"Open, I have business in town tonight, and I'm wet and cold." Nothing, not the hint of movement, neither a footfall to indicate awareness or any hint of comprehension.

The bastards can see me. "Open, damn you, I require entrance, it is yet early," but as though speaking to a rock it was to no avail, no sign of activity, and waiting for five minutes, I swore, "Open the gates, you bastards. I'm wet and need lodgings tonight."

Grimnir's a sod. 'I might watch and check they interrogate you correctly,' or words to that effect. I sat down and waited.

After an hour of my shouting and cursing someone came to the top of the left tower, throwing a chicken bone, or some such like at me, bidding me to be gone.

"Stop disturbing the night. The gate is shut and wouldn't be opened till half an hour after sunrise, so begone." He mumbled something to someone else; there was a short discussion. "We don't want your kind in here, why not live in a cave? Just sod off."

"I understand that you are in breach of your duties, I'll be settling this tomorrow, as I travel down in the caravan, and am much needed. I have been hired to assist."

"Piss off," came the clear reply, and for the first time there was the sound of others, listening, and encouraging their comrade, for tonight I was mild entertainment.

Sitting there, I considered whether I could use craft to gain access, but my ability in the spell was at the edge of my competence, and dreadfully unreliable.

Where the bloody hell is Grimnir? But it was approaching a half-hour to midnight, and I was concerned my lodgings would be shut or closing soon. *Sod it.*

I had always known that the entrance might cost perhaps two copper pieces, there were twenty to a small silver coin, and strangely I had not considered this option, having been reassured that they would open the gates.

Standing there, getting more angry, I bellowed, "One small silver!"

There was silence, yet not quite, for the man reappeared atop the tower, looking at me momentarily then turning, no doubt in discussions with his peers.

After three minutes there was a grating and the door slowly swang open, only three feet wide. Four men appeared, with swords drawn.

"Show me," said the lead man, as his comrades tried to look stern and serious, for I was clad as a warrior, and they knew there would be trouble if this came to conflict.

"It'll be a silver piece each, so five for all of you," he said, looking optimistic.

"All?" What the hell? For behind me shivering in the rain stood a family with a mule and looking bedraggled and in desperate need of warmth, a small boy stood there with three adults shivering.

"Sod them," I said, taking a half silver piece out of my purse as discreetly as possible and thrusting the coin in the man's outstretched hand. "They're not with me."

Entering the town, I enquired from the guard the whereabouts of the 'Haggard Hen', Grimnir had recommended the tavern as 'reasonable', yet where it was I knew not, and I hadn't expected the delays in gaining access.

Realising it was not too far, I strode towards the eastern wall, heading towards one of three market areas, now long since packed up, yet not devoid of activity.

Drunks, thieves and to be fair quite a few normal merchants and fellow travellers passed me by as swiftly as discretion allowed. Nonetheless, most people were secure behind shuttered windows with locks on doors, and only the hint of light escaping gaps beneath lintels and door frames.

Such it was, that when having threatened a drunk into guiding me to my destination and passing the dissolute and scum of the town I arrived at the Haggard Hen.

Three young men loitered outside; they appeared to have some wealth for their clothes were of a quality that was beyond the reach of most common folk, and noticing my approach nudged each other and muttered comments.

Let's get this straight, in no way do I look rich like Grimnir, nor by inference as powerful, but compared to the average man-at-arms, I looked rich. I stood six foot four inches with heavy build and muscles that only a lifetime of toil can produce. The cost of my equipment was close to one hundred and seventy-seven gold pieces or a little over thirty-five hundred silver. It was a price beyond the dreams of most. And I was pissed off.

The three fops, for they seemed that way to me, somewhat dandy and drunk with a confidence that comes from drink and ignorance, stood in my path, making very little effort to part ways.

"Get the fuck out of my way." I was tired and needed to eat and secure lodgings before it was too late.

"I think," said one, slowly trying to raise his posture, "The Old Swan is perhaps where you're wanting. Are you sure you've got the right place?"

"Ralpor, stop looking for trouble," one of the companions said, for looking at me, and realising the risk, he had stepped back, trying to grab Ralpor by the sleeve.

"Oh please, Kam, for fuck's sake, what's the world coming to if orcs can come in here?" He swayed, looking me up and down. The creature's obviously a thief, and it's just not right, allowing this sort in here, it's not right, not right that we suffer such company."

I almost laughed as I heard this. But my countenance was grim, and I didn't want trouble, not on Tam's doorstep. Anywhere else Ralpor would have had his manhood stuffed down his throat.

I stood there looking at the three of them. I growled, "If your friend apologises I'll forgive his insolence." The menace was stark for all to see; even the drunk Ralpor hesitated before drink and stupidity got the better of him…

"Oh please, this is ridiculous, I'll not…"

I swung my knee into his groin and he bent over like a man retching, and drawing my sword, swivelled the blade so the pommel drove sideways into his mouth, hopefully knocking a tooth out as he tumbled in ruin, crashing to the floor.

"Your friend is lucky to be alive," I said, looking at the two remaining companions, carefully checking for any attempt at retaliation. None. Thus, I walked in, lowering my head slightly, the doorway arch was low, the frame allowing for little headroom, and left Ralpor to the ministrations of his peers.

The inn was nearly empty, the barman and one of his employees, or daughter, were sweeping and tidying around customers in preparation for the shuttering of the establishment.

Walking now upright, my feet which were part shod with iron sounded a little like horse shoes over cobbles, smiting the floor with each step. I was certainly not inconspicuous, my presence caused most of the remaining patrons to turn and gaze.

Catching the eye of the innkeeper, and stepping in his direction, I said, "Say, it isn't too late, but I need to secure a room tonight, three pints of beer and food, bread, cheese, meats, anything that's good, nothing crap," and remembering not to fall out with anyone else that evening, added, "please," and, "how much?"

Observing my surroundings, I noticed the fire was slowly fading, but still produced heat, and there was room for my dragging a table closer, if one of the other patrons moved slightly aside.

"Yes, I have rooms. Good, average or," he looked doubtful, "expensive. Do you want your own or if you prefer you can share a dormitory, it's cheaper?"

"Give me the price for one night."

We settled upon the good room at two silver pieces, that included the beer and some broth, bread and cheese.

I exercised more manners, asking the other customer to budge up a little, as I dragged a table across the flagstones and stuck my boots up against the firedog to dry.

The innkeeper had disappeared, and the barmaid brought me a large wooden pitcher full of ale and pewter tankard. Smiling, she advised that the room was getting prepared, they hadn't expected anyone quite so late.

After half an hour there were five left in the room and the innkeeper said that he was locking up for the night, "But as most of you are lodging then you are welcome to stay and finish your drinks. Everyone else needs to leave, and that includes drunken cobblers like you, Arthur."

The innkeeper carried out Arthur, whilst the daughter started shuttering the windows and extinguishing the candles and occasional lamp.

It was warm, pleasant in the darkness, the tavern lit by the shadowy illumination of a lamp hidden down a corridor plus the glow of a subdued fire.

The innkeeper offered to show me my room, but I declined, instead enquiring as to the location. "Second right down that corridor." He pointed to where the lantern glow lit a passageway.

"The hound will not trouble you, but protects the barrels and entrance to the rest of the building." He clicked his fingers. "Ben, get," and a half wolf, half hunter dog walked to a pile of rags, settled itself down and turning its face, watched me.

Eventually, in the early hours of the morning I awoke. The fire had died down, I must have dozed off.

For a moment I sat there listening, wondering what had awoken me. Ben was alert, looking, but nothing further disturbed the night and getting up, I walked slowly to the corridor. Ben growled softly.

My room was shuttered, the bed was a mattress on

the floor. I locked the door internally and wedged the bolt with my knife. The window was closed, but not secure enough, so I placed my helm precariously on a hinge, a warning should anyone try to gain access. And lying on the bed, went back to sleep.

CHAPTER 4

In the morning I awoke listening to the sounds outside, there was work to do this day and I needed to meditate and learn the craft that might be needed quickly should trouble befall. What would be useful on the road to Hedgetown? Grimnir had said that with a certainty we would be attacked.

Three magic darts, one explosive fire and pondering a little I decided to choose a stun spell, useful against weak and unsuspecting opponents.

Crouching down, my hand clearing away the straw, I touched the ground almost with a caress, seeking the earth's music. Slowly I would be drawn in, listening and allowing the gentle eddies to engulf me, but this time it was different.

Clearing my mind of sounds and distractions and settling into meditation, I sank as a stone, an instant connection, faster and more powerful than I had ever experienced before, the intensity of energy, the whispering, but this time like a chorus, shouting.

Swept away I held on mentally as borne along a river tumultuous in strength, marvelling at the earth song, deep down I was drawn, riding the waves of rapture, searching, listening for the unique strands, the different ingredients for the fashioning of my spells, like searching in an apothecary for the parts of a potion, but the parts were all around.

Absorbing the energy, my mind incredulous for this was the most powerful experience I had ever had, and grasped emotionally and intellectually, absorbing an abundance of connective force, no longer seeking the mundane. Down I was drawn, intuition drawing me ever deeper. Voices in the deep spoke, no longer distant.

Now I do not suffer fear, but that morning I felt vulnerable, and after a while thought to draw my mind back, seeking to regain consciousness, I essayed to return to wakefulness to reach the ocean of perceptions yet floating across the subconscious mind. There was resistance to my return, like a gull tossed on the winds of a storm, seeking to land, but being driven aloft. Panic was setting in, the cold killer, devoid of reason, the secret terror of the mind. Breaking the meditation, I tried to recall the lessons Tam had given me.

"Sometimes masters of craft seek allies in the music, as guides to the way home, but you, Miller, will never need them."

Faster as my mind sought the air, the stillness of the

room, my mind sped back. I had already broken the meditation, but still consciousness had not returned.

Flashing in front of my mind I could see the cascade of music, hear each trumpet, each crescendo, shards of power whipping before me, the ocean or perceptions finally speeding beneath. I was getting closer.

I needed to wake up. I touched my nose, tapping my cheek, scratching my arm, till finally thumping my hand on the floor, I sensed a curtain descend, as a chemical barrier within the brain. I had resurfaced, the music had gone.

Drawing deep breaths, I sat there, my right hand clenching straw, my skin cold and sweat dripping across my face. *What the hell?*

I needed counsel. *Where's Tam?* I was scared.

After a while I dressed. My clothes were dry; the time spent in front of the fire had been sufficient, and sensing the abundance of energy in my body, I stepped out and grabbing some rags that were placed on a table aside the door, these to act as arse wipes for those paying for 'good rooms', I looked down the corridor. The inn was busy, yet still room to sit alone at a table.

The innkeeper espied me. "Did you find the room comfortable, master?" he asked.

"Yes, I slept well, and appreciate your accommodating me so late in the night. What time is it."

"Well! I guess it's some two hours before midday, but Magda can get a better answer for you in a minute."

"Yes please." I paused. "Where's the midden?" I held a rag visible so he got the point.

"End of the corridor, outside to your left, but you can use mine, just back here first right, and follow the smell."

I walked back past the barrels looking for a hound that seemed elusive.

The rags are always reused, boiled in a metal cauldron, as cloth is seldom wasted; only after it is threadbare would the rags finally be used to make char-cloth, and added to tinder boxes.

The cleaning of rags was typically the much-loved job of the youngest daughter within a family. I'd learnt some strange things in my youth. Never having rags, I was lucky to wipe my arse with dried moss or lichen.

Re-entering the common area, the innkeeper was arguing with a customer who was denying the cost of something as Magda walked up, folding a brass sundial.

"Hello, did you sleep well?" she smiled, looking up at me for I was almost two feet taller than her.

"Yes, it was fine, do you know the hour?"

"'Tis about two and a quarter hours before the midday. Will you be wanting anything else, master?"

Leaving the Haggard Hen, I made a point of exercising kindness and placed six copper pieces before the innkeeper and with considerable politeness thanked him for his hospitality, for the selective application of kindness as demonstrated in this instance was I was sure, an investment for the future. I think the innkeeper's estimation of half-orcs improved somewhat that day.

There wasn't enough time to seek Tam, but I would try and explain to Grimnir my problem, although even access to Grimnir would be problematic. In the meantime I needed better weather protection, probably a waxed hooded cloak.

Marching through town I passed various artisan shops, their shutters thrown back with doors wide ajar, some with their merchandise spilling onto the sidewalks. I started looking for a tanner or cobbler.

Passing one tanner displaying sheets of foul-smelling hides, I approached, standing in the doorway, blocking out the light so my arrival was instantly noticed.

"Yes warrior, what can I get you?"

"I need leather cut and fitted for this helm." Taking the iron helmet from my head, I tilted the inside towards him, asking, "It must be cured, cut and fitted within the hour, and using properly cured leather, properly thick and devoid of stench. I don't want to be reminded of your shop as I walk around."

He hesitantly reached out a hand. "May I see, master?"

"Should I go to a cobblers, or is this something you can do, and if so, how much?"

"Tomorrow it would be four copper, but I cannot do it in an hour."

We settled upon eight copper and I left the helm with him, carefully taking time to orientate myself, remembering the tanner's location.

The tanner had given directions to a clothes provisioning merchant, with the promise that he would have the job done on time.

On the way I bought some rations, a cooked leg of lamb, full water skin, and a small sack to hang at the belt, and arriving at the destination of the outfitters, I looked around. Was I being followed?

I sensed eyes upon me. No, not just the curious, something more!

Well, it was probable, every footpad had scouts, and I looked like a stranger, for with every glance to my left and right, with every hesitation at a junction, it was obvious to any would-be thug that I was unfamiliar, a visitor from out of town.

Well, it shows industriousness on the part of the local opportunists. Perhaps it was Ralpor, maybe he had hired some thugs to get his revenge; the toerags would rob me, and Ralpor would gain satisfaction.

The provisioner situated down a shaded archway had a plethora of merchandise on display – harnesses, ropes, hoods, boots, tack and wares for a multitude of purposes.

Stepping either side of displayed items, I was quickly noticed by a woman, tall and slender, greasy hair tied back, and wearing an apron replete with tool belt, knives and counting pole. She instructed a boy to enquire upon my needs.

"Get me the woman," I said, "for I don't want a boy serving me, I have silver and need a waxed cloak, complete with hood. I want to be dry in a storm, now go and tell your mistress."

The boy, somewhat scalded, left and spoke to the woman, who listened carefully and after a moment sent the boy on another errand. She approached, hiding her nervousness, this was after all, her domain. Nerves belying her confidence, she stood alone before a storm, a half-orc, and such creatures are notorious for brutality.

"Warrior, how might I help? The boy says you need clothing against the rain, what had you in mind?"

"A hooded cloak, waxed and made with quality material, I want to be bone dry in a storm, likewise it must cover me as you see me now."

I knew this would be a problem, for I was massive, and the chances were against me, but with considerable good fortune, three were found that fitted and seemed well constructed.

The cost was too much; six silver pieces with the least desirable of the three at five.

"Bloody hell, I'll be impoverished at this rate," but arguing was not getting me anywhere. In the end we settled on the least conspicuous of the three; it was dark green, almost black. I managed a modest discount, five and a half silver pieces.

"I need to borrow your boy for fifteen minutes, there maybe someone stalking me and I need a rear exit from this courtyard, and guidance to the tanner," whose name I gave.

"Six silver for you ask too much, the boy is needed," but she relented as I started to remove the cloak.

The boy led me through alleys and streets, quickly for he knew the way none better, and I bribed him with a copper piece.

The helm fitted, and after five minutes' adjustment I was satisfied.

My hood in place, I travelled with greater purpose to the square where the caravan would depart. As I approached, the streets became more congested, and with my cloak fastened tight around my body I placed a hand on the haft of my dagger. Where would Grimnir be?

The gates on the south side of the town lay open and a steady stream of traffic was moving in that direction. Whilst many trains jostled for position, giant shire horses scraped their hooves, anxious of the noise and clamour.

There were mighty wagons alongside smaller carts, the comparison stark, for these the largest wagons were owned by wealthy merchants or possibly partly owned jointly with others. The rich and those not so blessed. Some men-at-arms, though not many, tried to keep the peace as families streamed toward the gates, others seemed content to watch and wait without apparent activity nor readiness to leave.

Grimnir had said there would be hundreds in this caravan, and perhaps there were, but families sat on a cart or clerics riding mules, two hundred souls with their possessions produced quite a sizeable line.

This is too crowded. I didn't like being jostled. *There will be thieves in this crowd, and the tight, confining space would benefit their work.* Today, Cragtor would provide rich picking and I didn't want to be one of those targeted.

Most established trades had a Guild to promote and protect the interests of its members; thieves were no exception, being bound by rules and mutual support, for thievery was a profession just like every other.

Pushing back my hood, so that my face and helm were more visible, I hoped Grimnir might find me, though I suspected he wouldn't acknowledge my presence, at least not yet.

"Warrior!" said a man sitting on a mid-sized wagon drawn by two large oxen. He had a wife and three children with him, the wagon was unusually long with four wheels a large tarpaulin draped over the rear contents. One of the children, a small boy, sat at the back feet hanging over the side.

The man who had hailed me was encouraging the oxen to greater effort as fighting for space, the wagon laden with what seemed a lifetime's paraphernalia, moved slowly forward yet constantly jostling for advantage.

"My name's Nandrosphi, are you heading to Hedgetown?"

"What business is it of yours?" I asked, looking at him. His wife was scowling and whispering in his ear.

"None at all, sir." He leapt down, passing the reins to his eldest son, marching over, hand outstretched, a cheerful smile on his face.

"But it's a bloody long way, and if you fancy a ride, I could bribe you?" He was cocky and I didn't dislike his approach. "My wife's a bloody marvellous cook," he looked me in the eye, "but don't tell her I said so." He grinned, looking at me whilst hiding his doubt, for he was taking a chance. Glancing down, he observed my mail, and knew that such armour only came to those competent in battle.

"Now why would you want to do that?" I asked, though suspecting I already knew. His wagon would be one of the slower ones, and it was obvious there weren't enough soldiers.

"Can you raise the tarpaulin over the wagon, as shelter against the rain?" I wasn't bothered about getting wet, but even though my chainmail armour was lightly coated with oil, it was still made of iron, and yesterday's drenching had already caused a slight discolouration, the early signs of rust. Chainmail needs regularly rubbing down with sand and cloth.

"It does indeed, master warrior. Give me your name, sir."

So it was that I sat alongside Nandrosphi; we had agreed that I would be fed, and that one of his children would clean my mail each afternoon – half an hour's daily work was sufficient to keep rust at bay. I dared not be without it at night, so the boy would clean during the noon stop, or at other times when the caravan paused along its journey.

So not everyone hates my breed, I thought as I sat there, the seat mercifully sprung, for the wagon pitched and tossed as it remonstrated with every undulation of the street.

"It'll get easier as we get out of town, Miller." He passed me some weed, and asked if I'd tried it before.

I knew of drugs, of herbs and plants used for

medicinal purposes, and said that I needed them not. "My only vice is beer."

"It'll take three days to Hedgetown, shall I send Dan back to get more? For I fear there'll not be enough if you drink heavily."

Now that, I thought was a good idea; the sun was out, the clouds mostly parted, and I had by good fortune found someone that on the face of it might offer decent company. We were approaching the gate, but I could walk faster than this lurching charabanc.

"I'll go," and leaving my pack, sac, axe and cloak behind, for they knew their life depended upon not touching my equipment, I headed down a side street. I had seen the sign 'shambles', and wanted to enjoy this trip. After all, I ate a lot and was hungry.

Looking like a warrior, and I bloody well purposed to be, people moved out of my way, and striding into the slaughter house sought an employee.

"Give me twelve pounds of quality beef, and one cured leg of lamb. Wrap the leg up and the beef salted, you must have some already prepared… Now!"

"Err, oh, err…"

"Now! I'm in a hurry,"

In the end I paid one silver and three copper, whilst they fabricated the order as best they could, seeking out hung beef, and cannibalising another customer's order till mine was right.

I told them to fetch a barrel of beer. "You, lad, he works for you doesn't he?" I asked the older lad in attendance.

"Yes sir, but we don't sell beer, you could try

down the pathway, old Meg may have something to sell."

"You bloody well try down the pathway… and it better be good. Stop pissing me around." I growled and made it perfectly clear that I needed better service.

It was midday, when I set off with a barrel of beer under my arm – for I was immensely strong – the meat slung in a sack.

I couldn't see Nandrosphi's wagon, and after a few minutes a horn sounded and I heard someone say the caravan was underway.

A quarter of a mile farther, my arm was starting to ache but Nandrosphi was just ahead. Looking over his shoulder, he stayed his wagon until I caught up. The sack was loaded and the barrel more carefully heaved aboard.

"Your wife better be a good cook, for I eat like a horse, but I've one spare leg of lamb, and twelve pounds of beef. I've not tested the ale, but it should be potable."

I reached in my pack for the spare leg of lamb I had previously acquired; it was pre-cooked and sold by the same merchant that had provisioned my ration pack. A late breakfast, I offered none to my companion.

According to Tam, the distance to Hedgetown was some thirty-eight miles, but was that as the crow flew, or the road wended? Nandrosphi didn't rightly know, he just knew of it in days and hours. Already the faster parts of the convoy were spreading out. Nandrosphi's wagon having set off in advance of the main column was still near the front, but it was apparent that come nightfall we would be catching up.

His wagon was slow and as I suspected we were passed by all those more fleet afoot, indeed everyone walking was faster. This is why cities are built adjacent to the coast or adjoining a navigable river, overland travel is slow, especially transporting cargo.

Noticing that Nandrosphi drove slightly on the left and that we were being passed by all and sundry, I told him I wanted to sit on his right-hand side, "Better to observe my fellow traveller," but really to be more noticeable by Grimnir, who I feared might pass me and I would go unobserved, I needed to talk.

Nandrosphi explained that he was seeking to establish a fletcher's shop, that is one who makes arrows, for, "There is little need for many fletchers amongst the safe and civilised parts of Culanun." Arrows are required in times of war, which is why he was moving his family to Hedgetown. "Not much need when the enemy is far away."

He bemoaned that bribery and corruption had driven him to despair. "The least competent and most sycophantic have gained business at the expense of our struggling business." Though he assured me he was the finest fletcher in the kingdom.

Now in this I was mildly interested, not because I felt sorry for him, but I wondered how it was managed under Tam's administration, for she had mentioned the very same word when describing the characters that plagued her court.

We left around midday, with the sunset expected four hours before midnight.

"Have you travelled in a caravan before?" I enquired.

"Oh yes, a few, but this is the final leg."

"When do we stop?"

"When I was travelling to…"

"I don't need to know! A simple answer please!" I wasn't trying to fall out with him, I just wasn't that interested in the small talk, not that there was much else.

"Well, typically an hour before sunset, it allows for stragglers to catch up."

"So now?"

"Yes, I guess so. Look ahead, they are already positioning."

I could see the caravan corralling around the road, wagons and persons positioning themselves, none wanting to be on the extremities of the gathering, yet some, the wiser, seeking a good pitch, knowing that after the latecomers arrived they would be left with a fine location yet not belatedly too far from the centre of the ever enlarging camp.

A rider on horseback galloped past; he wore padded armour, and seemed to have a purpose. I stood up, looking back, trying to work out his destination, for this looked like a paid soldier, not a mercenary such as I.

The rider stayed his mount about four hundred yards behind, but it was difficult to see, different sized wagons and mounted parties partially blocking my view.

"Is it safe to leave my possessions in your care?" I asked, for the weather was dry, and I wanted to walk.

"You want to get down?"

"I do. There's no need to stop, I'll find you."

Jumping down, I watched as Nandrosphi's wagon lumbered on; he had experience of camping and it was clear that I would only be a hindrance.

Turning back, I shouted out to his wife. "I want four pounds of steak, it's in the sack." She watched me as I walked away.

Sitting atop a gentle sloping mound I observed as riders galloped to and fro, noticing with increasing certainty the arrival of Grimnir's entourage.

Why did people mass around him? Had they no business of their own, or were these the arseholes of his court? My would-be false friends, surely not all, for some would have relevant business.

My head turned, looking for the direction that Nandrosphi's cart had veered, for it would be easier in an hour or so to find him, all the while waiting for Grimnir's approach.

It took twenty minutes for Grimnir's party to pass, and the sun was setting. I had counted only twenty soldiers, even allowing for possible duplications.

Why were there so few? I would ask at the next opportunity.

"You there! Warrior!" I heard someone shout, but not being subject to anyone nor infringing any law, I remained seated.

"Me or someone else?" I replied, as a young soldier walked forwards, for what purpose I knew not.

Without respect of deference, he stood in front,

blocking my view, enquiring as to my purpose, along with confirmation that I was travelling with the caravan, that is to say, heading towards Hedgetown.

"The Lord Grimnir wants all warriors to attend him tonight, and that unfortunately includes you." Thus said the boy soldier, for he was very young and walked with a swagger, proud and arrogant.

"Clearly being a herald of His Lordship has gone to your head," I said, for I grew tired of insults caused by my ancestry. "But if you were anywhere else I would gut you and feed your entrails to the worms." I hadn't quite finished, but he reached for his sword.

Oh, by the gods, the child's a fool. Standing up, I towered over him, like a storm cloud.

"If you draw that blade you will die." My menace usually cowered most people, but this child soldier felt reinforced by his master's nearby presence.

It has to be said, that I was scarcely an adult, and being given to vanity and not fully immersed in wisdom, I also acted with petulance. A simple 'yes' would have sufficed, but I was an intellectual idiot devoid of wisdom.

The militia man-child drew his sword, waving it under my nose, for he was chastened, embarrassed, but knowing he was probably immune, protected by his master, knowing that no one would forfeit their own life, thus his bravery was reinforced and he felt less in fear.

"You are not welcome here, orc," he said.

And I felled him, muttering words that took three seconds to complete. The child soldier fell as though struck by lightning.

I sat down and awaited the consequence. "Bloody hell." But I knew he was unharmed.

By the time two warriors had dismounted and run the forty feet to my location, the child warrior was rising to his knees, totally bewildered.

"I didn't touch the child," I said most truthfully, for to all that witnessed the encounter my sword had remained at my side, and the art of craft is extremely rare, no one would automatically jump to that conclusion.

"Warrior!" Grimnir's voice rang out. "Are you travelling to Hedgetown?"

"I am, Lord," standing once more and speaking loudly, ignoring the two men with wrath emblazoned upon their faces.

"You are cordially invited to attend me, I am gathering all the soldiers and men competent with a sword, and seeing you, finely attired, would you be kind enough to joint me? For I know not your allegiance."

"Your Lordship is most courteous, it would be an honour. At what hour, Lord?"

The soldiers stood helping their comrade to his feet. For his part he was dazed, but no harm upon his body, for my spell had been to stun, not to kill. Indeed to kill is hard, at least with craft.

"Take the boy away, I think he's drunk," I said to the two soldiers and proceeded to seat myself once more, watching as they assisted their fellow comrade, angry but not sure of the foundation for their wrath.

CHAPTER 5

The meeting with Grimnir was set two hours before midnight. Time enough to rejoin Nandrosphi and be fed.

Before the encounter which I suspected would yet cause me trouble, I had judged with a degree of accuracy the location of my host's cart and heading that way, wondered if Nandrosphi's boast about his wife's cooking would be proven right.

"Ah, Miller," came my companion's voice as I approaching the cart, noticing his campfire thriving in the dry air. There were many such fires springing up, dotted around an approximately ten-acre site.

"What do you think of our position? Will we be safe tonight? Would you like me to change anything? I could…"

I held up my hand to silence him, we were only

some eight miles out from Cragtor, just past the ring of farms that sought protection under the watchfulness of the guards.

Tomorrow would be different; this conflagration, the multitude of smoking stacks were like beacons in the night. Every bandit and fell creature from hell could see this, or smell it. This caravan was like two men hunting, one being stealthy whilst the other sang.

"Tomorrow morning, Nandrosphi, you will be leaving an hour earlier than everyone else, but you are safe tonight, it is tomorrow that the peace will be broken.

"Now in about two hours I have to attend His Lordship, he's gathering the warriors together, and I for my sins have been summoned." Nandrosphi looked impressed, and I hadn't wanted him to be.

"Nandrosphi, everyone with a sword and knowledge of how to use one will be present, it's nothing special. When will my steak be ready? Oh, and by the gods, have you tried the beer yet?" I had forgotten about my cask. I need to get pissed."

"Err, before seeing His Lordship, master?"

"Especially so," but I wouldn't for my wits were finally returning. *Bugger!* I was a bloody fool, But I guess knowing it, is the beginning of wisdom.

During the meal served in wooden bowls, I wondered why Nandrosphi had taken such a chance with me. His two sons and small daughter sat halfway between his wife and the two of us, trying to listen to the conversation, yet whilst they wanted to sit closer, their mother being rightly cautious had commanded they stay clear of me.

"I'm half orc, you should know that we are violent and murderous, there is little to assuage our blood lust, and association with my kind is tantamount to suicide," I tested him. Why did he take the risk?

Nandrosphi looked at me. "You are half orc, for I perceive that, but also half human. Is that not so, master?"

I chose not to answer.

"Master, my family and I stayed last night in Cragtor, and I had the most terrible torment." He bent his head forward, whispering, "My death! Yet not by the hands of an orc, forgive me master, not by your hand.

"I fear I am to die, so terribly real were the shades haunting my sleep." He trembled. "I wish to deny the harbinger of death, for in that wretched sleep, with the nightmare prowling my dreams, you were not present, yet now you sit beside me. Can I thwart the machinations of the gods?"

He was ashen and looked downcast, shaking in the flickering fire light.

"Forgive me, Miller, you don't need the ramblings of an old man, but I just need to say, that when I saw you, my wife did indeed counsel against our association. I wish you no ill will nor mean to place you in harm's way."

I knew never to trust dreams, for a few bad mushrooms could precipitate the most horrendous of phenomenon. "Nandrosphi," he looked up, despair being replaced as he sought to control his emotions, "unless you have the gift of a soothsayer, I would not pay too much attention to shades that haunt us." I said this because I liked the way Nandrosphi addressed me, always respectful.

"We are all subject to torments of the mind." But was I sure? Only this morning had I not also been party to something wholly strange?

My hand touched the ground, with trepidation, but changing my mind, I stood up.

"I need to walk alone for a while."

I had thought to walk to the edge of the camp. I didn't know why, it was perhaps a desire to be away from the fires, smoke and incessant noise of people.

Whilst the camp was not particularly wide in a direct line, the necessity to circumvent each and every pitch doubled the distance travelled from Nandrosphi's location to the perimeter, yet it was interesting to observe the differing constructs of the caravan.

There was an unenforced social order, a separating of individual travellers into their respective social groups, an unsolicited hierarchy. Wealthy larger merchant wagons tended to station near their fellows, and the same was true regarding those farther down the pecking order.

Initially I took a great deal of interest in the techniques used to fasten and secure different types of loads, noting how some wagons were reversed towards the campfires and others longways. Even the pitching of shelter, either tents, or under canopies attached to, or above the wagon in question, whilst some forgoing any protection hoping for a dry night. This was my first experience of such group travel, being new even the most mundane detail had an element of interest.

Slowly arriving at the edge of the camp, I noticed that the deployment of wagons gave way to individual travellers, who camped in collectives, around large communal fires, and some, the more cautious, had appointed a watch roster, although most hadn't. Tonight wasn't going to be a problem, but tomorrow, well, I knew that would be wholly different.

Standing with the caravan encamped behind me, I sat down, the minutes passing by, trying to listen to the night sounds, but with little success. The noise of two hundred people, animals and crackle of fires made it impossible. Still, there was some comfort in the partial abeyance of sound, and then I saw them.

I was too close to flee. For a moment under a waning moon I had questioned whether the shapes in the woods were caused by the mottled effect of leaves casting their shadows as moonlight filtered down onto the heavily matted and bracken-strewn floor, or maybe a family of badgers were disturbing the undergrowth, but then as the seconds ticked by, and the disturbances became more widespread, I knew it was something more sinister.

My axe and helm were still on the wagon, and I cursed my foolishness. Drawing my sword out of the iron-ringed loop, I considered my options. For in front of me crawling, walking and jumping were perhaps a hundred creatures, the appearance matching that of goblins though I wasn't certain having never seen any before.

So it wasn't Nandrosphi's own death he had foreseen, it was mine, but by the gods I would die bringing ruination to these malicious, murderous creatures.

Slowly rising from a seated position, as a giant warrior ascending out of the ground, with my sword clenched firmly and a dagger ready to be drawn, I appeared as a shadowy silhouette to my enemies, a harbinger of death for I bellowed havoc and slaughter, shouting in orcish for it was a related language to goblin, ogre and other cave-dwelling creatures, cursing their miserable hides, warning them that the gods of the underworld had sent me.

Seeking an area where more were clustered together, I uttered my fire spell used once before against Grimnir himself. Speeding from my outstretched left hand a jet of flame sped forth, hurtling towards the group of twenty that were most exposed. It exploded and all hell broke loose.

In the darkness of night, the blinding flash was so bright it lit the night sky as lightening shooting from beneath a dark cloud. The immediate intensity was so great that I myself was momentarily blinded.

The flames engulfed far more than I had hoped, some fifteen fled screaming, carrying the flames throughout their ranks; they could be seen like cinder sparks from a fire, darting to and fro, seeking to escape their torment. This was real fire caused by magic, but no more than that, easily extinguishable, but no help came from their fellows, no succour to the wretched agony these fell creatures suffered, dying slowly as their clothes and hair roasted them alive.

Two more fell to my magical darts, and knowing there was no power of craft left within my body, I drew my dagger.

My bloodlust burst forth, the adrenaline pumping

through my veins, the joy of battle, the triumphant knowledge of skill against an enemy destined to be slaughtered.

Thundering in the ecstasy of battle rage I swang my sword with ferocity, charging the nearest three, for it was better to attack than be surrounded and picked off slowly.

I clove the head and part of a shoulder blade from the first that hesitating, had looked wildly around, seeking support. The blade carrying on its inexorable arc embedded in the breast of a second, both crashing down. Dark blood gushed from the headless goblin, though whether the blood was black, the grey vision that allowed us both to see each other would not reveal.

Running past these two fallen creatures, my left hand thrust a knife in the eye of the third. Panicking, he had tried to turn away, but I caught him in the eye; a scimitar of rusty iron fell from his hand as he bowed his ruined face in his dirt-encrusted hands.

This is it. Give them no time to flank you. Onwards I smote, slashing with such intensity and fury that my mind roared in approval. Another four fell, and they started to waver. Ridiculous for twenty-two or so, still left more than seventy-eight alive. No, not seventy-eight as my thrusting sword speared another. Swinging my knife down, an eyeball still imbedded hard against the quillion, but plenty of room for the knife to impale and crush the skull of the twenty-fourth. The foul creature twitched as I tugged to release the blade.

The group started to scatter, some running forwards, others back towards the wood from whence they came.

I cared not for those fleeing into the wood, there was greater efficiency in slaughtering those that had run forward. They had been abandoned, and in desperation they, turning around, saw death approach.

I ran, my chainmail crashing against my thighs, for there was an abundance of energy, so much strength, mail or no, for weariness could not slow me. The joy of slaughter; by the gods this was easy, as an arrow pierced my lower left leg, and neither stopping for the pain was absent nor in fear did I tarry. Three more were slain and sent to their petty gods.

Where were the rest? Looking around I couldn't see any, for all the others had fled making their escape to the nearest undergrowth.

Twenty-seven lay scattered around, dead or dying, spread over a considerable area as Grimnir, leading a charge of seven warriors burst out of the camp. Blasting his horn, he roared as he ran forwards, a torch held high, and then stopping some forty feet away, burst out laughing.

"Is that it?" He stood there grinning and trying to count. "Only twenty!"

"Fuck off, Lord! There's at least twenty-seven." And there were, for other men arriving with torches scoured the area and piled the dead as a heap; a small cart was summoned to carry me back to the camp.

Not a chance. "I'm walking, sod it," and I limped back, blood dripping from my leg, the arrow head still embedded, although Grimnir had snapped the shaft away leaving some three inches protruding from the arrowhead. It was starting to hurt.

Grimnir leaning over, whispered privately, "Men will think you're a hero. I can honour you, for that would only be seemly. Perhaps we can get drunk."

"Have you got any of Tam's salve?" I asked, not remembering whether I had any concealed in my pack.

"Oh, it's barely a scratch, stop making a fuss." He laughed, and after a pause, "We might have a spare scoopful."

Ten guards were posted and positioned around the perimeter, with instructions to patrol, and signal if trouble was forthcoming, yet Grimnir told me that this was only needed as reassurance for the merchants.

"They won't be back tonight, maybe not at all, but it is a worry, they are too far north. Tam will need to send out more patrols, this is her territory." Grimnir looked thoughtful. "You've done bloody well, your actions saved lives tonight, you gave them a frightful scare."

The meeting with Grimnir went ahead, albeit with only the most senior fighters present along with some ordinary mercenaries. He wanted to compliment me publicly and importantly wanted the other warriors encouraged and motivated by my skills.

My wounds were attended to in Grimnir's tent; the arrow was extracted, and a teaspoonful of salve applied, held in place with a bandage. There was really nothing more to do for it was the only place I had been injured, my left calf just below the knee and a few inches above the boot.

"Lucky shot," said Torak, one of Grimnir's more

competent soldiers.

"Doesn't feel lucky to me," I said but not ungraciously for I was glad of the cushions as I lay propped up against the centre pole of the tent's pitched roof, a pitcher of ale in my hand.

Soldiers and others chatted amongst themselves, a few complimenting me and asking for details of the battle, which I said wasn't a battle, just a small flurry of activity, scarcely a skirmish. "Nothing really." And boasting slightly, I said I had wished they'd fought harder and hadn't run away so quickly.

Grimnir plied me with beer and offered to let me rest in his tent that night. I cheerfully accepted though I asked if a servant might enquire of Nandrosphi, advising that I would be travelling with his family the following morning.

The servant stood in front of me and made notes as I dictated my instructions.

"Nandrosphi, you are to leave the camp an hour earlier than the main body, this is essential, without fail, it's important. Collect me from Lord Grimnir's tent before departure, you will be expected. No arguing, I will break camp with your family. Oh, and breakfast is required, your wife is indeed a splendid cook."

I insisted the brief message was spoken back to me, before dismissing the servant.

"Got a friend already?" asked Torak. "You've only just arrived in Cragtor, it must be hard to build associates."

"Torak, I have something to say to you."

"Please speak your mind, Miller." He looked slightly surprised at my priming of a statement.

"Some people are ignorant, rude and act like peasants, avoiding the company of half-orcs, but Nandrosphi isn't one of them. He has never disparaged nor insulted me for my ancestry." I wished I hadn't started this sentence, but now I needed to finish. "No, he's not a friend, just an acquaintance, but I'll see him and his family safely to Hedgetown, for I owe him a little and he will owe me a lot.

"Tell us, Lord," I said, looking at Grimnir, "is this typical, or can we expect more capable opponents before we reach Hedgetown?"

The other soldiers fell silent, for it was clear that they wanted to know the answer as much as I, and some were somewhat reverential in their attitude towards me, each man wondering how they themselves might have fared.

"Possibly similar, but goblins allied with orcs, better led, or wildmen with war hounds, it's unlikely that anything more substantial will trouble us. Of course, though I doubt it, we may have seen the worst."

"Miller, excuse me! My name's Charsin."

Charsin wore tired boots, a padded leather jerkin, and a sword, that seemed old yet serviceable. He was perhaps aged forty, his hair thinning, and he squinted at anyone farther away than ten feet. The poor fellow looked lean, but more from necessity rather than choice.

"I'm not in the employ of His Lordship, and am simply travelling down to Hedgetown to offer my services to farmsteads and anyone who will pay my board and modest remuneration. Some of the merchants have shown interest in hiring me, but with your achievements, and how you dispatched the goblins, I'm sure you would have no difficulty in gaining similar employment. What are your plans?"

Several soldiers shuffled their feet, embarrassed by the question. Did Charsin feel that he had a similar competence to Miller?

Torak looked at Charsin, and glanced at me, then stepped out of the tent. "Excuse me a minute, Lord."

He might as well not have bothered for we could all hear him trying to contain his laughter. People looked at one another, grinning yet better able to control themselves.

Now I, Miller, under normal circumstances would have sworn at Charsin, possibly thumped him and certainly would have laughed too, for the question was absurd. Not this time, for having only moments before gently rebuked Torak, I was not now going to align myself, besmirching this humble warrior of dubious skill and a limited future. So I answered the question with sincerity and directness.

"Thank you, but no, Charsin, if Lord Grimnir doesn't counsel against it, I will head for the hills and hunt down wildmen, kill their hounds, raze their dwellings and wrest back that which was plundered. A thief cannot complain when the honour is returned. But, I wish you success in anything you choose."

Charsin, still oblivious to his differing ability and status then went on to ask the one question I had hoped would remain unasked.

"How did you manage to burn so many of the goblins? For they seemed to have been roiled in fire." I wasn't prepared to answer.

After a long pause I stumbled, searching the lessons taught in my earlier studies, trying to recall stories of none magical fire. There was something, but despite my efforts it remain shrouded, my mind unable to recall.

"It was part of my, err… training."

"What!" interrupted Grimnir. "They taught you the use of phosphorous bags, those that explode and spout fire on impact? That was a profligate use of resource." Grimnir had understood quite well my dilemma for his many years of association with Tam had honed his guile. The discretion was perfect, and timing impeccable.

But gathering my wits, as an actor recovers his lines on a stage, I seamlessly reinforced the misdirection.

"But nigh on impossible to replace, unless you know a competent alchemist, Lord?"

"Alas, Miller, I don't, it's not really my field of expertise." He pondered, hesitating in thought, as though putting effort into the conundrum, a feint. "But they are as you have shown useful tools in battle."

Charsin seemed satisfied with the explanation as did all present, though he would have talked, more, for I suspected there was no end to his desire to control the conversation.

After a few more irrelevancies and opinions proffered by Charsin, I grew bored. "Enough,

Charsin! Lord Grimnir, has an agenda to discuss, and I have other matters on my mind." I shut him down. It was clear Charsin given any encouragement would talk incessantly.

Grimnir's tent was of a large hexagonal design, the central pole which I leant against being the only means of support, screens separated the main area from ancillary chambers, servants passed in and out, interrupting, till Grimnir bellowed, "Get out! And stay out until I give the word otherwise." And after waiting for everyone to leave, "Tomorrow, we can expect problems. The caravan consists of approximately two hundred and twenty souls and will, because of its size, be too great an opportunity for bandits not to try their luck."

"Were we not expecting trouble tonight, Lord?" asked Elranir, a sergeant in Grimnir's command.

I belched far too loudly, and mumbled some apology, remembering Thrandar's annoying counsel.

"Yes, its newly brewed, not stale yet," said Grimnir, looking at me with a slight scowl. "No, Elranir, they were totally unexpected, and as I mentioned to Miller earlier, the Lady Bluebottle will need to consider her actions. The attack was worryingly close to town."

There was a murmur of agreement.

"We aren't expecting serious opposition from the north surely, Lord," Torak spoke, "for with the troubles in the Marshlands and the constant potential difficulties with your brethren in the Grey Mountains, we're hard stretched in our facilities to cope."

"Torak, not every dwarf is hostile, and relations

with our eastern neighbours are not in jeopardy. Indeed we are more likely to be offering them assistance than worrying about any potential difficulties there."

"Nonetheless these, as always are difficult times. We must be vigilant, has it not always been so?"

"Err, if you say so, Lord."

It was clear that he didn't think so, and it was unlike Grimnir to gloss over difficulties. I was listening.

"...And I have found six additions, as you requested, wholly unconnected, new arrivals," finished Torak.

"Excellent, where are they?"

"Patrolling, and in need of remuneration," quickly adding, "they are, after all, new," to reinforce the reasonableness of his comment. "We could start recruiting locally, if the incentive is right."

"There are lots of ways to incentivise. How's the training course doing? It's been several months."

"Excellent, Lord, the militia are much improved. Roderick has been thorough and diligent, though men are looking forward to your direction, and we do need to sort out the rosters. Some leave has been delayed, and equipment needs to be sourced," and scratching his chin he added, "Zolpetre has been thrifty. There are, alas, issues."

I listened; the pain in my leg, annoying though it was, was dissipating. Tam's salves were possibly magical, although whilst I sensed no dweomer they succeeded in slightly numbing pain after a few hours, and the effects were second only to healing by craft.

I pondered… *Tam's cream must be sought after.* I learnt later that people travelled great distances and paid huge sums of money for what I had taken as abundant medicine available to everyone. It wasn't.

So easily had I transposed between a peasant with attitude, no social graces, no clothes, no boots to call my own, to one that sat in the company of the most powerful and joked about wounds and the cost of chainmail. Was Grimnir short of money?

I had one hundred and seventy-five half silver coins given to me by Tam plus about one hundred and forty-eight silver and sixteen gold coins, recovered from Joe's hidden stash. Approximately five hundred and fifty-five whole silver pieces, though much was broken down into smaller coins. Still a considerable sum. Did Grimnir need the cash? Whilst I had spent some of the silver, the majority was preserved.

Grimnir had given me a wealth of equipment, and Tam had said half of the armoury was probably his. I was perplexed. And tonight I had so many questions. Barely two days absence from his and Tam's company and I was already missing the ready ease of conversation enjoyed whilst ignorant, free in spirit, without deception, without the guile required to conceal friendship.

"Never run a kingdom, or a town," I said aloud. My subconscious had allowed the words to slip my lips, for it chimed with the environment and was not at discord with current discussions.

Elranir said he agreed, and hoped that he would

never be promoted, for being a sergeant allowed him access to his lord, yet without the complications of management or diplomacy.

"Ah! Yes Miller, for my part there is contentment being only an ignorant fighter in my lord's service. I am free from the burdens of administration and worry, bellowing at new recruits is satisfaction enough."

It was well said, for it flattered Grimnir, yet didn't require an answer.

The discussion then focussed on keeping the column together and with only twenty-two fighters, there would be difficulties; stragglers would need protecting for problems always arose and the sergeants needed to know their duty and options available, which protocols to follow.

"Tis a shame you will be out of action for a few days," Torak said, looking at me, "for you would make a difference in any fight should we become hard pressed."

"Well if the healer's work is well done, I will be up and about this time tomorrow, but regardless I'll not be leaving all the glory to you and the others."

"If you say so, Miller, but I think you are putting on a brave face, for that wound whilst not serious still looked nasty." He nodded towards my leg. "There's the chance of infection. Regardless, infected or not, I don't expect you to be running for a few days, maybe even weeks," and he added with alacrity, "I'll let you know how we get on, and how splendid I've been. After all, you've set an inspiring example tonight."

Finally, after rather mundane details it was sometime after midnight and the company bid me a peaceful night's rest, and took their leave of Lord Grimnir and I.

Waiting for everyone to get out of earshot, and refreshing my tankard...

"Well done, Miller," said Grimnir. "How was your first day of independence? I admit to being worried when that soldier started wagging a blade under your nose, and even more so when he collapsed in a heap. What was it all about?"

"Oh! He was rude, it was all a bit banal." I reached over and helped myself to some bread and cheese.

"You know, Grimnir, one of the things about not being confined, is that when you and Tam are not looking, I can really teach idiots like that boy soldier a proper lesson. I get fed up being on my best behaviour, it's really quite constraining.

"Tam said something along those lines, about freedom, liberty. I wasn't sure you would actually be joining us, and was delighted to see you perched on top of that hill. Is everyone giving you grief? Apart from your travelling companions, because a few more performances like today, and I bet the next time you walk into an inn someone will offer to buy you a drink."

"Oh yes! Talking of treatment, where were you when I tried to get back into town after Tam had transported me outside? Your bloody useless guards wouldn't let me in until I bribed them."

"Ha! Not my guards, but I suppose you didn't walk back with Tam; that would have defeated the whole point, so how much did they demand from you?"

"They didn't demand anything, bloody well ignored me until I made such a racket they told me to piss off." I scratched behind my ear. "I had to offer a silver piece, though I gave them one half... There were four of them. At least they drew their swords, I suppose that's something."

"I'll mention it to Tam. She will know who was on duty."

"Grimnir, are you skint at the moment? I know you are rich beyond my dreams, but I remember you telling Tam you needed to replenish your funds before we headed off to Castle Quay, which by the way, we still haven't been to."

"Well, only temporarily, but you needn't worry. Running a town is expensive, and Hedgetown tends to cost more than it generates, but yes, you're right, I'm not shy of funds, at least not when I get back."

"I have a few hundred silver if you want it." I owed Grimnir far more, even though he said he hadn't wanted paying for the armour. None other than Tam and Grimnir would have gained my money given without profit.

"No, no thanks, it's just better to let others realise that silver comes from mines and commerce, not grown on trees. People have a habit of asking for more if they perceive an abundance."

I shrugged, and...

"How the hell do you have a few hundred silver? Unless it's back wages from Joe. I hadn't realised he'd paid you anything?"

Grimnir looked surprised and suspicious. "Have

you been behaving badly?"

"Always," I joked. "But it was due me, so I took it."

"Aha! Well, it's to be expected. How much did you get?"

"Not enough, but sufficient to flee and survive had Tam not rescued me."

"Talking of which, when will you see her again?"

I explained my problem, the surprise and difficulty I'd experienced when preparing my spell.

The preparation can be done anytime, but being drunk was not wise so looking at my beer I decided to make this the last one, for in a few hours' time I would need to concentrate and wasn't looking forward to the experience.

Grimnir hesitated. "I can speak to Tam with ease when we reach Hedgetown, but in an emergency, and I take it that it isn't?" He looked at me questioningly. "I could try at other times, but only when critical." He coughed, grumbled, and said, "Magic, you know the sort, limited use, emergencies only."

"When we get to our destination, do you have any problems with my suggestion of hunting for wealth amongst the brigands?"

In truth I had no alternative plans, but didn't want to be under any headship. The urge to gain wealth and power was burning within, and tonight's skirmish had only reinforced the allure. The adrenaline rush, the fay spirit so long held back, desperately wanting to break loose.

"No, none at all, but please leave the farmers alone

and don't become a highwayman yourself, it's bad for me, bad for business, and I would be forced to confront you." He looked at me, seeking reassurance, hoping not to see an expression that might cause concern. "Any problem with what I've said?"

I smiled. "Such easy picking, that's why they all do it! Just a bad joke, don't worry."

"Worry? I've enough of that already, but it's fair to say any activity that causes distress to my enemies would be a blessing for me."

We talked about the risks involved in travelling alone, the likely inhabitants of the fells and hills both north and east of Hedgetown, along with allies that may be found; not everyone in the wild was deserving of slaughter.

"Oh, and I thought dwarves can see in the dark, like myself, so why the torch?"

"My eyesight in twilight is good, even in the pitch black of a moonless sky I can see better than men, though not as well as you I suspect, but it wasn't for my benefit, indeed the torch makes my night vision worse, probably the same for you? But men needed to see where I was." He downed his beer, and called for a servant.

"You can come back in, Miller will be resting here tonight," he said as three servants and a soldier entered.

"The caravan leaves early, about seven in the morning, so I guess you'll need waking an hour before then?"

"Bloody hell, that won't leave enough time." I

paused. "No, better make it two and a half hours before. I will need to meditate and prepare, err…" looking around, in the company of others it would be so easy to slip up, "err… my equipment," I finished.

"There will be little rest for either of us, Lord, but at least there's a chance I can sleep on the wagon."

"Sod all chance of that, Miller," Grimnir mused.

A creature let loose, destined to harm, to murder, to slaughter, yet perversely wanting to preserve the life of Nandrosphi and his family and trying not to bend my leg. Grimnir was right, there was no chance of sleeping, yet the leg was resting, allowing the wound to heal.

CHAPTER 6

Nandrosphi had arrived as instructed an hour earlier than the caravan was due to depart, and coming towards Grimnir's tent had become stuck fast between competing carts. Torak had ordered others to clear the way, and after a ten-minute delay we were lurching along the road, not the first to leave.

Sprawled on top of the tarpaulin which once again had been lowered flat, Nandrosphi having given the reins to his eldest son, was eager to hear the news.

"Apparently there was an attack on the caravan last night," he said, waving vaguely in the wrong direction. "Did you find out any more about it? His Lordship's men drove them off."

He seemed worried yet reassured that the battle had been so decisively won for rumour had spread around the camp that whilst the battle was hard fought, the guards had despatched the enemy with barely any casualties, and noticed my bandage.

"Oh, Miller," he looked sombre, "were you involved? What injury have you suffered? And…"

"Yes, Nandrosphi, I was there and it wasn't a big deal. My injury is very slight, and I don't want to talk about it… Have you kept me some breakfast?"

An hour later, I heard a distant horn, and saw two gallopers heading towards Grimnir's group, one with a very young soldier who spotting me, kept his head down. Other horsemen were heading up to meet them.

"Greetings, Miller," and I saw Elranir slowing his horse as he converged. He and five companions were riding slowly towards the front.

"Is there any trouble, Elranir?" I asked, for I was inexperienced with the concept of scouting.

"None yet," he said, "and perhaps we may get lucky, what with last night. How's the leg doing?"

"Fine, I'll be running after you within the day."

"Ha! I think hopping maybe, but all's well this morning." Je spurred his horse forwards.

Nandrosphi was listening, bursting with questions, but he restrained himself, looking around and periodically glancing at me, hoping I might become more loquacious.

My mood wasn't good, for once again the song had started as a hurricane, too deep, dragging me down into the rapture. The intensity had threatened to overthrow my mind. Lying on Grimnir's floor, and unbeknownst to all, I had endured a mental battle so wearisome, so exhausting, that having gleaned the threads and connections of my craft and escaped to consciousness, I would not be revisiting, not at least until Tam knew and gave counsel.

Dan, Nandrosphi's son, clambered over towards me, careful not to touch my leg, and asked whether it would be a good time to clean my mail. He could've asked without moving, but he was in awe of me, never having seen a warrior, nor a half-orc; it was the same curiosity that people show when they saw an elf for the first time. But it didn't bother me, even Nandrosphi's wife, who usually kept her distance and tried not to speak, was behaving herself.

On this wagon, I knew my place as did they.

"No, lad! I think today I shall keep it on," for regardless of the hour, my wits when combined with intelligence made a powerful concoction, and I was keen for battle. I relished the thought, and battle could come at any time.

As the day progressed it seemed to drag. I flexed my leg; the pain had gone but knowing from experience that twelve hours minimum was required, I resisted the urge to jump down and walk. It had started to rain, so Nandrosphi raised the tarpaulin over wooden arches that were themselves fixed to the sides of the wagon.

"Is it necessary, Nandrosphi?" I asked. "It'll restrict our view if trouble comes."

"Master, whatever you instruct, but I thought it was my duty to keep you dry?"

I left them raised, for the rain grew heavy and there were others around who would assist with spotting any potential enemy.

By midday, the rain eased and the hood was lowered yet Nandrosphi kept the wooden frame in situ.

"It'll be easier and faster should the weather turn once again."

People passed us by, and we were falling behind; the oxen though mighty in strength seemed weary and up ahead people were stopping.

"Is there a problem on the road?" I asked, standing to gain a better view.

"No master, I think it's just to allow people to catch up. The animals are tired, and we can use this opportunity to give them some feed and water, I've nosebags hung on the side of the wagon."

"Do we need to stop? I'm not happy delaying."

"The oxen need the rest, master, but I'll be as quick as possible, still half an hour minimum is best."

Master, he called me Master or Miller, as deference dictated, and for a moment I comprehended why Grimnir didn't always like being called 'Lord'.

Acquiescing to Nandrosphi's wisdom, I climbed down and tested my leg. Pleasantly surprised that the wound didn't hurt nor was the muscle tight, I strode gently around. Okay, it wasn't cured, not yet, but much improved.

Untying the bandage, I could see pink skin had formed over the arrow's entry point, only eleven hours earlier a jagged hole in my calf.

Torak and two others rode up and stopped alongside. "What the hell are you doing walking about?" He seemed stern yet not unfriendly.

"It's almost healed," I said, turning to show him. "It was after all only a small arrow."

"Crap!" He dismounted and walked over, looking down. "How the hell did you heal that fast? Are…" and he considered his words carefully, "All half-orcs blessed with miraculous powers of recuperation?"

"Not as far as I'm aware, just a little of Lady Bluebottle's ointment that Lord Grimnir gave me," I said nonchalantly, but looking at my wound, I was rather pleased if not surprised at the spectacular improvement.

"By the gods, that was generous. Damned expensive stuff, but I suppose," and he hesitated, "you earned it." He drew a deep breath. "Worth a bloody fortune."

"Really?" For never having considered the cost, I had no idea. "How much is a fortune?" I asked, slightly taken aback.

"Priceless! Too bloody much, I don't know, but more than I earn in a year, probably, that's if you can find any."

I thought to myself, *How ignorant am I? It's strange how you appreciate something more when the cost rises.*

Nandrosphi, aided by his two sons, was releasing the oxen from their yoke, whilst his daughter was filling two nosebags with grain and hay; his wife carried a wooden pail away from the road, she had spotted a small stream, some yards off.

"They'll need water," she said, noticing that I watched her.

There was no need for alarm, others were milling

around doing similar chores, and a steady stream of people walked across the heather, avoiding the gorse. Still I was wary, and climbing back on the wagon stood watching.

There may be no advantage in attacking a few people for monetary gain, but wild animals were entirely another matter.

Whilst watching and becoming reassured that no matters were amiss, I marvelled at the majesty of the mountain range, the Grey Mountains, home to dwarves, their white-topped summits forming a line, an impregnable barrier. What lay on the other side? Pondering, I tried to recall the stories clerics told during my years of captivity.

Nandrosphi's wife returned with the pail slopping water over the side, and I lost interest in the others. "Is it just the animals who get fed?" I asked as she watered each ox in turn.

"I'll find something, Miller, but we normally eat twice daily. If..." and she paused, "you can't wait"

Git! I thought.

Her comment whilst not rude, was inappropriate. Or did I simply resent normal interaction? After a few minutes sulking I considered my thoughts churlish. *Is everyone to either hate me or respect me?*

Patiently I sat watching the stragglers catch up, as Nandrosphi started to oil the yoke, hoop and harness, waterproofing the wood and leather. "It'll keep the wood sound, Miller," he said before scraping tallow on the axle, looking for signs of wear and finally finishing he turned in my direction.

"The trouble is," he said as he climbed aboard and sat next to me, "is that those in front will now be rested and eager to press on, whereas these poor souls," looking behind, "will need to wait and rest as we have done."

"I know what I would do," and noticing Elranir, some distance away, intended to suggest it to him, should he come closer.

"What would you do, Miller?" Nandrosphi scratched under his tunic trying to dislodge something that ought not be there.

"I'd tell the bastards that the soldiers are staying here for thirty minutes longer, and if they set off without us, they are on their own."

Watching and having calculated that we had travelled some seven to eight miles yesterday, approximately six miles thus far today, and another seven or so miles this afternoon, we would be midway to our destination, exactly where Grimnir said the greatest peril lay.

"You see around us, great wagons piled high with wealth, cloth, silks, spices, and suchlike. The horses and wagons themselves are worth a small fortune, regardless of what they carry. Where do you consider the greatest wealth lies?" I looked at my host, for I was calculating how I might rob this train, securing a fortune.

"Well," he scratched his chin, "I would suppose those three," he pointed off to the right, some three hundred yards farther up. "The large wagons that have stayed close to each other during the trip, they seem to have hired two guards of their own, I guess they might have the most to lose."

"They are certainly the most obvious," I conceded, yet wondering if it wasn't some of the single travellers mounted upon swift steeds. There were two or three that fitted that description, staying close to Grimnir's party, carrying what? Maybe gold, silver or gems, precious items that needed no showy display, and in the guise of pilgrims, holy men, or nondescript character. Their horses were fleet of foot.

If I were to rob this caravan, I would need to know who or what to attack before launching my assault. What would I do? I mused to myself. *Knowledge is power, knowledge is everything. I would already know what I was going to do, so the enemy must likewise.*

My host started to distract my thoughts, so I raised a hand, and getting the message Nandrosphi fell silent.

I'd sabotage my target vehicle, allow the caravan to be stretched, then create a diversion, a faint attack at the front, thus drawing off any guards. Goblins just wanted slaughter, hence the frontal attack, but men, even orcs were more cunning. Did I analyse too much?

"I need to walk."

"We'll be leaving in ten minutes." Nandrosphi looked down but didn't add anything else, knowing I was contemplative.

My helm and axe were with me, though the backpack containing my silver was left on the wagon along with the cloak. It's hard to conceal a war axe slung over your shoulders. My sword hung at my side, and a sheathed dagger.

There would be someone, or persons already in the train spying and ready to act.

The three largest wagons were the most obvious, and I headed towards them.

If it were me I would poison the horses, or disable a wheel. I'd already decided the individual riders would be hard to prioritise with any degree of certainty, but these great wagons were the ones. My host was probably right, they were the obvious choice.

Who would attack? Grimnir had mentioned wildmen, or orcs leading goblins.

Now whilst not disparaging my own parentage, it has to be acknowledged that orcs are not the brightest luminaries in the firmament, but a few orcs were also weak sorcerers, so not totally devoid of intelligence? However, of wildmen I knew nothing, they were men so presumably the least predictable.

As I approached the three largest wagons, they seemed to have assistants, servants of their own, or perhaps apprentices for they were preparing to leave and readying in a swift, practised manner.

Crouching down, there were about twelve in the party including the two hired arms, and watching, it was impossible to see if any of their party appeared less savoury than the others. Obviously the hired soldiers did, but that was expected. Eventually one of the merchants became uncomfortable with my watching, and crying out, challenged me.

"What's your business, warrior?" he said in a way that meant I wasn't welcome.

A perfectly reasonable reaction, I wouldn't want a

half-orc warrior staring at my possessions, eyeing up the situation, but I didn't reply.

I carried on looking, just watching until the merchant, becoming too unnerved called over the hired guards.

They walked over towards me, trying to project an intimidatory presence, and indeed the largest of them looked thuggish. He was about five foot five inches tall, which was average, but looked mean, ill-tempered and with scars and tattoos on his face plus a crooked nose, he was obviously used to using his fists.

"Draw your swords and you'll regret it," I growled, yet stood up.

He didn't draw a weapon, but walked up too close, menacing, only a foot from my face.

"What are you doing?" But without actually waiting for a response, "My master wants you to piss off, he doesn't like your sort," and predictably he added, "and neither do I."

"Frankly I couldn't give a damn about you or your master's opinion, but I'm staying where I am and I'll watch your wagons as long as I like." But I looked down at him and said, "I'll kill the first one of you that so much as touches his weapon."

He didn't like my confidence, for he was used to the situation being reversed and was wroth, loath to back down. He with his companion stood staring at me, and I thought, *'God, does my breath stink like that?* until after a few seconds his courage gave way, and he stepped back, turned and walked away mumbling something about 'security'.

The merchants carried on, glancing at me nervously until observing a small party of soldiers, one of the merchants called them over.

None of the soldiers were known to me but clearly I was the focus of attention for there were 'nods of head' in my direction, and the soldiers looked me up and down.

I started walking around the wagons observing the wheels and the draught horses, all looked fine, the horses showed no signs of ill health for I had knowledge of animal husbandry.

The soldiers left and another different merchant approached, introducing himself as Janras.

"Miller is it?" He hesitantly held out his hand, but I didn't take it.

"Don't shake hands unless there's cause," I said, but without anger.

"The soldiers say you slew the party of goblins that attacked the camp last night."

I ignored the comment, there was no point in answering, but instead asked, "Tell me, Janras, how long have you known your fellow travellers?"

In a little bewilderment Janras answered that all the party were known to each other for several years, they regularly travelled together. "For security, it's wise to stick together."

"And the armed men, you've known them a while?"

Janras sensing there might be a problem started prevaricating.

"Just answer please, it's possibly for your own

benefit."

"About three days, err, why?"

"Do you trust them? For I don't... How did you find them?"

Janras said they had introduced themselves and for a very modest fee and free food, had offered to provide protection.

He started to make excuses. "They were travelling down to Hedgetown anyway, it seemed a mutually beneficial arrangement for all of us." He seemed worried, and for well he might.

Idiot! So bloody easily deceived, I thought, but changing the subjected started reassuring Janras that there was nothing to fear from **me,** *Probably truthfully,* and after a little small talk left Janras's company and headed back to my wagon.

So that's probably where the trouble will start, I should warn Grimnir even though it's still only a fifty-fifty chance. I hadn't liked what I'd seen.

My small interaction had delayed the three wagons' departure, but not by much, and as I returned I found Nandrosphi had left. *Good.*

Looking around I could see his oxen struggling up an incline. The beasts were painfully slow but incredibly strong, and it would be no hardship to catch up, even with a leg not quite healed, but I wanted to find Grimnir, and at least report my suspicions real or imaginary.

Grimnir was as always surrounded by opportunists and some who actually had justifiable cause to be present.

"Lord! Have you a moment?" I said as I caught sight of him; he was climbing into a saddle. Grimnir turned around hearing a familiar voice.

"Is that the warrior who drank my beer last night?" he shouted over the din and cacophony of sounds.

"It is, Lord, and I return with appreciation and thanks for making a humble warrior so welcome. Have you a minute, Lord?"

"Aye, come over here, Miller." Approaching, he told everyone to give the invalid some room. I started limping slightly.

"Lord." He leaned down for our difference in height was not so great, and I recounted my meeting with Janras, admitting the circumstances and my suspicions, whilst not set in stone, were still possibly sound.

"Splendid! Miller, glad you're much improved, I'll be passing your wagon in a couple of hours. Have a sound and safe journey." He said no more, but I knew my concerns were not dismissed.

Allowing for Nandrosphi's travel at one and a quarter miles an hour depending on terrain, and my less than perfect walking style, it would be more than two hours before I could catch up. Grimnir would reach me too soon, I quickened my pace.

After an hour walking along the unpaved road, churned up by the passing traffic and earlier rain, my leg started to ache slightly.

Several wagons, those drawn by horse, were faster than me, yet none seemed willing to assist and I was developing a temper.

"How's the leg?" a voice enquired and turning around I saw Torak trotting up behind. "You seem to be limping."

"It's fine or will be in an hour or so, I started walking too soon, and my wagon is still some way off."

"Get a bloody lift from some of these faster carts," he said. "Like this one." He waved at the nearest traveller who scowled, trying to encourage his two mules to quicken their pace.

"You try getting a lift, I'm considered dangerous and half-orcs smell apparently."

"True on both accounts," he joked, "but I'll sort it."

He quickening his pace, caught the reigns of the one of the two mules, staying the animal so the cart slowed to a halt.

"You," he said, pointing to the man to whom the cart belonged, "will allow this man to sit on the rear." There was some protest about the weight and lack of room and fragile items, but Torak was firm and threatened to send his cart to the back of the caravan if he didn't comply.

*

Catching up and sitting once more on Nandrosphi's wagon, I tried to catch half an hour's sleep and whilst Grimnir had said such a thing was impossible, I did manage to doze off.

Three hours later I awoke, and much to my annoyance had missed Grimnir. *Sod it.* It was now approaching seven hours before midnight; we would be corralling in approximately three hours.

"Have you seen those three large wagons recently?" I enquired.

"They passed me earlier and will be well ahead of us by now, we have been a little slow. The haw ox is struggling, I'll need to take care these next four miles. I'm sorry Miller, we may be one of the last in."

That wasn't good, tonight we needed to be in the middle. *Shit!*

"What's wrong with the animal?" I didn't hide my concern. "Is there any way to speed up?"

"We rightly needed more of a rest at the noon stop, and unfortunately everyone is driving their animals as fast as they can, no one wants to be last." Nandrosphi looked at me anxiously for he well knew the risk and was hoping I could reassure him.

Bugger. And I was planning how to prepare for a lousy position. "When we arrive I want you to stay at the rear, but as close to the road as possible; the scouts will be patrolling and it's the sides of the camp which will be most hazardous." I looked him in the eye. "The rear road is the least dangerous." And then I thought. "But if you want to leave me here with the wagon and move to the centre, you can. There will be no campfire this far from the centre."

"But a fire will keep wild creatures at bay, and provide us with warmth, and…"

"And also signal your position. Can you see in the dark?" I knew he couldn't. "Well goblins and orcs can, so the fire disadvantages you, for you cannot see out. Creatures of the night will see you regardless."

I searched the sky. Would there be a moon? Would it rain? Just how dark would it be? *Bloody hell.*

Nandrosphi looked miserable; the prospect of sleeping in the open without a fire surrounded by the empty moorland troubled him, as well it ought.

Should I move him towards the centre? Nandrosphi, wife and children maybe a distraction, impede my judgement. *Yes, I will.* And I did.

At around four hours before midnight, we rejoined the body of the camp. Nandrosphi wanted to skirt to the left and try and squeeze closer to what he perceived as a more advantageous position, except I knew it wasn't and in the end he took my counsel.

We stayed the wagon ten feet from the edge of the road, the last in line. The most northerly, stranglers shuffled past us but I wanted to be near the patrolled road.

The oxen were allowed an hour to feed on the coarse grasses with particular attention to the least healthy animal. The beasts were watered using existing store, for there was no wandering off road in search of a stream.

Less than three hours before midnight, for I also insisted on being fed, the temporary fire was extinguished and looking up I observed the moon scarcely a sliver being obscured by passing clouds.

Nandrosphi fussed around his belongings, secured the tarpaulin to conceal most of his possessions, all he owned in the world, and I was patient understanding his anxiety.

Eventually I led them inwards towards Grimnir's

position, fully laden. My back pack and cloak were worn and I looked like a deformed character, a massive hunch on my back, but I cared not for my appearance.

After the first one hundred yards it became easier for other fires dotted around provided sufficient light for humans to see and reaching somewhere near the middle, adjacent to a soldiers' encampment and not far from Grimnir, I settled them down, telling the soldiers to leave them alone, someone recognised me, it was sufficient.

Few wished to leave their wagons unguarded and as I headed back fearful glances were passed in my direction; it was going to be a sleepless night. Some soldiers looked at me, one even greeted. I didn't know him, but I guessed they had all heard of the skirmish the night before. I wasn't going to be the only one not sleeping.

Arriving at the last campfire I found a priest with a slow-moving cart that had become stuck in mud earlier and was now paying the price for coming in last. In meditation, no doubt praying to his little god.

I looked up the north road from whence we had come. Nandrosphi's wagon stood alone as a forlorn sentinel, seemingly inviting, ready to be plundered, yet with the greatest protection of all, me!

It was slightly difficult to locate a dry area of heather on which to lie down but eventually I secured a suitably elevated spot, my back resting against a high-sided slab of rock, an overhang some fifteen feet tall. Draping my cloak over my mail and placing my great two-handed axe to one side, I settled down for a long night.

Now despite being quick to anger, I was actually in many ways patient, so as the hours passed I found my thoughts drifting but amiably through some of the lessons in craft that Tam had recommended I need to remember, 'So it becomes second nature to you,' she had said.

There was movement by the wagon. I had caught it in the corner of my eye, but watching it turned out to be a badger, followed by another and then a third. Good, for these creatures were wary and it boded well.

The night passed slowly and mercifully without rain. I could see across the moors, the far side of the road, and looking northwards there was nothing heading our way. Nothing disturbed the peace, the night was still, yet a small alarm sounded in the distant subconscious part of my brain. I became pensively engaged, attuned to the stillness; nothing was wrong, but that was it, there should always be something.

My hand hovered over the ground, so instinctively did I want to, not just touch, but listen to the song, scarcely caressing the ground as though testing my control. I could sense the power, the sensual pleasure, only needing to let my mind go, but I dare not, my mind had momentarily almost drifted, it would be so easy to fall.

Time passed slowly, and I must have been wrong for whilst all seemed too quiet I forgave my heightened senses. I had expected trouble and figments of imagination had sought to misdirect my mind. I had simply overanalysed; maybe Grimnir was right and we had seen the worst of it already. Tomorrow we would travel in day light, and by nightfall, we would be well within the guarded territory of Hedgetown's soldiers.

Looking around the road was quiet, the moors devoid of trespass, and the badgers had gone. An owl screeched overhead, its flight silent, just the cry catching me off guard. There was someone walking near Nandrosphi's wagon. I watched.

He wasn't a shadow, for I could see him clearly, albeit the details of his face too far away, but the manner of his circling the wagon, as a thief might stalk a provisioner, looking for opportunity. It wasn't Nandrosphi for the mannerisms were wrong. He stopped, looking to see if anyone was watching.

Oh well, something's happening tonight. I stood up one hundred yards out in the pitch black invisible to most, and grabbing my cloak, walked as quietly as I could. The campfires were subdued; many had allowed the logs to burn away unreplenished for none wanted to venture out looking for firewood. Yet as I approached I could hear a low-level background noise from the camp. Many had stayed awake this night, and now some half an hour before dawn they wouldn't sleep.

My boots, part shod with iron, were fairly noiseless, for I walked on the heather beside the road, watching the man. He re-approached the wagon and proceeded to untie a corner of the tarpaulin and remove some boxes and rope, laying them on the ground.

He touched something hanging from his hand,

what I thought looked like a lantern, and a narrow beam of light shone under the tarpaulin cover.

Half closing the door of his lamp, and walking around the wagon he removed several items hung on the side and returning to the corner, laying them next to the box, proceeded to crawl beneath the cover, a faint glow from his lamp, possibly a shuttered lantern.

Got the bastard. And I walked very quickly ready to run if need be, so that as I approached and my feet crunched upon the ground, the little shit would be caught.

The man squealed and protested, demanding that I release him, that this was his wagon and he had every right to be there.

I threw him to the ground, stamped on his leg, hopefully breaking it, and, whilst he screamed, drew my sword and with the flat of my blade knocked him unconscious.

Using the rope he himself had found I bound him by hands and feet and proceeded to return all the other items as best I could. Nonetheless, I was sure not everything was stowed correctly.

The camp had gone silent. "Now look what you've done," looking down at the trussed-up man, indeed he had his legs and hands tied together so I could have cooked him like a chicken.

Five soldiers arrived, running with swords drawn. "Late once again," I said, "I've simply caught a thief."

They looked around and then after perhaps half an hour enquiring of the details, they left. The greyness of early morning, similar to my dark vision, cast shadowy illumination across the moors. Dawn was upon us and heralded by the chorus of birds. We had survived without mishap.

As Nandrosphi and his family arrived, the thief was been carried away hung over the side of a pony, for I had indeed successfully broken his leg, and he had been unable to walk.

Nandrosphi looked with disgust at the man, and swearing, struck him in the face. "Well done Miller, glad you broke his leg, the bastard's lucky to be alive. You should also have chopped his hands off."

"Sorry! Next time I'll try and do better." I was slightly surprised by my host's animosity but nodded in agreement.

The camp was making ready, and Nandrosphi's wife was preparing my breakfast; last night's short-lived fire was resurrected. She seemed somewhat more willing, perhaps I deserved her dedication for she was frying sausages, the last of my steak, and bread dipped in goose fat.

"How's the ox today." I watched as the boys assisted with the yoke and hoop.

"Better, much better, but we need to have a proper noon stop."

"Are we free of attack now, and do we need to set off early?" Nandrosphi asked with a more cheerful disposition than he had had for much of the journey.

"Yes I think so, but we ought still to try and leave before the others."

I was wrong on both accounts.

CHAPTER 7

As the oxen were ready and we were starting from the back we set off before even the most adventurous, passing others only belatedly starting their preparations.

A soldier greeted me, a man scowled at me, others disinterested, we advanced through the assembling caravan. There was a mood of optimism in the air; fires were being extinguished, people weren't rushing as frenetically as the previous day, certainly there was less urgency.

Grimnir rode up and joined me as Nandrosphi looked on in admiration. "Another quiet night for you, Miller," he said, and, "hopefully this day will progress smoothly."

"You're up and about early, Lord." I swapped placed with Nandrosphi so I was closer.

"Well you weren't the only one who didn't sleep last night, I suspect half the camp was awake, although I caught a soldier sleeping on duty."

"Oh! What will happen to him?" For I'd heard of soldiers losing their lives, or being flogged half to death, for falling asleep on watch was a serious offence.

"He'll be beaten by his sergeant and thrown in prison for six months, then probably discharged, it depends if there are mitigating circumstances."

"Are there ever?" I asked curiously.

"Sometimes, but probably not in this case, I don't know."

We chatted about numerous issues and where I might lodge in Hedgetown, the 'Water Rat' was suggested, and of course the admonition not to get within ten feet of the hedge.

After about twenty minutes for the oxen were slow, and weaving between the various pitches slowed us to a crawl. I reached out and touched Grimnir's left arm.

"Lord, the troubles may have just begun." For ahead of us three large wagons lay stranded.

Grimnir tarried with us until we drew level; the merchants were shouting amongst themselves, for six of twelve draught horses lay on their side, unable to rise, and two others looked decidedly shaky.

Grimnir looked at me. "I agree, there will be a diversion, and the caravan must keep moving. Do you want to face the feint or the night-time defence? For I think I'll not be in Hedgetown by nightfall."

"There must be alternatives?"

"Janras," I stood up and bellowed. "Where's Janras? You there," beckoning to a man standing near, "where is Janras?"

"Janras is one of these merchants, I need to ask him something," quickly glancing at Grimnir.

Grimnir moved off to the side, seeking a better look, as Janras approached whilst simultaneously having a heated argument with two of his fellow travellers, but noticing Grimnir dashed away to meet him.

"Stay here," I said to Nandrosphi, as I jumped down and headed to where Janras had gone.

Four of the giant horses were sound, enough to haul one wagon, but of the others; two were in no fit state to haul anything, three had died, and the remaining three unable to get to their feet were possibly at death's door.

"You can't just yoke mules next to horses, it doesn't work like that," one man was saying, "and besides the harnesses won't match."

"Silence," shouted Grimnir.

And I, ignoring him, asked Janras, "Where are your guards, the ones I met yesterday?"

"Gone, Miller, I fear your suspicions were right." A look of consternation and despair was written across his face.

Rumours spread fast around the camp ranging from, 'Disaster, we'll all be delayed,' to, 'Well those rich merchants can afford it, they wouldn't have waited for us.'

Five soldiers were picketed around Grimnir to keep the merchants and others at bay.

"Miller and my sergeants are to attend me." He gave instructions for the caravan to proceed with caution, ten soldiers at the near front, and they were to head off.

Whilst Grimnir waited for his sergeants to arrive I spoke to Nandrosphi.

"Master, are you not travelling with me?" He looked worried and for once his wife sat closer, listening to what was being said.

"You know we discussed where the greatest wealth was in the caravan?" and Nandrosphi nodded towards the three stranded wagons.

"Well they're the target for what is going to happen." I briefly explained that there would be a small attack on the front of the convoy, but that it was deceit, a diversion.

"You must be near the front but not too advanced, better to lose ground, you'll still be well clear of any conflict." I hoped that it was true.

"There'll be ten soldiers most of the time plus a sergeant taking you to Hedgetown."

"But not you." He looked in abject misery.

"I don't know yet, but possibly, it depends upon His Lordship." And with that I told him to advance slowly, touching my weapons, checking I was complete. "All the better for my catching up with you." And I rejoined Grimnir.

Two of his sergeants had arrived, and as I joined Grimnir, he sent one away to lead at the front.

"Lord, can we not offload merchandise onto other travellers, or perhaps transfer the most valuable cargo out of the three onto the one remaining serviceable wagon?"

"We can and we shall, but I still want to face those bastards that did this, these would-be thieves."

There were numerous discussions about diverting resources between two sections but in the end Grimnir took me aside.

"If we send all the men to the front, and leave nothing here save ourselves, the caravan will reach Hedgetown, the merchants will lose their least valuable part of the cargo, although still considerable, and we would at least make a fabulous fight of it. What say you, Miller? You could prove yourself in a real fight. After all, goblins don't really count, not even twenty-four of them."

"Twenty-seven, you sod." And I laughed. "But if it's just the two of us we might lose."

"You think so? It won't be an army, just a handful of men, probably eight or so."

"Let's do it, but I gave my word to Nandrosphi I'd see his family safe to Hedgetown, I want him protected with two of his own guards."

"Sod that, Miller, why would you be so kind?"

"Don't be ridiculous, he'll owe me loads, and I need a place to crash out or store my possessions. After all, I can't knock on your gates and ask to speak to my friend Lord Grimnir."

"Ha! Yes I see, very wise, I'll give him two, you want to tell him, take the credit."

"I do."

Arrangements were made, the merchants remonstrated with Grimnir, and argued amongst themselves, but after an hour delay, for Grimnir had told them the grim facts. "Either cooperate of lose everything, for the caravan will set off immediately and you can take your chances." There was, after much angst, a resignation to their plight, an acceptance of reality and begrudging compliance.

The guards had been warned to expect a light but noisy attack at the front, but regardless of what might befall, they were not to return for the wagons, nor offer relief to Grimnir and I.

Torak and Elranir begged to stay behind and fight alongside their lord, but Grimnir, taking them aside had honoured their courage and impressed upon them that their greater worth lay in securing cohesion and discipline within the main body.

Upon reaching Hedgetown, they were to bring eight draught horses back, with suitable harnesses should size dictate and relieve Grimnir and myself with a force of men.

They were not to search for us, for if the wagons were not intact they were to return. Men must be preserved; there would be no heroic rescue, none at all, it was impressed upon them. They knew their duty.

Nandrosphi was introduced to his two guards, and whilst my authority was non-existent, Grimnir had graciously walked over and in no uncertain terms ordered them to the protection of Nandrosphi and his family, whilst kindly giving me the credit.

My host shook my hand profusely and even gave me a hug, which I didn't reciprocate.

"You'll always be welcome at my shop, Miller, I am indebted to you."

"Bloody right you are, I'm risking my life for you!" But secretly I was delighted at the prospect of fighting alongside Grimnir, far more enjoyable than sitting beside Nandrosphi, staring at the backsides of oxen.

The caravan was delayed an hour, yet under orders the slowest constituent parts were moved to the front and of the three mighty wagons, the cargo was redistributed according to value.

One of the merchants bravely requested to stay behind, but was refused, for his bravery came partly from a desire to avoid salvage fees. He had known there would be repercussions when they tried to secure repossession of their property. Or was he hiding contraband?

All the soldiers were in position, the caravan slowly set off, and standing completely equipped, save my cloak that was hung over a wheel, I turned to Grimnir.

"So what now? Is there anything more we can do?"

"No, nothing really, they will be watching us. With luck they might decide not to attack the main part of the convoy, after all there's only one fighter to worry about," he smiled, as I looked at him.

"Do you have a reputation, Lord?" I asked, hoping that they might make a mistake thinking we were easy to overpower.

"Not in recent years, but some might remember,

and we are dressed for war. They'll probably try to shoot us first, we shall see."

"Oh, bloody marvellous, can I hide behind your shield?" I looked at the wagons thinking they might offer enough protection.

Grimnir sat down in the middle of the road, an obvious target, and waited.

After two hours I was getting bored. "Why are they waiting?"

"I'm glad they are, it means the caravan is being ignored, they'll want to put a good distance between us and any help from the soldiers guarding. Give it another hour or two, nearer to midday."

I stood on a wagon, trying to look for anything unusual, any clue that might indicate an approach by enemies. Nothing.

Two hours later it was midday, and Grimnir was pacing the road. The sun was at its highest and he turned to me. "I forgot to keep some food back, we may get hungry at this rate."

"Well, being more intelligent than you, I haven't, I've got a ration pack stored away, but you'll have to drink water."

Then Grimnir whistled softly, drawing my attention, for a man was walking towards us across the heather, two hounds at his side. Then another ten appeared a little behind and more to his left, perhaps sixteen in all.

"Eight," I said to Grimnir, as we both watched.

"Sixteen," he said. "Though I had expected less."

"No, I meant eight apiece and we'll play the dogs as a quarter each."

"That's better," he said, smiling, "but remember these are likely tougher than goblins, just be wary."

The man continued as did the other, until some one hundred yards away he nocked an arrow, the bow at his side.

"I see you're guarding our wagons, but if you get your tail between your legs and don't look back, we will ignore you, for the alternative is far from pleasant, now piss off," the man said.

He was dressed for the outdoors – boots, cloth shirt, with light leather sleeveless jacket, a leather cap, and quiver on his back. He looked dirty with old tattoos above his beard and down his exposed arms. He probably had weather protection, but had left it some way off.

Grimnir said nothing but walked over to me. The huntsman took it as a sign of doubt, a discussion between two nervous adversaries.

"I'm protected against arrows, but you have no shield and can either crouch behind the wagon or take your chance, but allow me to draw their fire." He walked back closer to the enemy, making himself an obvious target.

"What is your name, stranger? For I am Lord Grimnir and whilst you are not on my land I am a good neighbour to the Lady Bluebottle whose lands you trespass. Why risk your lives threatening me?" He smiled and with mocking indecision, pointing at the wagons, said, "These are mine, you are much mistaken thinking them yours, do you have proof of ownership?"

"It would be better if you didn't die, Lord," and looking at me was about to add some comment, but carried on, "I have no quarrel with you or your..." he looked at me again, "servant."

"But I have a quarrel with you, for you're threatening me, and trying to steal that which doesn't belong to you."

"I suggest you go, Lord, for you are clearly outnumbered."

One of the other men, cursing, told his companion to shoot Grimnir. "Get on with it, stop playing games, Makus."

"Makus, is it? Now I have a name, so you'd better kill me, because when I get back to Hedgetown every bounty hunter will be seeking your head, even your fellow companions will be turning you in."

Makus turned to face his indiscreet fellow. "Stupid git, shut your bloody mouth.

"Lord, I will regret your death, for I have no quarrel with you, but you know my name so..." And with a swift and fluid professionalism he loosed his already nocked arrow. Grimnir not flinching, nor trying to evade, stood staring at Makus. The arrow missed by a few inches.

Makus let loose a second followed by a third, each missing. He cursed, studied his bow, doubting his ineptitude.

"What's this, dwarf, some kind of magic?" as a fourth arrow from farther back flew in my direction but with less accuracy than those fired at Grimnir, skidding on the ground a foot to my left, and striking a stone, flicked up in the air it spun, falling harmlessly away.

"You're dead, Makus," said Grimnir, as Makus turned to his peers, looking for reassurance. Grimnir was dominating the discussion, doubt gnawing at the lawless men.

"You'll have to fight by hand, and you'll die."

Makus loosed a further arrow, his fourth, but slowly this time, making sure of the target; he was certain of his skill.

The arrow flew past Grimnir's right shoulder.

Now Makus vacillated, unsure, for this was not how the confrontation should have started.

The wildmen started to come together, yet they were still spread out and too far away for my fire spell, but they would need to draw together.

"You could always attack us this evening," for I knew it would be a moonless sky, the sliver of moon from the previous night would be extinguished. "We see better in the dark," I goaded them. "There's nothing wrong with living in the wild, stealing from women and children and living caked in shit, what I can't abide is cowardice, but maybe you've lived with it so long you think worrying sheep is courageous."

Whilst farther away than Grimnir, my voice still carried clearly enough for some of the wildmen looking at me, nocking their own arrows.

Now I perceived that Grimnir had some ward against missiles, either that or Makus was a lousy shot, but if those others realised I was not likewise protected, that I was vulnerable, one hundred and eighty yards was not a difficult shot. An accomplished and skilled huntsman could easily strike with accuracy.

I stopped goading them, better that Grimnir take their wrath, for one shot had already missed me and I didn't intend to educate that I wasn't equally blessed with the same protection Grimnir enjoyed.

Grimnir walked over to me, and the wildmen watched.

"Take the shield from me, and step out. I like your insults, you seem to have developed a knack."

"But your protection, you will lose your defence against the arrows."

"No I won't," smiled Grimnir, "but you'll gain temporary protection, and they will assume I'm in jeopardy. Let's whittle down their arrow supply."

Reluctantly I slung my axe over my back and took hold of Grimnir's shield, drawing my sword. Grimnir and I walked closer to the men. "You know you do a pretty good line in insults," recalling my torment at the hands of the dwarf, the misery of Gledrill momentarily called to mind.

We stood about one hundred yards from Makus, and the others were closing, yet still about thirty-five yards farther away, not compact enough for my liking.

"By the gods you are ugly buggers, except that pretty boy over there. Do you take it in turns on cold winter nights, or has one of you got a wife, perhaps you two?" I pointed with the tip of my sword.

Five arrows sped towards me, and I raised the shield, but felt it twitch, tugging at my arm, dropping slightly, an invisible force realigning the area of protection. The arrows thudded against the front of the shield and fell broken at my feet.

All sixteen of them started peppering Grimnir; arrow after arrow flew at him, for perceiving that the shield had been Grimnir's protection, he was now exposed.

Dozens of arrows essayed to strike, but each missed, and then one final shot at me caught the edge of the shield, and spun me slightly sideways as the spent arrow tumbled away. Strangely I had felt no tug.

"May I try, Grimnir? Shoot one, or flame three or four, which would you prefer?"

"Will the one die? For I'd rather you got a few with your flame, better not to forewarn."

"The dart may kill, but will certainly incapacitate one of them, how about Makus?"

"Yes okay, go for it, Makus seems their leader."

"Will you surrender now, or am I to kill you all?" I bellowed. "For you will have to fight us in single combat, and there's only sixteen of you plus a few hounds."

They started to gather together, so changing my mind, and seeing they were planning to slip the dogs then follow with a charge, I walked forwards and loosed a fire spell, aiming at where eight were gathered together.

The flame, as some pent-up energy fled from my hand and exploded in their midst. The flash was not debilitating to the eyes for being midday the sudden contrast in light was not as grievous compared to the dead of night.

The smoke blown away on the wind, revealed six men lying on the floor convulsing in agony, whilst two more screamed, staggering back, trying to extinguish the fires that engulfed their clothes.

Dogs, terrified, laboured against their leashes and one who had moments before been loosed, fled baying as it ran.

Makus stared at the stricken, and turning back to face me was pierced by a dart, created through craft that smote him in the mouth, for these darts are unerringly accurate. He fell to his knees as blood poured from his ruined face.

"How was that?" I shouted over the din. Turning with a wide grin, I looked for Grimnir, but he had gone.

"Too easy," I heard the dwarf say.

"What the hell!" Grimnir had charged already, axe raised high. He, whilst not tall was streaking towards the enemy who totally wrongfooted were dropping bows and drawing daggers, swords, and clubs.

I ran after him, clumsily extricating myself from straps that allowed a shield to be held tight to the forearm. Cursing for this action delayed me, yet I knew the shield would prove a hindrance. I'd never learnt to fight with one, perhaps an oversight, but sodding hell, Grimnir was chopping at the enemy and I was behind.

The stench of death hung in the air, for despite the gentle breeze men exude fear, sweat drenching the body, shit and piss caking the inside of britches.

Several of the enemy attempted to rush upon me as I swang my own axe in swooping arcs, two handed, so much ferocity the axe blade whistled as it cut through the air.

Men screamed as they lunged, a release from fear, or as guide for their departing spirits, I knew not.

Driving my axe down, I smashed the skull of the first man, and leaning back kept the momentum of the arc, swing down the calf of a second, the cut so deep I could see his tibia.

Running forwards and peeling slightly to my right for I never stopped seeking my own path, men cursing, steadied themselves ready to parry or attack; their choice, but a poor tactic.

'Never fight your enemy on their terms.' The lesson driven home so often in training. So running wide, I hacked at an unguarded flank; three were down, the third caught in the kidneys.

One man braver than most, screaming as he charged, tried to strike as I pulled at my embedded axe but my training had been superb, and stepping slightly to my right, I drove a knee in to his side, causing him to lose his balance and tumble to the ground, yet with a swiftness unexpected he rose to his feet, looking at his sword, as though to angle a repost against me. I swang a bone-splintering blow to his forearm, smashing his sword arm. He dropped his weapon and tried to tumble away as I caught his foot, cutting off the last third of his boot, toes and all.

Other men were not so proficient; many were burned by my fire, for unlike the goblins and being tougher, had for the most part survived.

I chased down three of these who seeing the hopelessness of their plight, tried to flee.

In the end, finding myself three hundred yards away from the initial combat, I started walking back, watching Grimnir. He slew with a grim professionalism.

It was a joy watching him slay the remaining men, my approach had involved sheer terror, but with Grimnir it was more traditional, as a butcher cuts meat with practices precision, thus did Grimnir despatch the remaining outlaws.

One almost escaped, but running away from the dwarf and seeing his route cut off by an orc, he had been offered a choice.

"Be eaten alive by the orc or face me in fair combat, and I'll make a deal with you," said Grimnir. "If you best me, then you are free to leave, is that agreed, master orc?"

"Yes indeed," I said, staring at the terrified man. "If you beat the dwarf, I will agree to your freedom."

The man, shaking and incontinent, stood in front of the dwarf. It took only a moment. For whilst the man fought with some bravery Grimnir was a mobile slaughter house, and every man save Makus lay dead.

Makus died half an hour later, for I cut his throat; he had been crying and I couldn't understand what he was saying.

"That was a bit of an anti-climax," I said. "There weren't nearly enough of them. Perhaps next time we could avoid the fire craft. All the ones you fought were half dead to begin with," I joked, watching

Grimnir scowl at me.

"Do you suppose that's the end of the troubles today? Because we're not going to be rescued for a least a day and a half, possibly three," I asked Grimnir, with some sincerity. "I'm going to be so bored."

"Why don't you gather the silver and personal possession from those men out there, and remember swords, daggers and axes are all worth something. I'll start building a pyre."

"Really? Is it necessary? Can't we just pile the bodies as before?"

"Yes, we need to, they need to be burned, otherwise the rotting stench of death will draw animals in from miles around, and some creature are intelligent. I want to avoid further trouble." The dwarf stood up and set off for nearby trees looking around for fallen material, whilst I wandered in search of bodies.

I started some way off, noticing where the hounds had run, those that had escaped their masters' control, and after a while I found their camp, hidden in a shallow fold of the land.

There were large numbers of empty sacks, five hand-pulled carts and numerous packs. So using one of the carts I piled backpacks, half-full sacks and anything that could be examined during the time before 'rescue' arrived.

The cart was emptied adjacent to where Grimnir and I were based and I returned to search the bodies properly.

It took over two hours to thoroughly search every

corpse, for whilst I had quickly gathered the weapons, and removed one good pair of boots, and a decent belt, I had found no purses, no money of any kind, and imagined that the fallen had left their wealth behind.

Only when halfway through searching the bodies, and by sheer accident, had I noticed a round coin sewn into the hem of a vest, and cursed my ineptitude, for not being experienced in this work I was forced to restart afresh.

I stripped the bodies, even searching around the groin, for one had hidden money there. Well, I wasn't admitting to Grimnir how thorough my search was, but it was damn well thorough!

I piled the clothes onto Grimnir's pyre and hauled all the gleaned items into a separate pile next to the first.

"Did you look up their arses?" the dwarf asked, trying not to smirk.

"Really! You are joking?" I asked in incredulity.

"Oh no, that's the obvious place. Sorry, it's disgusting, but I've seen gold and gems shitted before." But the dwarf just couldn't keep a straight face long enough, and as I rose to my feet, he let loose a blast, a laugh so loud it nigh echoed across the wide valley floor.

"Git," I said, but it was a good joke, I'd fallen for it hook, line, and sinker.

"We need more wood, come and help me with these branches, two large boughs." The wood was a fair way off the road, and it took some time to drag and lift enough for the pyre.

So about four hours before sunset, we sat talking, sifting through the plunder, my first ever, well, excluding Joe.

The pyre was well alight, though the bodies had initially thwarted the advance of the flame. The fat bound in carcasses was dripping down and once that had happened the flames leapt some twenty feet into the afternoon sky.

Grimnir was explaining the likely cost, retail and second-hand value, and how condition adjusted each price.

"So these boots," lifting the pair I had extracted from one of the bodies, "these to buy new would be about three whole silver pieces, but you'll get maybe one whole to a whole and a half silver, depending."

"Depending on what?" I asked.

"Depending whether you're lucky and the merchant likes the boot, and what size they are. For all we know, the outlaw may have had different sized feet, in which case they're worth bugger all."

Lifting a stiletto, Grimnir judged the balance and quality. "The weapons you'll get about a quarter of their retail value, silver and gold, copper, full value, and jewellery and gems between fifty and ninety percent of retail."

"Why so little for weapons?" I asked, picking up a different dagger and weighing it in my hand, thinking it absurd.

"Well if a dagger costs five silver pieces new, what would a used dagger with slight wear and tear be worth?"

"Well at least half the cost of a new one," I exclaimed, as though victorious in my indignation.

"Exactly, and the merchant may take fifty days to sell it, that's why he'll give you a quarter, so he earns as well." Grimnir looked at me. "It's right and fair."

So in the end Grimnir, with greater experience said we had sixty-eight full silver coins in value, divided by two, that was, "Thirty for the orc and thirty-eight for Lord Grimnir, including tithes, taxes and tutelage fees, etc."

"Sod off, this isn't your land, you said it belonged to Tam, so I'll take thirty-eight and make sure Tam gets here share," and I meant it. The idea of tithes was known but totally unexpected.

The dwarf laughed and smiling, looked me in the eye. "We only tax travellers a copper piece and merchants two percent of cargo value.

"You'll get your share, plus royalties on those." He thumped his hand back at the wagons. "Don't worry, Tam will be thanking you for getting rid of these outlaws."

I smiled, for unwittingly I'd done Tam a service, and that was all to my satisfaction.

We rummaged through the wagons and decided the merchants wouldn't notice a missing wine skin. We broke open my rations, the night drawing in.

"How much will I get as a share on those wagons?" I asked, and the dwarf, pondering a moment suggested eighty to a hundred silver.

"That's good." I was learning. *Money is sometimes hidden, not just the obvious gold and silver.*

I told Grimnir that I could see a dweomer on his shield, the rings on his fingers, plus his axe and sword, "But not when the sword is sheathed."

"Most can't tell, not even sorcerers, so you have a talent, Master Miller, it may make you wealthy." Grimnir looked at me, challenging me to ask how.

"How?" I begrudgingly asked, for he had wanted me to ask and therefore I had been reluctant to oblige.

"Because magic is rare, extremely so, and the chances of finding another sorcerer is unlikely but magical items are rarer still. If you can see an item is magical just by observing it, the chances are that no one else knows, but be careful for not all magic is wholesome. Tam is the one to ask, did she not offer guidance on this matter?"

"That all magic can be dangerous and not beneficial? For a certainty, she gave counsel but…" Had I ever told her? "She may not know I can see the magic, I don't know, I will ask her if it's unusual."

"It is, I can assure you." Grimnir studied me, before looking at the sky wondering if they should fashion shelter against the rain.

Late the following afternoon ten riders arrived bearing the red hammer emblem of Grimnir emblazoned on their shields and embroidered on their uniform cloth capes.

"Hail, Lord." And turning around and seeing our fire still burning plus the ash remains of a larger conflagration, he said, "I suspect we arrived too late, though we rode through the night. The caravan should be safely within the town by now." The soldier nodded in my direction, for it was Roderick.

"Did the convoy suffer any attacks?" enquired Grimnir.

"None I think, for they reported nothing and were in good order when we passed them."

"And the draught horses?"

They're ten hours behind, lightly guarded, there was trouble down at the marshes," and he looked at me, and said no more.

"Don't hold back, Roderick, say what I need to know." Grimnir noticed the hesitation, discretion, and bade Roderick continue.

"Two dead, Lord, the reptiles attacked and the third marsh outpost was nearly overrun, but they held to their duty, and with reinforcements we drove them back. The area is secure."

"Good, I'll attend them the day after tomorrow. Miller and I will take two of your horses, and two other men, and will meet the draught horses in a few hours," and pointing at two young lads, "these two will come with me and reinforce the others. We dispatched the brigands and you will suffer no further trouble here. See to it that the wagons are unmolested, Roderick."

"Aye Lord, we'll be in town within two and a half days."

With that I set off with Grimnir. I chose a large grey horse, for some were scarce larger than ponies, and my weight was considerable.

The journey to Hedgetown was uneventful, and passing the relief haulage party and leaving the two soldiers that had accompanied us, we pressed on alone.

"It would be a great boon for me if you did cause mayhem in the fells and moors, Miller. I've better things to do than handhold merchants against marauding brigands."

We approached Hedgetown from the north and I could see Grimnir's stronghold as a towering castle, on slightly raised ground a little off centre yet deep within the town. "Has the town grown much in size since you have been lord?" Curious, for as we approached the farms seemed less extensive than those around Cragtor.

"Oh, about fivefold in the last thirty years. Most of our trade comes from the north and westwards from the sea, we are a trading point, we sometimes get dwarves from the mountains and occasionally a rare halfling, though there are a couple near Cragtor."

"Really? I hadn't noticed any before, apart from Tam."

"They keep to themselves. I think they are more abundant overseas, but I'm not sure. We do well through the taxes collected, and provide a safe haven in the middle of the wilderness." He looked at me. "Even cut-throats and thieves need somewhere safe occasionally. I just wish they didn't piss on my doorstep."

"What's the punishment for defending oneself in Hedgetown? Do I need to behave myself?"

"Same as Cragtor and anywhere else, but I guess I'll be hearing reports of you, just make sure you didn't start the fight. Seriously," he stayed his horse, alongside mine, "it's a lot rougher here, you need to store your wealth safely. There are merchants who provide that service for a fee, and I strongly recommend you avail yourself of their facilities for you will get robbed," and he emphasised the point. 'Not if, but when.'

"It's best to wear your studded leather jerkin rather than mail, it'll draw less attention, and less attention is better, but at least you know a few of the soldiers."

"Will I see you again? For I would like Tam's counsel on the craft problem."

"Ah yes, I'd forgotten, can it wait a few days?" As I looked disappointed and anxious, Grimnir suggested that I meet him the following morning about two hours after sunrise.

"Just present yourself at the main castle entrance."

"What, like last time, and lose a silver coin?"

Grimnir didn't reply for we drew near, approaching a line of travellers seeking access into the town, some blocking the road.

Two guards noticing their lord approach rushed out and started pushing the crowd aside. One grabbed the reins of my horse and pulled my animal away for he perceived me as just another man to clear.

Grimnir laughed as I was led away, and spurring his horse forward he shouted down to one of the guards, but loud enough for me to hear, "Make sure the orc pays his due."

So being sent to the back of the queue and scowling, but secretly appreciating the joke, I paid a copper piece and entered the town.

It occurred to me that I sat on a branded horse; the guards had been dilatory in allowing my unfettered access. It was a shame, because I might have sold it and given Grimnir something to think about.

Whilst I knew how to look after horses, for I'd tended enough during my time at the farm mill, I had no idea of the cost and wouldn't steal from Grimnir anyway.

Plodding through town, trying to avoid the alleyways and side streets, but being caught out on several occasions, I occasionally needed to back up or dismount, the lack of width or headroom impeding my progress, but this was a new location and unfamiliar.

There on the side, between two thoroughfares stood a soldier, no shield but a red hammer on his breast marked his affiliation, one of Grimnir's men in the employ the town's master, unlike myself now enjoying my freedom.

Making my way towards the man I jumped down and asked him to hold the reigns for a moment, then, as he complied, I walked away.

Initially he stared, bewildered, before protesting and shouting after me.

"Very valuable, don't lose it," I said, "or woe betide you," replying without turning back.

Free of the horse, I wanted to find the Water Rat; it was only the early afternoon, but my armour needed attention for it had started to rust and I felt strangely dirty, plus dropping off the backpack, helm and axe would allow more freedom to explore the town.

Best walk around the corner, I thought, for I could still hear the soldier cursing and he might yet pursue me.

"You," I said, pointing at a fellow carrying bread, "which way to the Water Rat?" He looked at me and nodded, turning sideways, said it was three hundred yards towards the hedge, that way, gesticulating to my left.

The town was indeed rougher than Cragtor; merchants walked with protection, people seemed uglier, uncouth, the language was coarse, more bravado, the inhabitants choosing to wear basic attire; certainly there was less wealth on display.

Except of course for me, marching in full war gear, perfectly reasonable, yet an obvious display of wealth.

As I approached what I hoped was the Water Rat, or at least within the correct district, a man, a beggar, bumped into me and I felt a tug on my belt, no more than that.

Now any reasonable person might allow for circumstance, a chance of error, an unfortunate encounter, nothing mischievous, but I wasn't so charitable and grappling him by the back of the neck swung him down violently to the floor, such that he grunted and exhaled due to the severity of impact.

Reaching for my knife, seeking to draw the blade, I felt air, the haft easily accessible was absent, stolen by this, this scum of the street.

In an instant of awareness, understanding my danger, for he was armed and I wasn't, I rolled away fluidly. In the same heartbeat as the act of drawing my non-existent dagger the would-be thief swept the blade, my own dagger, striking me in the face. I felt the impact and knew he had struck with partial success, the helmet providing protection against the worst of the cut.

Blood trickling down my face, as rain or a tear might fall, reaching the corner of my mouth, I knew there would be a scar.

We both rose to our feet, but my falling and rolling away gave the advantage and recovering my balance moments before my adversary, I kicked his leg, driving him down.

For the second time he essayed to rise, twisting away with remarkable dexterity but his efforts did not avail, for I drove my sword into his flank and groaning as he fell he desperately tried to catch me once more with the dagger.

He stared at me and knowing he was damned, spat insults before my right boot struck him in the head, and pulling my sword free and with a skill of precision forced the blade down into his neck, the wound widening as the broad blade pushed deep, tissue rent aside.

Without thought for those nearby nor witnesses to my crime I watched as blood splayed out, filling the gaps between cobbles.

The dagger was forced from his clenched fist and quickly turning I ran away towards an ally, only allowing myself a moment to look back. His body was being plundered, people were searching and stealing anything of value as he lay dying.

Blood fell from my damaged face, the cut beginning to sting as I touched the wound and ran through several streets, likely away from my destination. A stranger with nowhere to go, no alternate destination, no acquaintances, and potentially a fugitive, I suspected crimes including murder were not rare in Hedgetown.

Seeking a place to hide, for an hour or two at least, before resuming my search for the inn, I steadied myself, momentarily resting against a street corner, looking to see if I was being watched or pursued.

This wasn't really a problem; people weren't squeamish, and passing between small houses, hovels, and single occupancy trade premises, the sort that has a room or two behind, blood continually dripping to the floor, I remained vigilant, needing attention.

At least I fitted better to the surrounding ambience, for I was now simply one of the crowd; all here suffered under mishap and the vagrancies of life. No longer was I the swaggering warrior devoid of unfavourable circumstance.

Slowing, I approached a woman nursing a child, no consideration to modesty for both breasts exposed, the child suckling on one. Reaching within my belt I withdrew a half silver piece, a day's generous wage, saying, "Woman, I needed your ministrations, but out of sight, somewhere private."

Seeing the coin, and with amazing lack of care for her child she abandoned the infant, grasped my right hand and drew me inwards, closing a curtain behind, so threadbare you could see the street outside.

Stood amongst the trappings of poverty she wrenched an old man out of his chair and sat me down, commanding the old man to sit outside with the infant.

"Master, I'll look after you, would you like some ale?" Reaching for a beaker made of course clay, scarcely shaped into a vessel, she proceeded to pocket my silver coin and proffer a sour ale, whilst dabbing my wounded face.

The bleeding stopped after half an hour, for she applied a mixture of honey and spiderweb bound in goose fat. But I chose to tarry, not wanting to leave her apparent sanctuary, thus allowing any potential pursuit to falter.

"What is your name?" I asked, for she was a useful woman and knowing her might come in handy, I knew not.

"Why sir, what name would you like? For I have not asked yours," she smiled. "But if you're after business I could, for another silver piece, keep you warm tonight, there's never any trouble in here."

I hadn't a clue what she meant, and after explaining that I had accommodation already planned, it dawned on me when she cheerfully replied, "I'll be happy to travel and attend to you wherever you like, are you sure I can't oblige?"

I was so innocent!

Eventually I found the Water Rat nestling between an old weir complete with derelict water wheel, and a former levee now overgrown and long since obsolete.

The inn was a union of several buildings having expanded over the years such that it had two arches and an internal courtyard. Standing at the head of a narrow cul-de-sac, the whitewashed walls in need of renewal showed signs of lichen stains, but overall the place looked prosperous and capable of a variety of services, it seemed Grimnir had advised well.

Approaching, it was refreshing to see an eclectic mix of travellers and tradesmen disposed to argue their cause. Horses, ponies and mules stood in the courtyard, either being attended to and stabled, or made ready for onward travel.

Numerous people loitered outside, for the weather had held off; the threatened rain failing to materialise encouraged people to assemble outdoors, some arguing heatedly over aspects of trade and miscellaneous trivialities.

Placing my backside on a spare bench and resting a foot on one of the stools tethered to each bench so they couldn't accidentally be removed, I sat and watched for a moment, checking to see if anyone had followed.

Arriving approximately three hours before sunset, I wasn't impressed with my first day in town.

The innkeeper scowled for I looked dishevelled; the goose fat had started to run down my face and the stains of dried blood suggested that turning me away might be a good idea. Yet I held out silver and after a moment's hesitation the landlord thought better of it, accepting me as I was and becoming more agreeable when I chose the most expensive room and added additional services to my bill.

"I'll need my armour scrubbed and oiled, my boots cleaned along with this jerkin and vest, oh, and I want to bathe, er, please."

The cost of five silver and three copper pieces proved too much of an incentive, and the landlord gave instructions for his servants to attend, but he took the silver in advance as I followed him into the building.

The room being situated on the first floor was extremely secure with bolts top and bottom of each shuttered window, the door triply so, but I wondered if all rooms were better protected for this wasn't Cragtor, and changing into my studded leather jerkin, still immaculately clean, and spare vest, I walked barefoot into the common area.

My bath was preparing and knowing it would take at least an hour for heating the water was the slowest part, I ordered several beers and a board of meats and bread.

Parking my backside on a rocking chair, foot on a table, I belched and waited whilst time passed, staring at everyone, observing those in the room, who for the most part pointedly refused to return my gaze. It didn't help that my balls were on display.

I wondered upon my current circumstance, contemplative, introspectively studying, knowing my destiny, getting better at self-analysis!

My goal wasn't the amassing of wealth, though that would come, but to be a lord like Grimnir, yet greater, for I couldn't aspire to be like Tam, my craft was far too weak, yet I had silver and could live well, but this freedom of mine was merely a release from bondage, a stepping stone to the rule of people and lands with iron and slaughter.

Build an empire, a kingdom first, and hold power over all that I could see; the dreams of children, but as I clenched my iron fist this would not be a dream, slaughter couldn't wait.

Sitting there, a peculiar contrast of blood, sweat and partial cleanliness, a formidable orc of unknown talent, people watched through the 'corners of their eyes'. Had they any idea their future lord and master sat amongst them?

I wanted to slaughter them all, start the tenure of my reign but I was drunk, and it was well that I was, for being so fay of spirit I could have wondered into the market square and declared myself lord and master, except it belonged to Grimnir. I wallowed in dreams imagining the dwarf doing obeisance to me whilst Tam watched approvingly.

"Another beer!" But rather they helped me to my bath, and then staggering to my room I had just enough wits to spike the door and fall head first onto my straw-filled mattress; it wasn't late and that was fortunate.

CHAPTER 8

By the gods. I awoke with a massive hangover. It was dawn, the sun had not yet risen, the common area was deserted but the front door stood ajar.

Stepping outside, my mail coat slung over my shoulder, I sat down, breathing in the chill air of dawn and thinking, *What a bloody awful headache.* There was no art in craft for such things. *Shit.*

After a considerable breakfast of ham and eggs and downing two more ales I started to recover, the hair of the dog, a traditional cure for the previous night's excess.

"How far is the castle from here?" I asked the innkeeper, for although Grimnir's keep was large, still amongst the narrow street it was not always easy to spot.

"Tis about half an hour, past the…" and he

paused, for suspecting rightly that I knew nothing of this town, and therefore related landmarks were an irrelevance, he gained his bearings and pointed, "a quarter west of the rising sun." He meant northwards.

Along the route I secured storage for my possessions; the innkeeper had allowed his son to guide me to a merchant who agreed a rate of a quarter silver a week to protect my belongings, with a charge of one copper each time I required temporary access.

As I approached Grimnir's castle, the town became more active and wearing now only my studded leather jerkin, sword and cloak, I looked far less conspicuous.

Now the thoughts that had stirred my heart the night before were subdued, as I sat on a giant stone fifty yards from the mighty gates. The stalwart defenders of Grimnir's castle, two great oak doors, each leaf stood wide open and in the corner of the gate house, two massive beams lay propped and chained against the wall.

Soldiers dragging prisoners bound by ropes; wagons and hand-pulled carts lining the roadside, some gaining access whilst others waited to be called; scribes and servants hurried through, nodding to guards, others having their papers read before being allowed entrance. It was clear that the soldiers couldn't read for a robed official stood flanked by two of the guards, documents were checked and cargoes inspected, allowing the merchandise to be counted and checked off.

This monster that consumed revenue, the workings of a minor kingdom for Grimnir's rule prevailed in these parts, despite nominally part of the greater kingdom of Culanun. Everyone seemed in the pay of Grimnir and each had their grubby hands in his pockets.

I mused that I would rule by terror, yet thinking it I knew instantly it was the least efficient form of government, spawning corruption at every turn.

Still I sat contemplative, trying to work out the most efficient and the least corrupt way to manage a kingdom and looking back I knew I was trying to fathom a relationship between efficiency and order, or effort against reliable return.

Was it a contradiction in terms? A realisation that ruthless equity was the most profitable.

Flukaggrrr, a future lieutenant, would accuse me of being an intellectual prat, but, he was chosen because he had just enough comprehension to understand that brutality wasn't always the answer, and he was well regarded whilst being immensely loyal.

Was that my calling, to rule efficiently driven by commerce? Sometimes troubled dreams sent possibly by my enemies in craft sought to portray such a position as a pawn under the control of Tam, but there was a connection between Tam and I unbeknownst to every enemy, hers and mine.

She had given me life as a mother births a child. Damn them, I didn't mind that in future years when my kingdom was expanding, Tam, and to a point or extension, Grimnir, were left alone, unmolested, even protected. Loyalty counts, my only virtue, but I was still lying to myself. Grimnir was wrong, as the reader will discern; I was half human, after all.

"Lord, you are too kind," Flukaggrrr and others would say, but none opposed me for they knew my strengths and much was achieved. "Ignorant pig-loving peasant!" He liked the insults and above all the cruelty and plans for conquest; he and others grew rich, and never before was an orc hybrid kingdom so successful.

But I transgress…

My hood was cast back, the sun had risen, and estimating it was perhaps a quarter hour before I was due to knock or more precisely, present myself, I waited, observing. A soldier walked past looking at me inquisitively. Was I recognised? For good or ill?

Rising to my feet, I walked towards the open gate, and seeking the official studying papers and without regard for etiquette walked in front of a line of merchants waiting to be called forward.

"You must wait your turn, get back in line you'll be called shortly," said a soldier, trying to grasp my arm and turn me around.

"My turn is now for Lord Grinner ordered my attendance at this hour," as I shrugged off his hand.

"Wait your bloody turn!" he bellowed, for from commoners he expected absolute obedience. His curse caused others to look around as I glared at him and presented a swiftly drawn dagger to his throat. There was a pregnant pause.

"Miller?" I heard a voice shout from above the gates; a soldier peered down. "He's expected, Hengel, allow him access." I couldn't see who it was but someone had recognised me.

Hengel, feeling the cold steel pressing against his neck stood temporarily immobilised, and then for I had not pressed home the attack, with absolute precision he edged his neck away, carefully extricating his body from harm. He was terrified and had not the grace to look at me, but eyes cast low, gently turning, he walked off as though other duties beckoned.

"You're a lucky bastard." I wanted Hengel to piss himself but needed another minute for the terror to reach his bladder and the time was denied to me.

The official checking papers looked up and said, "Miller, is it? Please wait a moment, I'll be with you in a just a second," and he was.

Leaving everyone stood waiting, he walked over and greeted me with due courtesy, giving his name although it sounded unpronounceable. 'Izziguyurp-yuk' or something similar.

"I'm to look after you, His Lordship is breaking his fast but we are to interrupt."

The castle grounds if anything seemed busier internally than externally, for as we walked between walls there were fletchers feathering arrows, bending wood wrapped in leather between weights or held fast in vices, blacksmiths both shoeing horses and fashioning weapons, bakers, tanners, hoopers, and the ever present brewer.

Yet always administration, men tasked with the distribution of produce, the counting of numbers, bloody bureaucrats and my heart sank; there must be a better way for this seemed like a town within a town.

As we gained access to each level in turn, the depth and magnitude of Grimnir's stronghold became more apparent and impressive. Gates protected each ring of fortification like a giant maze, designed to hinder any attack should an enemy breach the outer walls.

People stared at me as I walked with my guide, and even more so as we entered the living quarters and approached Grimnir's great hall. A young fop stood to one side of oak doors.

"I'll not enter," said my guide, "but this man will see His Lordship is aware of you arrival." He offered his hand but not reciprocating I nonetheless muttered a 'thank you'.

Looking at the young official, my guide informed him, "His Lordship gave instructions that this gentleman be admitted immediately upon arrival."

So he left and I watched as the courtier looked at me, and especially my sword.

"Get on with it, open the bloody door." For he stared at my sword too long.

Turning away he knocked, and without waiting entered, closing the left partition in my face.

"Sod that!" I wanted to walk in, and with my customary brazen approach, did.

The courtier jumped as I followed, unsure of his protocol, a scared rabbit. He may have said something but standing there I paid no heed for never had I seen such a great hall. Vast with towering ceiling spanned by mighty wooden beams, sconces along the walls, rough but impressive wood carvings outlining each high window.

In the corner men gathered for I could faintly see

the outline of a door leading to an annexe. Gathering his wits, my would-be escort commanded me to wait for he was certain of his duty and allowing a half-orc access to his lord whilst armed was probably not high on his agenda. I ignored him and walked towards the throng of people.

"Doesn't a lord get any peace even when he's eating?" I said, and flapping behind me the courtier rushed forwards determined to announce my arrival, though the deed had already been done.

Grimnir, raising his voice bid me welcome, and in undertones told those present they had better scatter for a wrathful, life-hating, murderous orc was now amongst them.

"That's better, tell them to piss off," and I honoured Grimnir by bowing, all part of the act that there was no common friendship between us, then falling to one knee I requested an audience.

Of champions appearing before their masters, I had heard stories of bowing three times, scraping noses upon the ground, but alas I was not skilled and told everyone to fuck off.

Grimnir was a breath of fresh air, he had been right to discourage my association with fawning courtiers for I would have suffocated.

But still play acting, I placed my sword before his feet and begged his forbearance.

"I have private news for my lord, such that your enemies will quake, fearing your wrath, and dread will haunt their waking hours for they will not sleep."

It's how everyone would approach me and I was

happy to practise the art.

Grimnir greeted me and bade me stand, whilst he finished some business, for he was, as I knew, heading down to the marshland.

It was obvious that having walked through his town he had business to discuss, the town was a shit hole of depravity and the oasis of calm in this his court, belied the work or perhaps simple maintenance needed to keep the town functioning. A bit less decorum and a bit more blood would sort these characters out. I was young and naive.

Grimnir, having dismissed everyone, led me to his inner chambers and drawing my attention to a mirror, he swept back the silks that shaded the surface so I was faced with polished silver surrounded with gold and electrum, studded with jewels. A powerful dweomer shimmered and it seemed as if mist reflected upon water, yet having no physical depth.

This, he assured me, would allow Tam and I to communicate.

"I'll excuse myself, you have private matters to discuss and I need to inspect some men for I'll be gone within the hour. Keep in touch. Will you be here when I get back?"

"I don't know, probably, and, thank you for everything." I meant it for being ungracious by birth and learning I was glad to have the dwarf as a friend.

"Oh, before you leave ask for Zolpetre, he's got your share of the bounty." Grimnir walked out leaving me looking around, but ultimately focused on the mirror wondering how it worked.

Pacing up and down but being inexorably drawn, fascinated by the mirror, I studied the arcane words inscribed along the edge, seeking any keyword that might activate the device, giving clues as to its operation.

My study of arcane craft had been thorough but because the language was truly ancient I struggled at the inflexions and verbs used throughout the millennia. Elvish and the language of men were easy, as was the ability to speak Orcish and I could even speak a smattering of Dwarven greeting. But of the most ancient of arcana, well, I was on shaky ground. The context could either hinder or assist in fathoming the words beautifully written, each swish and flick, each dot and missed vowel, the context of words was as important as the words themselves for the language had evolved over centuries and I was not proficient in the most ancient of writings- and this device was ancient, probably more ancient than I would ever touch again.

After what might have been half an hour I grumbled but not in anger, for I was enjoying being in the presence and trusted with one of the world's oldest historical artefacts, the workmanship superb.

Still as I pondered... A voice clear and yet remote, whispered, "Try as once before, for there are always ways that the earth can assist."

I was elated to hear Tam's voice...

Now I'll stop, and explain to the reader.

In the future I would murder, plunder, and build an empire, but every time my heart was hardened against Tam, every time my counsellors persuaded me to strike at the only free kingdom on my doorstep did I falter, my heart misgiving me. Not until Tam and Grimnir were facing ruination would I permit my men to encroach upon their lands.

It wasn't love and I know it sickens you as a weakness demonstrable by my words, but she was inviolable, the only standard that I adhered to, nothing else, for I would kill and maim people who begged for mercy, yet even in those future times there were complications, matters formed as a barrier in the mastery of the gods.

Standing in front of her image, or was it an image, for I suspected a gateway where she could step through, she listened as I told her my experiences, and in so doing my synapses fired recalling the exhaustive battles, as scars on my brain triggered by the recollection.

"I dare not, for I cannot listen any more and I tried to remember your counsel that only those more accomplished in craft needed a guide." She said nothing, other than encouraging me to describe more.

After a while, Tam said words that I did not expect.

"What you describe, the troubles you face, are not known to me," and pausing as though considering a busy schedule, "I'll need to share your experience, as we did in the earliest of your training, but it cannot be now, for…" and choosing her words carefully, "I'll visit you at your lodgings, the Water Rat, tomorrow morning."

Other matters were discussed trivial in nature, but after about three quarters of an hour the mirror gradually became opaque; Tam's image faded.

"Tomorrow at first light." Her voice trailed away, and she was gone.

She didn't know! Of all the omnipotent people in this world, of all those wise with knowledge and experience, she was uncertain. I had assumed she would have had an instant answer, that she would assuage my anxiety.

So it would be tomorrow she would join my mind through craft and together we would plunge once more into the violence of the earth's song.

I spent the rest of the day walking around Hedgetown, trying to seek Nandrosphi's new fletcher shop, but to no avail. No one had heard the name and it was probably far too early for any meaningful progress in establishing a business.

So having secured my silver from Zolpetre, and rebooked my lodgings for another night, I bought fresh rations and proceeded to circle the outskirts of town, it would fill most of the day and I wanted to observe the legendary hedge that gave the town its name.

This living monstrosity, carnivorous in nature, stood nine feet tall and about twelve deep, encircling the whole town save where two stone towers spanned the main entrance, a lethal guard against invaders. Its broad dark green leaves swaying gently in the breeze belying its foul nature.

Today like most days there would be an execution. A poor wretch, a prisoner guilty of some heinous crime would be cast within, and I was delighted to find that I had not missed the spectacle.

Whilst patiently waiting I spoke to a man whose job it was to tend the hedge, this meant using large scythes to cut away on the internal town side of the hedge thus making more space for housing as the living abomination grew outwards.

About two hours before sunset, a crowd of people started to gather outside of the town adjacent to the hedge and I was curious to note the number of children clustered around parents, an afternoon free from work whilst mothers kept an eye on those too young and foolish. Old men with little to entertain themselves sat huddled in small groups, some playing cards, copper pieces thrown in the middle, small winnings and an agreeable pastime.

Guards formed a cordon around the execution site, keeping the curious at a safe distance, remonstrating with any that ventured too close.

"Tis always sad when a child is caught unaware," said my companion. "But these executions serve to remind the inexperienced and unwary." He examined his boot for his right sole had started to come away and the welt needed resewing. "We encourage mothers to bring their young to witness the savagery and danger."

Eventually a slight murmur spread amongst those waiting, heads turning towards a group of soldiers leading a small cart with a man bound cursing and swearing.

"He was caught forcing himself on yonder girl." The cutter nodded away towards the gate, but I couldn't make out to whom he referred.

"The father rightly refused compensation, even though the bastard's relatives tried to bully him, so now he is to die. Bloody good riddance," he spat on the ground, "I'd have castrated him and fed him piece meal, bit by tiny bit."

My companion walked away, he had duties, and the guards didn't prevent his approach, as I sat enjoying the spectacle.

Two strong teenagers under the supervision of guards pulled the cart, undoubtedly receiving a small payment, pocket money undeclared to parents or perhaps they were married, new wives struggling with an infant whilst the boys would get drunk on cheap beer, but they enjoyed their work, grinning and passing comments to the condemned. The prisoner cursed and no doubt reflected upon his miserable fate.

Ninety yards from the gates and parallel to the hedge the boys who struggled over the uneven surface, careful never to come within fifteen feet of the foliage, stopped. Lying flat on the back I could see the condemned trying to free himself.

The crowd now silent watched as guards proficient in their task attended and unceremoniously grabbed the man by his feet and threw him to the ground. He wriggled, desperately aware that his life was nigh over.

A man wearing nothing to distinguish himself stood next to an adolescent girl, both staring at the prisoner, the only other towns folk allowed within the cordon, she the victim, and he her father.

The condemned man cried, begged and pleading to be spared, imploring the girl to forgive him, apologising and trying in vain to secure her sympathy and watching I smiled as the girl spat at him, sure in the knowledge that he had shown her no such compassion.

"For pity's sake, she wanted it, she was willing." He turned, appealing to the crowd, who jeered and shouted insults, none appearing to offer any succour. Once again the prisoner pled, beseeching the girl and her father, imploring the two for mercy; he was shaking, desperation written across his face.

One of the guards kicked him in the side, and bid him be silent before placing a hessian sack over his head.

The girl about fourteen, of slight build, whispered something to her father, and for a moment I wondered if she was relenting, that her resolve had wavered and the worm would be spared. The father spoke to one of the guards who in turn ordered the sack removed.

Shit, he's being reprieved. But I was wrong.

The man screamed for having momentarily hoped the same came to the realisation that her revenge was absolute, he wouldn't be clubbed unconscious. Even animals led to slaughter were usually unaware before the knife cuts the throat, but no, he knew with a deadly certainty that he was to be cast into the hedge without mercy, conscious and aware to his very last breath.

The hedge cutter, my brief companion, walked towards the condemned man, and with the aid of two guardsmen hauled him to his feet. He wobbled, screaming, his feet buckling so that the guards near carried him upright and then without warning, thrust him violently forwards; he fell perpendicular head first about seven feet from the green foliage.

Immediately the hedge shivered as entwining

tendrils reached out faster than a man could draw a sword. The plant with amazing dexterity gripped the prisoner, squeezing as he vainly squirmed.

Slowly the man was dragged inwards as more tendrils shot out like ivy that winds around a tree, thus was the man consumed, the hedge becoming more animated, thrashing and quivering twenty feet either side.

I watched fascinated as the prisoner's flaying feet disappeared, drawn within, but the screams continued for perhaps three more minutes, and I wanted a scion of this plant.

Could it be grafted or planted in a pot of blood? I would buy the cutter a few drinks, and waiting, I watched until he had finished his business, and followed him.

CHAPTER 9

Mountains rose in the distant west, scarcely visible through the trees, and an open fire made with some skill and ringed with stones was placed at the entrance of a temporary makeshift shelter. Primitively constructed thatch lay atop boughs bent down and fastened with ropes, the fire slightly under cover of the awning was protected from the light rain and prevailing wind.

Three goblins tended the flames, a deer skewered on a spit dripping fat and being roasted, rotated by the smallest of the three.

An orc belched as he wiped his jaw free of fat and beer, chunks of crudely cut venison lay on a clean rock that served as a plate and he looked at the sky, it would be night time soon. The crescent of a new moon could faintly be seen.

"We'll pack up in a few hours," said the orc, "we need to rejoin the others." The goblins dressed in animal hides grinned and one, getting up, disappeared into the undergrowth.

The orc's clothes were of a decent hard-wearing quality, leather britches, filthy cloth shirt and a sleeveless wast coat made from well tanned hide, a deep and broad belt, boots in need of waxing and a fine iron scimitar. He needed a wash, but would brush up well, for living outdoors was hard on clothing.

Flukaggrrr had a reputation for keeping discipline, and he had captured these goblins who like wild animals could be trained and thus it had been one year since they came into his service. They had prospered, the four of them, raiding farmsteads, murdering stragglers and picking on travellers, gleaning a modest living; even the goblins were allowed to keep some of the winnings, albeit of no great value, but they lived reasonably well and didn't starve.

Now they had allied with another larger but less efficient band of some seven orcs, who fought and quarrelled amongst themselves so much that they succeeded in very little, but Flukaggrrr was a proficient warrior and was trying to unite the party, albeit two within the larger group resisted his leadership, and he intended to get rid of them.

Tonight they would attack; joining forces, he would cower most and suggest a good plan. Ultimately they would agree, but discord and ill discipline would hamper their success. The goblins, knowing they would gain little without Flukaggrrr's leadership always stayed close to their master.

They were in this area spying on a group of woodsmen, who lived within a fortified palisade, comprising an earth bank ringed with stakes, normally too formidable to assail, but Flukaggrrr had captured a boy, one of the woodsmen's children scarce eight years old and he lay bound with a cloth gag stuffed in his mouth.

The small group delayed until it was dark, approximately three hours after sundown. The campfire having been extinguished and all provisions packed and made ready, they headed north east, the four of them with an infant walking tied by his hands to a rope so he couldn't flee, terrified for his future. The party could see with perfect night vision, better even than half-orcs.

Flukaggrrr would ransom the boy and ultimately betray the men, it would be a night of slaughter, but he also intended to be rid of his two quarrelsome and rebellious peers thus he hoped to gain the mastery of an enlarged group.

Stalyk and Crar along with the others hid watching Flukaggrrr's party return, but, and Flukaggrrr cursed, they were so damned inept that he could smell them downwind.

"Crulzoll will be furious," he muttered. The orc god of cunning would be apoplectic, for Stalyk's group were useless, badly led. Even despite the wood fire that they had failed to hide he knew of their location, so bloody incompetent.

Still, they had their captive, and the woodsmen knew that two orcs would appear offering to ransom the child for six silver pieces and various provisions.

For Flukaggrrr had betrayed Stalyk and Crar, informing the woodsmen of the exchange but adding that the two orcs would suddenly draw weapons and try to murder the twelve fortified men.

If the plan worked, and he was sure it would, the six silver pieces would be the least of their plunder, plus it solved his leadership problem.

Stalyk and Crar were to be the sacrifice, the feint, whilst the rest of the party would attack from the rear. They would die hard, taking a few of the enemy with them, all to the best, and their greed meant no one else would be allowed to parley, especially Flukaggrrr the goblin-loving orc.

So it proved to be, Stalyk and especially Crar were formidable warriors in their own right yet lacked intelligence and wisdom. Even a fox with the wits of a frog could sense danger, or treachery, yet these two insisted despite Flukaggrrr's feigned pleading to be allowed to negotiate as he had captured the boy. In the end the two forced the issue with threats that only they would secure the reward.

To their credit they managed to kill five woodsmen and caused such a stink and commotion that the nine led by Flukaggrrr attacking from the rear were unopposed, scaling the fence with a proficiency enhanced by adrenaline, blood pumping, fear clenching their guts. The woodsmen, realising their mistake too late became surrounded.

In the end half of the woodsmen escaped into the night, taking women and children, for Flukaggrrr wanted to secure his group knowing he would lose orcs and goblins in a fight he might not win.

Perversely, in spite of the bloodshed the child survived, at least to that point. What became of the woodsmen was an irrelevance, they weren't worth pursuing, for their wealth was now Flukaggrrr's. He had five orcs, three goblins, himself, and a small stronghold.

CHAPTER 10

The hedge cutter couldn't be persuaded to sup ale with me despite my attempts to bribe him with a fine meal and as much beer as he could drink. In the end it proved to my advantage, at least financially, for he explained that many had essayed to cultivate the hedge without success.

"It's like chopping your arm off, and hoping your body will become two," he laughed slightly, "two mighty half-orcs where only one existed before."

"So the hedge is a living creature, not a plant?" I asked, for his explanation seemed reasonable.

"I don't know, perhaps it's magical, but many have tried, it can't be done."

And with that knowledge, I headed back to the Water Rat, satisfied with the day, but mindful not to get too drunk, for tomorrow would be difficult.

During the night I awoke to the sounds of a disturbance outside but being on the first floor I fell back to sleep, content when someone shouted for the night-watch and declared themselves a victim of robbery. I cared not for troubles that hid in shadows, it was a reminder to be careful.

It wasn't a great night's sleep, and as a cockerel crowed I sat awake. These birds with the slightest hint of dawn seem to compete with each other to be the first to declare the new day, yet as I opened the shutters looking down into the street for any remnant of the night's troubles, my vision still in greyscale, I wondered if the bird had simply pre-empted dawn for the sun would not rise above the horizon for at least an hour and the damned creature was surely premature.

Tam had said 'first light' so I dressed, although as winter was fast approaching I hadn't slept naked and making myself fit and ready for the day poured water over my head, flattened and combed my hair, and wondered whether I should remove my weak and scant beard.

The innkeeper like in Cragtor had opened the door, so stepping outside I sat on a bench, and watched the town come to life. I wasn't the first to stir.

Guards would be changing shifts, bakers would already have stoked fires for their ovens, the scent of wood smoke lingered over the town as the air was cold and still.

A boy ran round the corner, a bridle in his hand; others were tending horses and tack, rubbing down and feeding animals. The activities of the day were pressing, for daylight hours were reduced and much needed to be done in the shortened time.

Pulling my cloak tight and looking for a cord that would further protect me from the chill dawn, I waited patiently.

Tam arrived flanked by two guards, men in the employ of Grimnir for they wore his emblem, and seeing me she thanked the men who bowed low, quickly glancing in my direction yet taking their leave of her.

"Hello Miller." She touched my face, running her hand over my new scar, greeting me with affection and enquiring as to my well-being. "Is your accommodation on the ground floor? For you know we cannot hear the song in rooms above."

I didn't know that, though with hindsight I had merely forgotten, yet it rang a bell, there was something her words reminded me of but I couldn't remember till later in the afternoon.

"No, I'm on the first floor, sorry! I hadn't thought you would come here, security was my initial concern."

"No matter, we can hire a room for the day." She pulled her hood down over her eyes, hiding her face. "Will you please make the arrangements? We mustn't be disturbed."

The innkeeper didn't hesitate as I paid silver for a room with no intention to stay the night. It was hardly unusual, though he looked at the size of my guest and wondered if it was appropriate.

Entering the room, I closed and bolted the door, secured the shutters and lit the sole, solitary lamp.

Tam placed a cushion on the floor and sat down, throwing her hood back and facing me, the light of the lantern dancing across her face, like so many times before when she had taught me craft by the light of a candle whilst visiting at night.

"When you're ready." And she held my left hand, sensing my trepidation. "I'll go first ready to catch you, I am prepared, you won't fall."

I watched as she became still, aware that even with her advanced skill she maintained but a slight conscious awareness of her surroundings, knowing that that was more than I could achieve for when listening to the earth's song I would be oblivious to this chamber and the passage of time.

My mind prepared, steeling myself for the experience I had always until recently enjoyed, my right hand reached down, palm pressed flat. The earth murmured to me and I let myself fall.

Down I was drawn, oblivious to space and time, no longer part of the room but now surrounded by beautiful sounds. Swiftly I flew across oceans of thought, my mind capable of the most magnificent imaginations, music playing in visual symphonies of colour, sound becoming combined with my senses so that I could hear words as colours, the power of craft, the energy contained in the earth spoke to me, imploring gently to be gathered. I could see how to fashion spells, joining parts that formed an array, the intricate connecting energies that when combined created the power needed to actions spells upon awakening.

There were also voices deep down, I could hear

them, living entities speaking to one another; I could sense their presence, distant yet alluring, strangely fathomable, yet two others travelled with me. I knew what they spoke, one was Tam's yet the other I had no experience nor comprehension of, yet I knew a name… 'Sandy'. There was an intense bond between my two companions.

Tam's mind enquired as to my comfort.

This wasn't it, the differences to my last experience were profound; this was normal, perhaps a little stronger, but not like the dread experiences I'd felt in Cragtor nor on the road to Hedgetown.

She knew my thoughts, and I with partial comprehension of hers felt an emotional tug from the earth, as we started our ascent. Passing altered realities, I emerged into the room, happy yet perplexed.

Tam took a few more minutes, and waking she smiled, she always smiled.

"Not what you were expecting, Miller?" she asked as I looked her in the eye. "You did seem to have an improved synergy to the music, did it trouble you?"

"No! No, it was almost normal." I looked earnestly at her. "You could sense I was comfortable, you read my thoughts," and worried that I had summoned a friend needlessly, "Cragtor and Grimnir's tent were wholly different…"

Tam, got up stretching her legs, and asked me to explain once more the difference. "Was it speed, intensity, lack of control?"

"Oh, Tam." For I was dismayed the experience hadn't been repeated. "It was all of them, but ultimately yes, lack of control," and then I added, "but you were with me, you must allow me to fall, to see how terrible it is."

"I didn't exercise any resistance, neither constraining, nor interfering with your journey." She spoke with sincerity. "You were unencumbered, I simply observed, travelling with you, you and I."

"And..." And I pondered whether to say a name, knowing that I knew a secret, but she was my ally, and there **was** something wrong. "You have a guide in craft, don't you?" And I knew that was expected as a safe bet. "If I knew a name would it upset you?"

"It would depend on how discreet you were, for I doubt anyone but myself knows." She was curious, not angry. "If you have a name," for she sensed my thoughtfulness and care, my concern for her well-being, "I would allow you to say it."

"Sandy." And as I said the word, I sensed a presence, yet deep within the ground, and Tam laughed.

"Oh, by the all the gracious spirits, Miller, my most wonderful of young friends, and I hold you as a friend." She grinned and looked glorious. "How remarkable. Yes, I have an ally by that name, though it is not his true name, a fabrication on my part."

She held up her hand, "Wait, a moment," and laughing some more, she touched the ground and I sat there watching and waiting for her return, a return to wakefulness.

Ten minutes passed, and Tam opened her eyes once more. "Say the name again, please Miller."

And as I did, I felt the presence once more, and Tam held her hand up. "Did you feel that?"

I nodded, and said I did.

"Remarkable, truly remarkable and unexpected… Watch, but do not be alarmed, do not worry or feel afraid," and she whispered so gently, "Sandy!"

Without cracking or disturbing the stone flags, yet pushing rugs to one side, rose a shape as of a giant roughly hewn man, corporeal, fluid, yet like molten lava without heat, quickly forming and filling half the room.

The massive creature had an appearance of falling earth and rocks cascading down a mountainside, a bank of scree let loose as tumbling water over the sides of a cliff, yet never landing, continually replenishing itself, shimmering as the outline changed ever so slightly, bewildering the eye.

"This, is Sandy, my ally, who you can strangely sense…"

Sandy spoke, and as he did the earth shook, words were so deep, so long in uttering he seemed to rumble as an earthquake. "Under the ground in my domain…"

"Sandy…" Tam interrupted, "we'll meet in Cragtor, in two hours, in my deep room, we'll talk then, or you will raze this building."

I watched in awe; this tremendous elemental of the ground, who towered over Tam and to some extent myself was incredible to behold, yet I sensed the intimate affection they held mutually between themselves. Even now whilst I couldn't hear thoughts, I could sense an emotional empathic connection, that they would never forsake one another.

Sandy tarried for a moment and as he drew back into the ground an arm like a tree trunk touched me, as granite rubbing gently on the heel of a foot it felt course yet not cutting; he slowly slid down into the earth.

Tam and I talked about assistants, allies in craft, and how they're found, how initially friendships are formed, of how the empathic link is forged, tenuous at first but growing stronger with the years.

"Sandy had been scarcely a heap of earth little more than a mole hill when first he appeared above ground," Tam said, and dwelt for a while in thought, reminiscing, looking back, as recalling a distant memory.

"Yet now he's an elder amongst his kind, venerable, though he will live for many many more years, for the connection was made whilst we were both young."

"There are benefits for both." And Tam explained that each gained a longevity of years beyond their kind. "But more for the companion than the sorcerer."

I wondered for she so seldom used the word 'sorcerer'.

"The sorcerer's companion must be willing, and of a like mind, for whilst it's not a marriage, each must nonetheless be content, more than content, and more than comfortable. Sandy had to be eager to share my company." She became silent, deep in thought.

"And what type of companions are there?" I asked, for whilst I had asked this question before, it had seemed like high craft and not likely to affect me.

Tam pondered, wondering how to answer, perhaps contemplating if she imparted too much information.

"Most are elementals from the ground, others of wind and fire, yet some are hidden entities from different worlds, and rarer still are those that walk with you during your dreams." She looked at me and said, "Others are on different planes capable of craft, some are demons, and even rarer and fortunately scarce," and she faltered, "some are so evil, so wretched and filled with hate... enemies of life, seeking to consume, even their... even such as you," and I could see she was troubled in the advice... "yet most are spirits of the earth."

"Are they a form of familiar?" I asked, worried it might be a stupid question, for until now I had imagined such creatures were simply the fancies of children's stories, and not for the first time would reality be hidden in tales.

"Really Miller? There are no such things." Her laughter broke the seriousness of the discussions.

Now I wasn't going to let the matter drop so lightly, and I pressed home my question. "Are there no such things as witches? And even in children's tales there is sometimes a modicum of truth."

"Witches or wise women? Who happen to own a cat? There are no familiars, but yes if you like, entities that assist with the earth song might be considered such. But ultimately no!"

This surprised me, for I thought there might be

weak practitioners of craft, capable of simple conjuration.

"How does one befriend an assistant?" And my eagerness was hard to hide, especially from Tam, who seemed to read my mind as well as Sandy's.

"You don't, they do, and I've yet to be convinced of your need." Tam, realising she had spoken with a degree of tactlessness, added, "Forgive me, for I spoke ungraciously, but allies are found because you need them." She went on...

"You can hear their voices in the earth song, I know you can hear them, you've said it before."

"Those voices deep in the bowels of the earth are entities, like Sandy?" I asked.

"Miller, have you forgotten my lessons so soon? There are many different forms of living sentient beings, energies, spirits elementals, even shades and demons."

"Why would any ally seek such a friendship? It's hard enough to find companions in my world." I couldn't see myself as desirable material. Tam yes, but not I.

"Ah! Now that is a good question." And she knew why I asked. "Are you not drawn to the song, loving the experience? Perhaps the reverse is true, maybe when you were born, a companion was likewise? And if you join when you're young, there's an affinity to the association, a connection, a symbiosis, so that each gains." And she faltered... "I guess too much, for the meaning of things, the why, is a subject for philosophers and... but, well, it was mutual for Sandy and I."

Now I didn't consider myself a child nor a youth, yet I clearly was. It was simply that I had passed from being thirteen, to very slowly approaching fourteen, from an idiot, arrogant in mind but powerful in body to someone who had undergone life-changing experiences.

Knowledge is power, knowledge is everything, and having studied I was sometimes slow in recalling lessons learnt during the night when the present bright daylight overwhelmed the senses.

Tam and I spoke of lands to the east and west, of failing kingdoms, and the ultimate collapse of Culanun interspersed with the need for me to study the crafting of my spells, for I had in truth fallen behind.

"My mind is growing in confidence, and maturity, I can concentrate so much more," and I would have discussed with Tam the collapse of kingdoms, but I was only a child.

To the reader I must reiterate that orcs are mature by thirteen; our lifespan is so much less than other races, yet I was half human gaining what I believe to be the best of both races, the strength and stamina of my father, with the versatility of my mother's human blood, yet at the time my arrogance was unsurpassed. Now in old age and looking back, there never was really a time when I was perfect, but having to choose and given a choice, twenty was probably the best for me, although my hands would be red with blood before that time.

We talked for an hour, perhaps longer, and I was aware time to meet Sandy was reducing.

So Tam walked to the door, and unbarred the

room; it was a little thing, something I would not have thought to do, or rather not have bothered about, but she was a standard bearer, a light of decency, for eager to depart and having little consideration for others I would have left the room empty yet internally locked, much to the consternation of the innkeeper.

"Hold my hand, when you're ready, it will take but a moment."

And unlike in Cragtor, where Tam had without spoken words transported Grimnir and myself across one hundred and fifty miles, this time she spoke. Twisting her voice, her vocal cords stretched, uttering words of a convoluted style, difficult for humans, and presumably halflings to utter.

The world stopped, sound muted, and we stood in a room devoid of colour. Normal tapestries hung on walls, and gradually movement returned; shades of men could be seen walking as though they interacted perfectly with their surroundings. I tried to speak but my voice was muffled, and Tam, turning round looked at me, and raising her voice bade me wait.

I watched fascinated, these shadows couldn't see me and I stretched out a hand trying to touch one, but he moved out of reach, nonetheless an ink quill lay resting on a table scarcely two feet away, and reaching out I tried to grasp it.

Tam for a moment held my hand back as though to ward against my actions, but changing her mind withdrew her arm yet her aborted action forewarned, instinctively I became wary. The quill totally incorporeal could not be felt, though an icy chill passed through my hand as though holding snow too long without gloves.

My hand recoiled without conscious thought, and the quill which had seemed no more substantial than mist, fell to one side. I had influenced it, yet had not felt any physical contact other than the intense cold.

Tam, squeezing tight around my other hand, muttered one syllable, a meaningless sound but probably a power word, a short spell, similar to the three second words I had used to stun the child soldier.

And the shades vanished, we were in a room identical in dimension but desks and furniture were different, arranged differently, and the quality was much improved. Colour and distant sounds returned, as in the blink of an eye all seemed normal, yet we were far from Hedgetown.

"What do you think happened, Miller?" asked Tam, sitting in a chair suitable for her size, and watching me closely.

"Are we in Cragtor, were we in Cragtor?"

"Yes on both accounts, you saw a different application of craft, for we stood awhile in a parallel plane of existence."

And I wondered, for having heard Tam utter words rather than silently transporting us I had considered Tam's powers reduced, at least for a while. The casting of craft is easier when words are spoken, less energy is used than the silent application of a spell, and I had thought Tam preserved her powers when we left Hedgetown, a hint of her limits.

"So you found that plane by accident?" I asked. It

was an educated guess.

"You are clever!" She watched momentarily, slightly surprised by my perception. "Yes, it was found by the failure to complete an incantation many years ago."

"And the final word completed the journey, finished the spell?"

"Yes, that was how it happened, but it was interesting don't you think?"

I question Tam on so many matters, sitting on the floor, for even one of the larger chairs seemed too fragile for my weight, and Tam's furniture looked fabulously expensive.

"Grimnir said that Hedgetown didn't really pay for itself, that the taxes generated were insufficient to cover the upkeep?" Now my real question and Tam already guessed, was the amassing of wealth, and how she must be able to acquire or steal anything she needed.

"Is that what drives you, Miller? I never thought it would be."

So we understood one another, and I didn't really know how to answer, not given to self-analysis, introverted thoughts, or cross examining my motivation. Though that was also a lie, on occasion I did, but never dwelling too long on such matters. I wasn't sure how to answer yet she deserved a reply.

"Having lived in poverty my heart is seduced, but I will add more to the answer, perhaps respect…" And I faltered.

"You will find your way as a warrior, and build a

kingdom, and many will come and give you that respect, but not yet." She looked seriously at me, yet with understanding and empathy.

*

I had forgotten she had spoken those words, only now as the story is being retold, scribes sitting on cushions before my feet, ink upon their hands, do I remember. Under normal circumstances those words would have been indelibly imprinted upon my mind, but overshadowing events were about to follow.

My throne is made by a craftsman probably no longer alive, carved from the trunk of a mighty tree and inlaid with silver runes, and sitting I observe, whilst watching scribes write, for my story includes this remembrance.

Yet, recalling those memories has precipitated a desire for solitude and rising from my throne without dismissing or explaining my actions I leave the hall and sit in my study, contemplating my wealth and power, brooding in the quiet shadows of my mind, comforted by my ally in craft, memories reinforced, seeing the events being discussed in clearer focus.

My private chamber is strewn with books and scrolls, religious reliquiae, cabinets with locks, runes of power scribbled across the walls, secret notes of journeys and the pitfalls thereof, this room a sanctuary and impossible to enter, warded against any save myself, and not cleaned for more than a year.

Sitting in secret emotion, thinking I could have done more.

"Flukaggrrr, get me Flukaggrrr!" I bellow, sticking my head into the corridor connecting my library, study and chamber, and an orc ran away, despatched to summon my lieutenant. It would not be too late.

My scribes will sit for an hour, waiting, wondering whether they are dismissed, and eventually returning I will continue. Flukaggrrr, with duties he disagreed with, too soft, too sentimental, and they are, steels himself for his disagreeable task ahead.

*

Tam and I waited, each deep in thought, and after a while she looked up, and informed me Sandy was approaching, and shortly thereafter I also sensed his presence.

The room has no windows yet there is light carried by shafts that are carved between the stone walls and the grounds outside; a gentle breeze ruffles the leaves of an open book, and a lamp emits a golden glow, yet seems not to be lit for there is no scent of burning.

Tam rose to her feet, walking around, and said we should try again and, "If this fails we shall go back to your room at the Haggard Hen, let's see."

"It will be right, for I've remembered listening to the song whilst resting in your chambers, you said it wasn't possible."

"You heard the song, when you first arrived, the first floor?"

"I know I'll need your support." For my hand had brushed against the ground, and whilst such actions normally don't precipitate the meditation required, I knew the ground would envelop me and I would hate this experience.

"Sandy's ready, I shall go first as before," Tam said

after a minute or two, and sitting down on the floor, she touched the ground without fear.

Watching and waiting, allowing time to pass, for I knew there would be distress, Tam and her ally would be needed, my hand felt the ground and concentrating as an unwary swimmer enters a fast-flowing river unsure of their skill, I entered my meditation.

There would be no caress, no listening, no seeking the music. I would fall, and I did, racing across the ocean of altered perceptions, being sucked down as falling from a cliff yet elated and fearful, glad that this was it, no misdirection on my part, Tam would see.

The energies became intense, the music tumultuous, the speed of descent accelerating for this time I didn't struggle, determined that she would see the reality, allowing the journey to unfold until sounds too strange and alien caused my anxiety to rise and I started to resist, my descent slowing yet not arresting entirely. Then I stopped; the rapture of sounds still played but the figments of energy no longer sped past like sharp knives, instead floating gently around ready to be harvested.

Enveloped by Sandy, cushioned against calamity, Tam entered my conscious thoughts, calming and counselling against fear.

"We will ascend, and talk." Her words trickled across the music, my mind relaxing, and gently, as carried upon a wave I was washed ashore, waking once more in the depths of Tam's castle.

"Wasn't that wonderful?" said Tam, as Sandy rose from the ground.

"Err, no!" I looked at her askance. "I'm drowning,

I lack control, surely you jest Tam?"

We sat, or rather Tam sat, as I paced around the room. Sandy whilst immense was not too confined for this chamber was larger than the accommodation at the Water Rat.

"Why is the experience so much more intense here yet not at Gledrill nor Hedgetown?" I asked the question that was on everyone's mind, certainly mine.

"I don't know," said Tam, but she looked at Sandy, who growled and nodded, but more a rumble, not a sign of discontent nor malice for any sound seemed as thunder underground.

I focussed on Sandy. Moving over and touching him, I said, "But Sandy has an idea, doesn't he?" For my intuition and the sideways glance between the two suggested they suspected something and as I placed my hand on his arm I could feel his strength, almost understanding the way he existed, his affinity to the ground, that he preferred certain mediums yet was capable of assuming other forms, not being bound in stone but comfortable in the shape he adopted, sensing that even his presence above ground was a slight discomfort not quite an affliction.

"Sandy doesn't like air," and looking at him, "isn't that so, Sandy?"

Sandy said nothing, but I knew he communicated with her. I couldn't hear the words, like listening down a corridor, knowing a discussion took place, not close enough to separate the sounds.

Sandy turned his head and looked down at me. "It is possible you have a synergy with the earth, like and yet different to mine." And as he spoke the earth shook, the walls resonating with the modulation of his voice, and upstairs, farther above servants in Tam's castle wondered at the vibrations.

"Surface dwellers cannot normally feel as you do." He spoke the words soothing to me, marvellous as I could almost leap in between the syllables, he spoke so slowly.

"If you wish I will journey with you at your next attempt, but Tam will understand my inability to support." He spoke to me, but I didn't understand the implication, his meaning, not yet, not until later that day.

"We will try again," said Tam. "There is a chance. Sandy has proposed an experiment, an idea, but it's just a suggestion, possibly nothing."

"What? Please explain." Yet part of me didn't care, I just wanted to journey with the two of them, for when Sandy had cushioned me from falling it was how I imagined a child would feel wrapped in the warmth of their parents' arms, though never having experienced that security and love.

Tam disappeared for an hour for she had duties to perform, and perhaps for the very first time I accurately appreciated how limited her time was.

During my association with Grimnir and witnessing his responsibilities, the incessant demand of courtiers, advisers looking for guidance and support, the very real complexities of running a small city, I marvelled that Tam managed her time so expeditiously, it was clear that when my kingdom was established the choosing of competent and wise administrators would be as important as strong and loyal captains.

Sandy sank lower, the rough outline of a head appearing above the ground, like a giant caught in quicksand. He looked at me, inviting questions.

"Sandy, if a question is too intrusive, tactless or private, excuse my curiousness, but... when you appear, you have the form of a hewn man carved from stone, is that you, or for Tam and my benefit?"

He rose a little, changing shape, appearing as a simple rock. "Is this easier on your eye?" The sound was not emitted from a physical mouth for there was none. "But it seems convenient to have legs that walk and limbs and hands that can grasp."

He, for that was how I perceived him, told of the marvels of the great deep, places of the world, of might caves, immense heat, rivers of lava, and of wonderful panoramas, of other creatures that lived underground, many living, with flesh and blood, but staying hidden.

"Like dwarves and goblins?" I asked.

"Like fish that live in the ocean, yet are not created through energy or consciousness, but sentient nonetheless, the world below is varied like yours on the surface."

He told of journeys that he and Tam had shared, of dangers they had faced jointly, mainly above ground, but also of expeditions barely scratching the surface, a mile below the open air, in passageways and mines.

"When you are underground can Tam see as you do?" I tried to understand the experiences they shared.

"No, only in thought, for..." He stopped, mindful of her privacy careful not to reveal too much. "She has joined me deep in caves miles below the surface when I wanted to show her caverns of great magnificence. In physical form she would join me.

"There are fires and waterfalls below the earth, great vistas, perhaps she might show you one day."

"How old are you? Were you born, or bourne of the earth?" And to my surprise, and yet not wholly unexpected, Sandy explained that he would spend many years on this plane, the world I knew, but that one day he would cease to dwell. When Tam died, he would be drawn back to his original plane of existence; he simply existed, extant forever.

"When Tam leaves the world, I might linger, the choice would be mine, but probably not, and eventually I will return ultimately with the passage of time. I will have no choice," he rumbled. "I suppose I die, but not really."

The stories Sandy spoke were enhanced by very faint, intangible yet perceived emotional feelings that passed from Sandy to myself, my mind forming pictures, imagining the splendour.

The hour of Tam's absence flew past. I was glad for the time with Sandy, hoping Tam would be delayed, but she wasn't.

Entering the room, Sandy rose and returned to his humanoid form. Tam apologised for her absence, and suggested we would need two or three more journeys.

Standing between the two of us, I was surprised that Sandy would be transported with us, her application of craft not inhibited by his size, and grasping her right hand, her left hand surrounded by Sandy's massive roughly hewn fingers, she uttered no words, and we vanished.

It was about an hour or two past the middle of the day, and we appeared near a shepherd's hut, built upon a headland, surrounded on three sides by the sea, the huge expanse of the ocean dark blue, with white-topped waves breaking around rocks below.

Sandy stood looking at the sea whilst Tam opened the door of the hut and entered, leaving a silver piece on the threshold, and bade me follow her. Sandy, remaining outside, sank slowly into the ground. A gentle breeze blew and seagulls cried to warn against our presence.

"We'll not be disturbed, yet we are sheltered from the wind, and any rain that might come."

I remembered her words that practitioners in craft had sometimes been absent so long that their physical bodies suffered injury.

"Surely you and I will not be absent too long?" I asked.

"It's a good habit to have; never assume, always be prepared, we talked many times about protecting your physical body." She closed a shutter and locked the door by sliding a wooden peg through a hoop. "Just because I'm with you is no excuse.

"Now Sandy will be waiting, but if he's correct, your experience maybe different. Are you ready? I'll go first."

Watching and no longer dreading the experience, I waited as Tam settled herself, touched the floor and closed her eyes, and waiting a moment longer I began my meditation.

My mind drifted slowly, unaware of time, seeking Tam, searching for Sandy, slowly crossing the ocean of altered perceptions, aware of the strands of energy gently floating past, but still below.

Concentrating more, I sought in sensual awareness for the earth song, listening yet barely hearing, struggling to descend, buoyed as a cork floating atop the ocean of perception, moving slowly, trying to gather speed, but meeting resistance.

Tam's mind reached out to mine, a muffled voice, the awareness of Sandy muted, unable to connect. She pulled me deeper; the connective forces so easily harvested seemed elusive.

Down Tam drew me, her will pulling me deeper, enquiring as to my comfort, and I could faintly hear the earth song, like rain falling upon leaves, so faint.

I wasn't engulfed in the rapture, far from it, as Sandy's thoughts came into my mind, distant, devoid of clarity, like trying to hear someone shouting across two fields. I was so disappointed and struggled trying to follow Tam, fighting the impedance, seeking greater synergy, for Sandy was requesting I break the meditation, and return to consciousness.

Opening my eyes, I brushed the dirt from my hand and staring at the shed, gaps in the walls and roof reminding me of Joe's barn, my misery less than a year before, I rose and unbolted the door for Sandy was outside, asking if I was present.

"So now we know, and it is good for you," said Sandy. He towered over me, there were no features on his face for his shape did not allow for smiles, frowns, or any expression, even my slight awareness of Sandy's emotion was absent. There was no connection, nothing. "Tam needs to descend, she will be an hour or so."

"How do you know, and what is there that's good?" For me there was nothing positive. "One day, I'm normal, then tossed around within a storm, and now barely able to meditate." I felt thoroughly forlorn and diminished despite Sandy's comments, conflicted in thought, this latest experience upsetting.

Sitting on the headland, my thoughts such as they were, melancholic, despondent. For half an hour I tried to get Sandy to explain, but to no avail.

"We will travel twice more before this day is spent," and as he said that and before I could question him further, he gently merged once more into the ground.

Lucky bastard! Sitting alone, I wondered if I had driven him away, probably.

Time marched on and after two hours, longer than expected, Tam spoke, making me start for I sat outside watching the gulls wheeling overhead, the roar of the sea and the bitter wind distracting my miserable and melancholic mood, for the weather was fast deteriorating, no longer a mild and beautiful day.

"It's getting cold, I thought you might shelter whilst waiting for me?" Tam looked slightly up, for I was seated and the difference in height was not great.

"Please come into the hut, and I'll explain, it's possibly interesting news, but we need to test a theory." She walked ahead. "Sandy suggests that although you have a remarkable ability to sense him due to your affinity to the earth you are hampered by the proximity of water. Unexpectedly you are polarised in your ability to cope with the earth song, dependent upon where you are." She looked at me, judging how I might react to this revelation. "That would explain your enhanced ability the farther away from Hedgetown's marshes, or the sea at Gledrill."

Having a disability or benefit that was predictable, that was the most important aspect of her explanation, for my anxiety was heightened and augmented by my lack of understanding. Knowledge is everything.

"So where is the farthest point from any body of water that you know, and please," I almost implored her, such was my desire to remove ambiguity, to settle once and for all the cause of my differing experiences, "can you take me there?"

"No," and for a moment a shiver ran down my spine, "but Sandy can." I must have shown my relief.

"Will the driest place be best? For you saw how I struggled to control myself even within your castle."

"Don't worry about that, but we must find your potential limit. After all, your strength and ability is finite. Craft doesn't grow exponentially, there will be limits, even in the middle of a desert."

It wasn't a desert, neither was it devoid of life, for even upon sand, there is water scarcely dozens of feet below the surface.

"Where are we?" For I'd held Sandy's great hand and Tam had allowed her power to be directed by the elemental, his knowledge forming the destination.

Faithfully Tam had unquestioningly allowed Sandy free control, never doubting for a moment his loyalty, yet he could have cast us into solid rock.

"I don't know."

As Tam spoke, Sandy rumbled, "Five hundred and forty leagues from whence we were, on a mighty land mass, the largest in this world, and many miles from water, either as you judge distance on the ground or below."

And now I was fearful, not in dread fear, for as I've said before I am not easily intimidated, nor easily given to panic, yet this was it! If Tam and Sandy were correct, this would be the peak of my synergy with the earth, my greatest journey ever, immersed in the rapture.

I could meditate as I stood, for were my feet not adjacent to the ground, but meditation is as much about preparation and familiarity, and I sat down, not observing my surroundings, the temperature warmer than earlier, the wind gentle.

Tam would have none of it, and she rebuked me for my haste which I normally checked, but that day I was desperately eager to clarify my position.

"I'll not be your guard, Master Miller." It was the first time she used the honorific, and she asked Sandy to check for animals and humanoids within a few miles.

Sandy sank lower, and barely four minutes later rose, counselling no humanoids, but arachnids and snakes, plus several quadrupeds, small in nature. I wondered how he knew, a skill I had no comprehension of nor would know how to learn.

Tam needed to rearrange her powers, so we watched over her as she meditated for an hour. I was bursting with impatience, but subject and in debt, which to friends was allowed.

Upon returning Tam cast spells around the border of our non-existent camp, spending extra agonising minutes checking that no creature, never mind how small, could gain access and finally she paused, and looked at me.

"So you want to see if Sandy's hypothesis is confirmed?" And sitting, we both prepared for meditation. Sandy glided into the ground, and Tam gently reassuring me, closed her eyes.

My heart beating quickly caused my meditation to take longer as I steadied my mind, breathing slowly and deeply; a minute passed before placing my hand on the ground, a trigger for connecting, so well practised over the years, I fell.

Racing across the sea of altered perceptions, the ocean scintillating as it sped beneath, the music already audible, and falling like a stone, Tam clutching at me, her spirit flying alongside yet failing to arrest my descent, keeping up, but not grasping successfully.

With power and immense experience, she sped closer, fleetingly steadying my fall but failing to secure a permanent connection and slipping from her grasp I continued my fall, accelerating faster. She drove ahead, diving down, protecting me from the shards of power, her energy shinning in the darkness, despite my mind being aware of colours and sounds, a contradiction, yet it seems best at describing my experience.

The rapture of music around me, in beautiful clarity, each instrument capable of being isolated. I could pinpoint every chord, the sounds of the earth, the sighing desert, the groan of grinding rocks deep in the bowels of the earth, all the senses harmonising.

Sandy offered to help, for he was exalting in power, an elemental of the earth; he too was unencumbered by the absence of water, so that his mind shone like a beacon in the tumultuous music.

Placing her mind in front of mine, and deflecting the shards of power, Tam finally steadied my fall, as the chorus throve and the trumpets brayed, slowly exerting her influence she and I slowed to that of a feather fall. The connecting energies of the earth floated harmlessly around.

Sandy enveloped me, he and she, buoying me as I rejoiced at all I perceived, feeling each sound, tasting the music, all my senses combining, so that none stood alone, yet all complementary.

How my mind rejoiced, triumphant in accurate knowledge, knowing that life, or more importantly, my life, was splendid.

Tam and Sandy spoke to me clearly, without obfuscation; their chosen thoughts rang clear and true above the music, so I could hear every intended word.

For they proposed to allow me to descend deeper, Sandy reassuring me that the voices were safe, for I could make out words, enquiring of me. I had been noticed.

The shards of power now gentle mists of connective energies seemed different, more complex, and of a higher order, like fish deeper in the ocean, larger and pursued by fishermen risking their lives seeking the greater gain.

Slowly we descended, and after a while I asked to be released, my mental acuity prepared to furnish its own break and control. Sandy agreed. Tam pressed ahead, always protective.

Slowly, with a care I only expected from Tam, Sandy set me adrift, gently loosening his hold so that I fell, in freefall, yet the natural resistance was building and the experience was not wholly without control.

I fought against the fall, almost stopping, before allowing myself to slip the break, exhausting my concentration, knowing the journey back might prove impossible.

The connecting energies thinned, and before me I saw colours change, a purple hue formed, 'eyes' watching me, and observing Sandy, like sharks avoiding dolphins, 'tales told by fishermen', I also was observed, but initially left alone.

The energies down here were intelligent, some malevolent, others benign, so many disinterested, but all aware.

Visions played across my consciousness, some of the tiniest of energies, like shoals of fish, seeking to enquire, wanting my address but not in a physical way, studying my thoughts, others scurrying away, less than curious. But as I descended still deeper, my progress slowed; the small energies were replaced by more powerful wills, having greater strength, formidable intellects.

Descending, a voice entered my head, and was thrust out by another; it started questioning, followed by a third, and increasing in number becoming intrusive, possibly similar to how demons might possess a man, some seeking to connect, others less genteel, and a few nasty, but all curious.

Their minds focused on mine, fleeting questions, scarcely time to register, whilst some were persistent.

"Will you come again?"

"Who are your friends?"

"How do you know a name you don't recognise, and can't pronounce?"

"They will betray you, you'll be forsaken!"

"How will you get back?"

"Why?"

"Why?"

"Why?"

These creatures of energy and intelligence were of differing types. I hesitate to use 'species', for whilst a few repelled me, many were spirits of wind and fire or strange beings I couldn't fathom and yet rarer still, of dreams which I found fascinating. Most though were like Sandy yet none had the intensity of his power. Occasionally one of greater strength would enquire directly with Sandy, I heard their thoughts.

Always he would advise of my gift, the ability to connect, to hear the words they spoke, it was a warning against revealing secrets.

Slowly natural resistance increased until I stopped falling, and floating in meditation I could enjoy the spectacle of a new world, probably within my dimension, but unreachable by all, save a handful skilled in craft. Tam would say later that maybe only ten people in the whole world could journey so deep in thought.

"Yet descent is not power," she would later caution, for I was young and needed protecting against vanity.

There was a hierarchy here, an acquiescence to authority, and I wondered how that was maintained.

"Tam, could you ascend from here? For I doubt even with my mind enhanced through panic, could I summon the strength. I think I would be trapped."

"We shan't need to try." Allowing a while longer, we were borne aloft, carried by Sandy, even Tam choosing to ride with him, enveloped, so that the difference was a man carried on horseback across several miles would arrive before his walking comrades. I was brought to wakefulness faster than I could ever fashion myself.

Elated, I smiled for ten minutes, marvelling at my experience, being watched by my companions who talked privately, their minds as one, so I could not understand with accuracy what they said.

Time passed, and I was allowed to contemplate, my thoughts becoming reconciled to my new potential, able to understand the implications and risks, to formulate a clear understanding until I eventually asked, "What would have happened if neither of you were present?"

"You would have been unable to rise, and your body would either have died from malnutrition, or erosion, infracted upon by the coming winter," said Tam, being herself careful to impress the risks of my synergy.

"Or," and Sandy's voice rumbled, slowly uttering syllables, "you would have been driven insane, tormented in mind. Not everyone allows trespassers unhindered access."

"I trespassed?"

"At shallower depth, it matters not," Sandy spoke, "but deeper, you became a tolerated visitor, for a while, so yes, you trespassed."

"Once across the Ocean of Perceptions, your return is extremely difficult if unimpeded by natural resistance. You must be careful where you practise your craft, Miller! You ***must*** understand your peril." Tam looked earnest. "Being cautious is essential for whilst you can learn greater mental acuity, greater control, you will never learn to recover from that depth. Would you jump from a wall if it were ten feet? But not one of a thousand. Think of it as a cliff, sheer, with death before you."

So now I knew, that my mind had tremendous potential.

Sandy returned to the ground, wishing me good fortune, and unbeknownst travelled amongst his kin, sending word to fellow spirits of like mind, bidding that they offer aid and succour should chance encounter allow, for being like Tam of a wholesome nature he was considerate and honourable.

Of this I knew nothing, only months later learning of it through third parties.

Tam transported me back to Hedgetown, and offered to advance my training in craft, but having had my fill of tutelage I declined, determined to configure my own understanding based on failed experimentation. Nonetheless as a parting gift she left me a scroll, the second in my possession, yet different, and knowing what it contained I lifted her up in my arms and hugged her. A first for me.

CHAPTER 11

I bought a mule, a ten-week-old hunting hound, tent and winter provisions. Placing my mail, and helm along with most of my secondary purse in the care of the merchant, I paid for six months' storage.

With mule, hound, provisions, tent and three silver pieces I set out walking into the wilderness, east-north-east of Hedgetown away from the road to Cragtor, for I needed to be alone, distant from the marshes, yet not too far.

Travelling perhaps eight miles, a mile or two beyond regular patrols, still considered under the influence of the town's guard, yet in practical terms far enough away to avoid people, I sought a place to stop on the edge of trees, a large deciduous wood, and fashioning a refuge, a tent with awning covered in foliage and invisible to any cursory glance, I made my camp as comfortable as possible.

The mule, its use now superfluous, was slaughtered, and butchering the animal I hung its flesh on ropes to dry, although the hound ate well for a few days.

Expecting to tarry into the heart of winter, I sought the hoof fungus and bone-dry rotten wood to replenish my tinder box, storing a large volume of surplus in cloth bags hung near the entrance, a few feet from the open fireplace. The fungus could carry an ember for a considerable time, whereas the rotten wood when powdered, crumbled as dust blown on the wind, was excellent fire-lighting material.

There is a skill to storing large logs, stacked outside, so that the rain doesn't soak the whole, and my time on Joe's farm proved useful.

My immediate surroundings were searched, for I needed to know which animals inhabited the area; an animal absent or an animal disturbed, a sound out of place, all would forewarn. I was at one with my habitat.

The mule had carried casks of beer, weeks of dried rations, bandages, wax, and a plethora of miscellaneous items, including blankets and pots, bought cheaply, and unlikely to last, but there would be no returning, the equipment to be abandoned when the time was right.

The tent was spread amongst poles cut from sycamore trees and bent and secured to the earth, resulting in a larger living area than some might imagine, and comfortable for ferns had been cut and dried above ground and placed layer upon layer. I would share my dwelling with ticks and fleas, but that was not unfamiliar to me.

The hound who I named 'Git' learnt obedience, learning the hard way through several severe beatings, such that after five weeks he was trained. He never again resisted my will and accordingly was never struck again, well, at least not severely.

Git paid close attention to every inflexion of my character, a click of a finger, a whistle, a nod of the head, never missing direction, constantly seeking my approval, watching his master until he came to anticipate my desire. He grew in companionship, and would remain loyal for many years and a guard during my meditations.

Remembering Ben, the hound at the inn, and Tam's admonitions about protecting the body whilst the mind was absent, I had complied.

The first time I used craft, Git nearly jumped out of his skin, a magical dart sent streaking towards a deer, some one hundred and forty yards, striking the animal in the head. Git had taken a moment to gather his wits, before bounding across the heather, gleefully tossing the dying animal from side to side, and dragging the doe back slowly, but determinedly. He learnt to steady his nerve as I practised my skills.

Thrice a day, I meditated, gathering my energy, seeking the connective forces, learning my craft, both through vocal incantation and silently, building my powers of concentration, trying different conjurations.

I learnt that natural resistance, this far from water, steadied me just above the voices, and I could force myself a little lower, a reverse of my will to ascend, for I enjoyed the company of the little spirit creatures, milling around and talking to me.

These tiny entities probed my mind, many fascinated by my ability to speak and communicate with them, and I would dwell in their company for as long as my mental concentration allowed. It was an effort, and after a time I would ease my thoughts and gravitate upwards, resting once more amongst the strands of power before journeying back and speeding across the ocean of altered perceptions.

I was learning daily, and after a month had succeeded in reliably transporting myself five hundred yards using words, the silent application of this particular craft still eluding me.

Magical wards of protection similar to those Tam used on the headland were established around my camp, thinking they were high enough above the ground until one day Git nearly killed himself. Somehow he had managed to break one of the invisible lines, and suffering a systemic shock to his body, it took several days for Git to recover, a little longer before his natural enthusiasm and confidence was restored. He would forever avoid the area where the 'shock' had occurred, not understanding quite what had happened.

At night my hound rested within the tent, the fire stoked so that it provided warmth. His hearing acute, he would lie by my side, occasionally venturing out, but less so as the snow arrived.

The night became a time of unconscious meditation, reciting the lessons learnt, considering how different spells might be crafted, the strands of energy like joining letters in a word, creating differing sentences. So much was complicated, and practitioners of craft had spent millennia guarding their discoveries.

Why had Tam furnished me with this knowledge and kindness? Grimnir had asked the same, but there had been clues in their discourse, of past friendships and failed support, I knew not, but I counted myself fortunate and blessed. Whilst I stank and was covered in fleas, this time alone with my hound in the wood and hunting across the moors, free of obligation, was the best of times.

During the second month, whilst preparing to diminish a squirrel captured the day before, Git growled, glancing at me, so that I crouched down, hushing the hound and listened, watching.

Two men approached, yet each from different directions, no doubt smelling my fire, for we were within the wood, and the smoke dissipating through the branches was not discernible. There were no wards against trespass; not seeking to place my hound in further jeopardy I had avoided using them. So I watched as the men converged on my camp, some eighty yards away, ignoring convention that strangers always announce their arrival, never walking into someone's camp unannounced; the bastards meant trouble.

The men, dirty, rough, yet equipped for the weather, signalled to one another, the nearest man approaching would pass within fifteen yards unaware they were observed.

Sodding hell! I had left my sword in the tent and my spells were inappropriate, for intending to reduce and enlarge the captured squirrel, the practising of craft, I had grown complacent.

Shit. I rushed towards my tent, the element of surprise lost, and reaching under the cover, Git running beside me, collected my sword and started to lace up my studded jerkin.

"I noticed your fire, how are you?" And without waiting for an answer, the stranger enquired whether I was from these parts, all an irrelevance. He referred in the singular, no mention of his colleague.

Stepping out in front of my shelter, "Who are you, and do you travel alone?" I asked, testing his motives, for there was still doubt, it might yet be innocent. "It is unfortunate you did not announce your approach."

"My pardon, I meant no disrespect, but only now have I seen your camp, for it is well concealed. May I approach and introduce myself? I travel alone."

He was a lying bastard, and I was not in the mood to reveal anything to him. "Piss off, I don't want visitors."

He argued awhile, protesting that my manners were typical of an orc, and cursing he appeared to withdraw, saying, "I'll travel where I like, and no scum such as you will hinder me," yet he withdrew nonetheless. I couldn't see the other man.

Git, my hound, sensing my heightened alertness sat outside, watching the man walk away, and finishing the lacing of my jerkin, with a dagger in one hand and my sword in the other I summoned Git to heel. We headed through the trees and bushes in the direction I hoped the other intruder might be hiding.

"Where is he?" I hissed at the hound, more the eagerness of the words. Git, sensing the hunt was on, bounded ahead, sniffing, seeking a clue, for this was a game, and he loved his service to me.

After five minutes I heard Git growl and bark, and the bushes burst alive as a I charged in the hound's direction, movement apparent ahead.

The second man could be seen running away through the trees, Git leaping at him as he thrust a knife down, wounding my hound in the flank. Git yelped in pain, falling flat to the earth, whining in distress.

Bastard! And I chased him for quarter of a mile, before he turned and essayed to nock an arrow, having to drop his knife in the process.

Charging, he loosed his arrow in haste, yet it struck my arm, a successful shot, but he had no chance to launch a second or recover his knife, for closing the gap my dagger skewered him in the stomach, and he stared into my face, my blade twisting up though his diaphragm, cutting and gouging deep into his ribcage, lungs torn and ripped apart, my left uninjured arm lifting him off his feet such was my strength.

"That was my hound, you bastard," and I pulled out the dagger, searching for his neck, as he fell lying on the ground in shock. My blade struck again; he was too traumatised to evade, though it would have availed him not, for he was already mortally wounded.

I stood over the dying man, looking around for any counter attack, but none came, and after five minutes of listening and retrieving my injured hound, I headed back to my camp carrying the poor creature to the tent.

The arrow was pulled from my arm, the cloth vest torn, so I poked and tried to retrieve as much embedded material as I could – it hurt like shit – aware that cloth carried into the body could fester and possibly cause mortification, gangrene.

Git lay there, still whining; he needed attention, and I walked out of my tent and bellowed a warning to the first man, certain he could hear, yet actually wanted to intimidate, not ready for another altercation, my hound's injuries forefront on my mind.

A year's wages? Bugger that! I opened my single jar of Tam's salve, and applied a quarter to Git and the same to myself. Twelve hours, and I knew we didn't have the luxury of time, the first person would be back.

I wanted to cast wards, the type that had disabled Git, but couldn't take the chance; the power of craft could be manipulated, energies already fashioned could potentially be changed but I doubted my skill, and it would be foolhardy to meditate trying to collect the right forces, an unprotected hour.

So I lay Git deeper within the tent. He turned his head, dutifully anxious, worried that he could not accompany me, so bidding him, "Stay," I hid in bushes twenty yards away, waiting and watching, my sword arm aching, strength lessened yet still I could wield my blade.

All for a bloody hound? But it wasn't true, it was my hound, my pride, my tent, trespass against me, plus the lack of respect.

Patience, I knew how to be, and crouching down, seldom changing position, for an hour and a half I watched; three men approached.

One closed and as luck would have it passed adjacent to my location, scarcely six feet away. He died without knowing his opponent, a knife in the back, it matters not, for I am no coward.

His screams filled the air, thrashing around, his back bone half broken, his limbs uncontrollable, contorting, he died and moving aside, I hid again, waiting and watching.

One man headed to the tent, and I burst out determined to defend the hound; he turned around with a sword already drawn, a grim determination written across his face. He looked strong, yet I knew very few people were actually trained in the use of swords.

Fathers may have taught sons the simple art of parry and thrust, some acuity in observing the opponent, common tricks to be aware of, but there were few trained warriors locally, even fewer capable of defeating me, yet likewise there would be no need for this stranger to suspect my greater skill, and knowing this I wanted to kill slowly.

A voice rang out, "He's killed Sem, knifed him in the back."

My opponent steadied himself, watching my blade and circled slowly, turning his front towards my tent, angling himself towards where he hoped his companion would appear, losing the only advantage he had, that of flanking me.

Lowering my sword, I looked him in the eye, exposing my body as undefended, but really pensive and coiled like a spring ready to snap back. "Why do you lose your only advantage?" I asked, almost sighing. "You've just turned your back to where your companion may join you, so now I can see you both." As I spoke as if to confirm my comment, the second man came into view, some fifty feet immediately behind my opponent.

"We're well known," he said. "We kill for a living, scum such as you will be easy, though I'll confess, I've never had an orc before," he snarled, and swearing, he called his companion forward. "This orc bastard killed Sem, we'll have his eyes and tongue cut out before he dies."

"Really?" I said, as I feigned a stumble, yet rolling in the opposite direction, thrusting my knife into his ribs, as he plunged his sword down to where he imagined my stumble would leave me, striking empty air.

Looking at me as I rose to my feet, my knife still embedded in his side, his eyes were wide in shock and disbelief, gently touching the haft, hoping that somehow reality was not as grim as it looked.

Stepping away, allowing the pain and despair to eviscerate the man so he would cease to be a threat, I walked towards the third assailant, who had up until a moment before been running to support his fellow.

"You do know that I will not allow you to escape." I played with my sword, allowing fear and doubt to sap my opponents courage.

"Bastard, half-orc!"

"Oh I am, you are correct, but unlike you I'm a live bastard, though you have me on the half-orc bit." Walking towards him, I wanted to smell the fear, see him shaking.

"I'll kill you quickly if you like, for I've got your companion over there; he'll live for a few hours. I think he was planning to pull my eyes out?" And I had an idea, a way to torment my new opponent.

"Do you want to pull my eyes out?" I wanted to judge his doubt, understand just how confident he was. Did he think he could win? He didn't reply, thus not confident at all.

"You go first, please," I asked. "I hope you are better than the others."

He snarled at me, looking for an opportunity to strike, seeking any sign that might show a weakness in my skill, and finding nothing but hopelessness and despair he started making excuses, anguish setting in.

"It wasn't my idea, but if I have to fight you I will."

"Oh you do, I'm afraid, sorry. I know you know, you'll die."

I took a step back and looked behind, catching a glimpse of the other man clutching my dagger, not knowing what to do, unable to move for his breathing was becoming impaired and pain was taking hold.

The other lunged, thinking he would gain no better advantage. But my stepping back had been calculated, and a further half step sufficed for his blade to miss by a few inches.

I ridiculed him. "Pathetic… Is that it? Is that your best? Not very original."

"Why are you such a bastard?" he enquired. "You know I'll lose."

"Because your party injured my hound, and you lied to me."

He fought me for ten minutes, not because he was good, but because he was useless, and I was being cruel, cutting him and bruising, poking with the tip of my sword, and he started pleading. Begging and becoming incontinent, his stomach twisted in knots, sweat dripping from his face and neck, despite the chill air.

In the end he turned and fled, but limping, he fell, my sword swiping down on his neck, felling him to the earth. Crashing half into a bramble bush, he turned slightly as I pushed my sword into his groin then slashed his torso twice. He twitched a little before dying.

The other man was tortured, only a little, I had no desire to rip out eyes. His breathing laboured, he didn't know what to hope for, but nonetheless he confirmed there was no further threat, their camp two miles away behind rocks aside a fast-flowing stream, and giving directions I had a good idea where it lay.

The four bodies were dragged clear of the wood and burned. Snow was falling again as the fire took hold, and having stripped the bodies of anything of value I was beginning to regret not keeping the mule.

Their camp was searched the following day, for I wanted my hound with me and my wound needed proper rest. I can fight two handedly but preferred my sword arm truly unimpaired.

Their camp contained a wealth of plundered merchandise and two ponies, a cart and broken harness. *What were they planning to do with this? Perhaps secure a replacement through plunder.* I answered my own question.

I used craft to successfully mend the harness though due to its size it took two applications. The ponies needed proper care but snow was falling and due to lack of shelter they would have to manage the day's journey back to Hedgetown.

Before setting off, I returned to my woodland camp and secured the tent against ingress by creatures or snow, concealing the entrance with branches and gorse, before heading into town, Git sitting on the wagon, for he was ill equipped to struggle through the increasing snowfall, and on several occasions I needed to assist the ponies through ruts and past hidden boulders.

Arrived about seven in the evening the gates to the town were closed, yet only moments before as I approached I had seen them ajar. The shorter winter days caused towns to bar access after sunset, and with the usual pigheaded stubbornness of guards that seems universal, they resisted my request to open.

Sod this, my ponies were in distress and it was still five hours till midnight, I had no intention of waiting under a lean-to temporary shelter provided for those caught outside after nightfall.

Normally I would have bellowed and sworn, but I knew names, and my voice rang clear across the rampart, my manner exuding confidence, demanding they summoned Elranir or Torak, and bloody quickly, or Grimnir himself would be wroth.

There were a few men who considered it a bluff, but others dissented thinking discretion worthwhile, thus, after discussing amongst themselves they opened the gates. We were still haggling over the tariff when Elranir arrived, one of the junior soldiers having been despatched to enquire as to the veracity of my statements.

"I should pay a bloody copper piece," but had conceded that one silver would be my limit, an equitable payment for all the recovered merchandise. Elranir walked up.

"You look bloody disgusting," he smiled, "have you gotten a permit for bringing all those fleas, ticks and lice into town?" and laughing, told the men to allow my passage, no charge, for he lied, saying I was employed on His Lordship's behalf.

Elranir, flanked continuously by soldiers, bombarded with tasks that distracted his concentration, was always keen to inspect and correct his men, yet never maliciously, he simply could not be in all places at once and I thought him competent, the sort of sergeant or captain I would seek in future years.

After remonstrating with guards, yet not particularly concerning me, and they for their part wishing they hadn't summoned his presence, I said, "Walk with me please, Elranir, a couple of your men too if you would be so kind. I can reward you with a good story, and if you fancy, a drink or three in a few hours' time." I needed to go via my factor, the merchant, whose address I gave.

He agreed for it lay within his remit, also he suspected I got on better with Grimnir than was meant to be apparent.

I had a guard for the securing of my equipment

and sale of everything else, and Elranir, liking the story had offered to keep Grimnir informed. "Less trouble on the northern road," he said.

Elranir declined my offer of free beer, he was on duty and men fared well under his command for he was a good leader, setting an example in honesty and diligence to duty that included not getting drunk.

The merchant was watched as the goods were appraised, the items separated according to value, one or two items surprising for I had no idea that tin ingots were worth so much yet disappointed that the rolled linen was declared too water damaged to be of any value.

The ponies and cart were sold, a branding on one of the ponies' quarters apparently not difficult to hide, and an amount of one hundred and thirty-one silver pieces would be added to my inventory. I demanded a receipt, a scrip of the whole. He made a serious mistakes on the scrip, and was surprised I was competent in reading and he apologised profusely, saying it was an honest error.

"Let's be having no more," and I left with ten silver, and headed for the 'Water Rat', saying farewell to one of Elranir's guards who had overseen my safe arrival. Git walked close to heel, ignoring other animals less well trained, who when approached were kicked away. "Leave my bloody hound alone."

I didn't enter, but catching a boy by the arm told him to summon the landlord. It was cold, snow lay on the ground, and I needed attending to.

The landlord came, and looked at me, worried that I would infest one of his better rooms, and saying as much, it was agreed that I would stay in a stable whilst two hot baths were made, and my clothes nigh boil washed whilst leather was treated to remove all signs of infestation. I stood naked, scratching my balls, until rags were provided, wondering if they had anything as effective as Tam's lotions derived from plants, for lye probably wasn't enough.

I tarried three days in town and spent nine silver living well, my accommodation on the ground floor, but meditations whilst beneficial weren't as deep as I would have liked, unable to fall near the little spirits; even when trying to push myself down I was still far too high to enjoy their company.

However, my dreams were visited by a small spirit creature, one of the entities, of a type that dwells in the subconscious mind, darting into and playing with my imagination, changing the direction of my thoughts, especially when I slept. But I couldn't communicate with him nor could I read his emotions, just knowing he was there at night when I slept, and upon awakening there was a residual awareness he was still travelling with me.

The weather started to improve, and I had mainly waited for Git to be sufficiently able to traverse the snow, which still lay on the fields.

There was a small caravan setting out and securing a ride with the help of a soldier who vouched I was safe, and exchanging the last of my copper pieces, Git and I sat on a large open-topped wagon carrying fleeces rolled into bales.

Thus we departed two hours before midday, the wagons making their usual slow progress trundled up the north road heading for Cragtor and after some seven miles I left the caravan heading off into the wilderness, the moon hidden by clouds. My sight better than Git's, we walked as quickly as the ground allowed, Git staying close to my heel.

We laboured four or five miles across rough ground, and it was bitterly cold; Git wasn't happy, and remained distressed until such time as the fire was lit. Eventually we reached camp and moving aside the branches concealing the opening I was pleased to find everything undisturbed.

It took a while for the larger logs to catch alight, even after scraping the damp bark away and making feather cuts to the wood, but after thirty minutes the fire was established. It was approximately an hour before midnight and the sun wouldn't rise until four hours before noon.

Waking at the crack of dawn, the morning chorus muted, I made preparations for the day ahead; the fire needed stoking, I searched for animal tracks, fed the hound, and generally inspected the camp.

Git wandered through the trees chasing the odd rabbit, but he was doing according to my will, for whilst he scurried around, it reassured me that little of danger or hazardous to my health was nearby.

Finding the trapped squirrel still alive, I decided to continue with my earlier plan, the energy to enlarge and reduce along with a limited portal spell, powerful, indeed my most powerful remained charged in my body. Later I would try to convert higher powered spells into weaker applications. It was certainly possible but I didn't know how.

The sun was scarcely above the horizon, its weak light filtering through the branches, now devoid of leaves. I settled down to begin my meditation, keen to revisit the small entities, yet as I sat ready to touch the ground something disquieted me, something in my mind that I couldn't 'place my finger on'. Had I forgotten something? I couldn't fathom what it was, but my feral senses were aroused. Could the little spirit entity be trapped? Was I receiving a warning?

Pushing aside my caution, and getting ready to continue, alarms were sounding, and I couldn't ignore them.

The hairs on the back of my neck stood up, and rising to my feet, I grabbed my sword, already wearing my studded leather jerkin and touching the haft of my knife. Very quietly I went outside; Git bounded towards me.

"Get inside." I gently clicked my fingers and pointed; he sloped off, not understand what he had done wrong, but something was disquieting my mind. The hound looked from within the tent, eyes peering out, and changing my mind, I pointed to my heel, and Git followed me into a thicket, near to where I had hidden before, lying down silently.

I waited in the cold, half an hour, and then something caught the corner of my eye. Something ruffled the side of my tent, but I had seen no one enter.

Slowly, with little sound, for my feet tread gently on snow, I stole up and peered into the gloom. A small cloaked figure was searching through my possessions, opening my backpack, gently taking out items and laying them on the floor, but perhaps noticing a fractional change in the light coming through the doorway, he looked up, and seeing himself watched, darted out through a hole he had cut in the rear of the tent.

Chasing after him, shouting for Git, I plunged into the undergrowth. My adversary was incredibly swift, difficult to keep up with; he was about four foot ten inches tall, fleet of foot, wearing dark clothes, a hood blown back revealed a mat of grey hair tied in a ponytail, and as he ran I saw a belt with pouches, a knife, and cord or thin rope.

He ran so quickly, jumping into foliage and emerging at an angle, Git would run onwards in a different direction, and after three minutes he had eluded us.

Returning to my tent I went through my backpack and was relieved that nothing seemed to be missing. The two tiny scrolls were there, and repacking everything, I grabbed rations, and set out, kicking the fire into the sides of the tent so that it caught on the edges, and soon the campsite was ablaze.

Whoever it was that gained access, did so with neither my hound nor myself being aware and whilst he may not be deadly the camp was now compromised. We were heading for the road and I suspected we were being followed.

We ran, the hound enjoying the change, but I was alarmed, never having imagined anyone could sneak up so successfully and then evade me with such professionalism.

How could we be found, unless followed last

night, but then why wait for the morning? Too many questions, and I just felt vulnerable. Perhaps I should turn and fight, but this person would probably avoid a confrontation, or seek a time of his choosing; he was potentially lethal.

We pressed on and sliding down a long but shallow valley we entered a freezing cold stream. I grabbed my hound and uttered a spell, transporting myself and a bewildered hound less than a third of a mile down the ravine.

He would see where we came in but not my departure, tracks would be lost, plus a little distance gained.

We ran and walked, the hound flagging after two miles, its legs impacted by the freezing snow. So I carried him, sometimes slung over my shoulder, sometimes under my arm, either way I encouraged the hound to run where the snow was thinnest for it was uncomfortable for the two of us.

It look three hours of hard slogging, for the ground was covered in melting snow and underneath coarse heather, boggy in places. Eventually we reached the road, some seven more miles north of Hedgetown and walking southwards for three miles came upon a patrol, and I felt stupid.

Not knowing any of the soldiers, I continued to walk the rest of the way; we would reach town before the light failed, and I would secure my room and place wards on the door. Git could sleep in the stables.

I had no money, and the guards reluctantly agreed to accept two copper in an hour's time, for one remembered me from a few nights ago, mentioning

Elranir's name.

Hammering on the merchant's door, he looked surprised to see me and handed me twenty silver pieces, adjusting my scrip or chit as he called it, before I secured lodgings at the Water Rat, with scarcely a flea or louse on me.

A lad was found to deliver the two copper pieces, receiving one for his services. Both I and the hound ate well, though I retired early and changing my mind, allowed Git into the room, though I made sure the shutters and door were secure, and spiked one of the door locks, a double protection.

In the morning I headed towards Grimnir's keep, needing to leave Hedgetown for I couldn't reach my spirit entities, and during my sleep had become more convinced that the warning received the previous morning had originated from the little entity that visited my dreams and even now I vaguely half sensed was present.

Was this my ally in craft? Not what I expected, but I needed to know.

Nervous as I walked through Hedgetown, even early in the morning, I wanted to avoid close contact with anyone.

Approaching the castle I noticed that the gates were half open, and only a couple of people stood outside, possibly arriving early and required to wait inline.

"Lord Grimnir," I bellowed. "Torak, Elranir, Roderick!" Not in the slightest of hope expecting Grimnir to hear or reply, but I wanted to be noticed.

My hound and I approached, meaning to walk unimpeded through the gates, a forlorn hope, yet sometime confidence gets you halfway and it worked, a man looking over whispered to another, and then a third, yet I was still denied access. Bloody right I should be, or someone is incompetent.

A guard less aggressive than he might otherwise have been, came down a spiral staircases as I stood in the archway and asked after my business.

"Lord Grimnir wants to see me immediately." But, I added, trying to sound plausible, that, "In his absence, I am to see Zolpetre, without delay," and without pausing added, "my name is Miller, it is urgent... May I sit there?" A bench just within the outer courtyard.

I had learnt that one allowable act frequently reinforces a proceeding less agreeable request, and I was trying it for the first time. Some turd of a cleric had talked about manipulating minds, and he had tried his skills on me without success, but his reasoning had seemed logical, and remembering his advice from years ago I sat down on the bench, not waiting for permission. All about confidence and control.

Interestingly it seemed to be working, but as I sat waiting, Git at my side, I doubted I would ever study such matters. Nothing focusses the mind more than a sword scratching your enemy's scrotum.

Ten minutes later an official arrived, and I thought, *Shit, I'm going to be kicked out,* but I was wrong, and was shown into Grimnir's hall.

Grimnir was sat on a stool in front of his throne, though he called the throne his high chair, for thrones rightly belonged to kings and he was only a lord.

"I prefer it here, it's more comfortable than that pompous seat." He thumbed his hand behind.

"Why do you have the damn thing then?" I asked, already feeling relaxed in his presence.

"It's expected…" And he marched around the hall, shutting doors, and shouting down one corridor, asked that his breakfast be doubled, for he had a guest.

I explained everything to Grimnir, except my application of craft and the meditations with Sandy and Tam, although he knew an awful lot about craft for one who never practised the skill.

He cross examined me about the men I killed and the words they spoke, of the recovered merchandise and where I had sold it and approved of much that I had done, even commending Elranir, and the guards at the gate.

Only when I told of the shrouded figure did he become serious; over and over again he asked for the most exacting of details, and after twenty minutes of talking and eating he shocked me with words said so nonchalantly.

"How did you know that an assassin was stalking you?"

I looked aghast. "I didn't know… not until now."

"But you sensed the danger, so you must have had some inkling… Have you got a helper in craft, Miller, or does your hound commune with you telepathically?"

Laugh? I did, but it was no laughing matter, and

Grimnir thought not too.

"You know that every large town has a small Thieves Guild, and larger towns such as this, have one for assassins, though in all locations they are hidden, impossible to fully eradicate and at the moment an ancillary office of the thieves."

I looked surprised, and questioned how he combatted such lawlessness, and when he said he knew who the current guild-master was, "Though he would never admit it if I arrested him," I looked incredulously at him.

"Just do it," I said.

"And then another springs up, yet I have no influence?" Grimnir's tongue was contorting trying to eject a seed caught between two teeth.

"So I will keep the status quo, and find out who hired the assassin and have the contract voided, or would you prefer me powerless and unable to influence? Which or what would you have me do?"

"Bloody hell! Towns and law are complicated... Does Tam have an assassins' network operating in Cragtor?"

"No, she expelled them all, and now I've got them, but I don't have her skills in your craft. Besides, my town is on the frontier, she understands that my location disadvantages me."

"So just to be clear, you know the Thieves' Guildmaster, he knows you, and you can talk to him and he won't try to assassinate you?"

"Exactly." Grimnir was trying to impale a fried mushroom that was left on my abandoned plate.

"It's a symbiotic arrangement, he knows I would kill him; his whole family, cousins, nephews, aunts and uncles, his children and friends, and that I, not he, command in Hedgetown, he operates under duress." Grimnir succeeded in skewering the fungus.

"He avoids infracting upon my court and officials, at least whilst they are in my employ, and occasionally he ingratiates himself by giving useful information.

"It works because he's not allowed to get too powerful, he knows the town needs to function, he doesn't disturb the goose that lays the golden egg, he's the carrion breeder, the rat that clears garbage, and for the most part avoids upsetting me."

Some people are industrious, others not knowing where to start, but a fleeting thought crossed my mind, a jest to myself... "Bloody hell, I've missed my vocation in life."

"Would you like to meet him, Miller?" Grimnir smiled, a play on my emotions, knowing I learnt whilst he imparted knowledge.

"What! The man who agreed my death? Too bloody right I'd like to meet him."

Grimnir belched, and asked to be excused, but before departing, he stuck his head through a door and uttered some words I couldn't hear, and leaning into the hall once more, "Just visiting the shit hole, back in a minute."

I waited, walking around Grimnir's hall, looking at statues and carvings, examining how dust settled, and soot marked the carved woods farther above, noticing a fireplace and peering up, wondering if a thief could shinny down.

Three minutes later Zolpetre entered the hall, and took a seat ten feet from Grimnir's stool.

"Hi Zolpetre!" But he had not the grace for small talk, and I desperately tried to fart, but couldn't.

"How much does an assassin cost to hire!" I asked, but he with the crass aloofness of all bureaucrats said he didn't know, and I thought he was an ignorant lying turd. "You have never heard of assassins? Or that they work for money?"

"I know of them but not their fees." And as I stared at him, he deigned to give a little more information. "Apparently it depends upon the difficulty."

"Er, huh, no shit!" What an obvious statement. "So someone like you wouldn't cost much?"

He was now more than ever convinced he didn't want to talk to me, so we both waited for Grimnir to return.

"Ah, Grimnir," as he walked into the hall. "How much does an assassin cost to hire, say, to kill me?"

"Five gold pieces, but they would charge more if they knew you better." He walked over to his seat and mentioned to Zolpetre that I would be staying within the castle grounds for the next day, and possibly until the day after, and that quarters on the ground floor would be needed.

Like hell I will, I thought to myself. *I'm off to Cragtor.*

Grimnir also gave instructions to summon Guildmaster Jambeedee, for lunch, immediately. It would be business, and he wasn't to be unavailable, the point impressed.

"Miller is to be given unimpeded access to **all** parts

of the castle, now and in the future, no hindrance."

I spent the rest of the morning helping Roderick train Grimnir's recruits, but I wondered if I actually encouraged or demoralised, for being a brutish opponent, even when Roderick confiscated my wooden sword, half the recruits were in disarray and leaving me with a wooden dagger no larger than a twig, I fended off one attack after another; all the recruits were battered and dejected.

Sitting on the outer ramparts, watching the industry within the grounds and observing guards at the main gate, I wondered what a Guildmaster thief would look like. Merchants and others entered and left the castle; could I guess who he was amongst the many who passed below?

About midday, I received a summons to join Grimnir, and gathering my normal attire marched into the main hall, telling the door warden to piss off, when he objected to my weapons. "Unencumbered access, you turd. I'll be encumbered without my sword." And by the time he'd worked out the nonsensical words, I was walking across the floor.

Sat around a modestly large table lightly covered in food with wooden plates, a wiry individual was talking to Grimnir, but turned to observe my entrance.

"Good day, Jambeedee," I said, as I walked towards him.

As I crossed the hall, I had an understanding, I instantly knew who had trespassed against me, and why.

Jambeedee stood up and offered his hand, greeting me, but I refused to reciprocate and observing him noticed the quality of his clothes, that whilst drab and subdued, upon closer inspection had subtle quality, the material being finely made and expensive.

With considerable grace, all a conceit, Jambeedee spoke. "I apologise for any perceived infraction upon your health, Master Miller, but Lord Grimnir has asked that I use my influence, modest though it is, to secure your peace."

There would be none, I thought.

I suspected the merchant, my would-be factor had arranged my death, for I had six hundred and ninety-two silver pieces in his care, and my equipment amounted to an additional thirty-five hundred. Sufficient motivation for murdering an unknown itinerant half-orc, and I wondered if the Water Rat's innkeeper was also complicit.

"If my efforts prove successful, my lord," for Jambeedee looked back towards Grimnir, "Miller's safety should be restored within forty-eight hours. I'll need to speak to my friends and so forth." Jambeedee was careful to carry on the pretence that he was only a go-between, it was all polite conversation, but I had no intension of waiting forty-eight hours.

"Grimnir!" I said in front of Jambeedee. "I'll be collecting my equipment from my factor in two hours' time, woe betide him if there's any problem, perhaps a couple of guards might accompany me?" And Grimnir, understanding, called for one of his sergeants.

Jambeedee, keeping his expressions neutral was quick to comprehend the risk, for he wanted to access the merchant first.

"Master Miller, your safety is paramount, please allow me to collect the items on your behalf as it seems some of my friends may have misbehaved. It's the least I can do, you are after all, a guest in His Lordship's house?"

But I wanted the merchant dead, and with Grimnir watching, I agreed to Jambeedee's kind offer.

"That's extremely generous of you, Jambeedee, and I gratefully accept, nonetheless in a couple of days I will be paying him a visit; he'll squeal like a pig for he probably arranged the assassination with someone."

"Oh, you think your merchant was involved? Well, I don't know! If you like I can try and find out?" Jambeedee remained expressionless.

I showed Grimnir my scrip, and then offered the paper to Jambeedee.

Within two hours my possessions were returned and not unexpectedly the merchant had mysteriously fallen head first onto stone flags, breaking his neck, slipping whilst repairing the warehouse roof, strange as his wife reported he was scared of heights.

CHAPTER 12

"No wonder this bloody horse was lent to me, no one else wanted the damn creature!" My arse was sore, for riding three days on a horse with a peculiar wallowing gait had proved too much for my backside.

Persuaded to protect a small caravan, between the towns of Hedgetown and Cragtor, I Miller, a half-orc bastard, rode alongside Riklor, a junior sergeant in the employ of Lord Grimnir.

"Bloody hell!" I looked at Riklor, for in front of me stood a man I intended to murder – Krun. "Surely this turd's not in the employ of Lady Tam?"

Krun was one hundred and fifty miles from where I had seen him last and seemingly on patrol, and Riklor being a sergeant in the employ of Lord Grimnir, had a tenuous authority over low-ranking Cragtor militia such as Krun.

Dressed in chainmail, a sword at my side, and a battle axe strapped to my horse, I dismounted and stood six foot four inches tall, formidable, and I so wanted an opportunity to slay him.

"Krun, you stinking bastard, what a pleasure it is to see you still poor and unpromoted. Why aren't you where you belong, or did you get caught fornicating with a pig?" I walked up to his horse desperately trying to antagonise him. "Still paying whores for your entertainment?" I drew my sword as I approached, and poked him none too gently in the groin.

"Oh, by the gods! It's the ignorant half-orc slave. Who did you steal that armour from?" And looking at Riklor, "Is he with you, Sergeant? For the last time I saw this ugly bastard, he was pleading for his life, begging for my mercy."

I swang my sword, blade turned flat, striking Krun in the mouth. He fell from his saddle, though his right leg was caught in a stirrup.

Five militiamen surrounded me, and above the cursing Riklor bellowed, "Put your bloody weapons away. You as well, Miller."

Walking back, I remounted my horse, and rode past the other men, kicking Krun's horse hard so it leapt forwards ten feet, and Krun who was trying to release himself from the stirrup was dragged along the ground, his head hitting small rocks.

"My duty's done!" I shouted back to Riklor, for the caravan was now well protected. "And I know if I tarry in Krun's company I'll do something stupid."

What the hell's Tam employing Krun for? I wondered as I galloped along the north road, heading for town, Git racing to keep up.

It took me a few hours to arrive at the gates, and dismounting paid two copper pieces toll. Cragtor was more expensive than Hedgetown.

"You need to pay extra for the horse," said one of the guards, and I told him he could "Whistle up its arse," for the beast belonged to Lord Grimnir, and I wasn't paying, and leaving the beast outside the gates walked through, much to their consternation.

"I'll inform Glamdrun, your captain, when I see him. You should give it to Sergeant Riklor, he'll be here within the day." For I didn't want to deprive Grimnir of the animal's value, even though it was the shittiest horse I had ever had the misfortune to ride.

My battle axe now carried in one hand, I headed for the Haggard Hen and hoped the landlord would remember me for I wanted to bathe and secure lodgings for the night.

Pushing through town, one hand on my axe, the other ready to grasp my dagger, I was conscious that I had far too much silver in my possesion and would try and offload some with Tam.

The 'Hen' as it was known locally, offered various standards of accommodation, and being somewhat richer than the last time I visited, I intended to sleep well tonight. As I entered my iron-shod feet clattered on the stone flags, reminding me of the last time I visited.

Heads turned, for the common room was packed with the better off in society, who weren't accustomed to seeing a road weary warrior spending serious silver.

Nonetheless, the landlord remembered my last visit; it was after all hard not to, and securing the best room in his establishment I paid for a single evening, to be bathed, my mail scrubbed and clothes cleaned.

It was late afternoon, the sun low in the sky, and keen to get on with my mission I headed for Tam's castle.

This time before dusk was interesting in Cragtor, for many traders were still open for business, lamps hung above open shutters, people buying cloth, pins, oils, herbs spices, women browsing, though most determinedly accomplishing tasks whilst time allowed.

The smells and sounds of Cragtor were in contrast to Hedgetown, the place felt more secure, the rich were not restricted in their showy display of wealth and children seemed more ready to run ahead of parents, forming small gangs and running through the streets and alleyways. Individuals were generally less wary of each other. Guards walked singularly whereas in Hedgetown the patrols tended to be in groups of two or three; people were for the most part relaxed and at ease.

Tam knew I was travelling with the caravan, yet the hour of my arrival wasn't known, and unlike Hedgetown, only Glamdrun and Tam could vouch for me, so approaching the castle, I was braced for delays.

The castle doors smelt of fresh light tar, a form of creosote designed to preserve the timbers but also flammable and of doubtful benefit in times of conflict for the doors could be set alight, burning for hours depending upon how recently the surface had been treated.

Men on wooden scaffolds were repointing the lime mortar, stone masons were lowering blocks of stone and dressing large stone blocks newly set within the walls. Below them, on the green grass in front of the ramparts, roughly hewn blocks brought from quarries were being chiselled into differing sizes. Tam had seemingly begun repairs on her stronghold, though it had always seemed well maintained.

Although I didn't know it then, the upkeep of a castle is an ongoing chore, yet there seemed a lot of activity.

Approaching, the main gates were almost closed, and I was rightly challenged; an overweight man wearing banded mail hindered my access.

"Halt! I need to see your permission, or know the nature of your business." He seemed slightly wary of me for my armour signified competence and he rightly considered caution and deference was due. Appearance makes a huge difference when dealing with guards, and he knew to exercise his authority with care.

"Now then, guardsman! I have business with Lady Bluebottle, I'm expected."

"Yes, I was told someone of your race would be seeking access. What is your name, master warrior?"

"How many half-orcs do you see trying to gain access to Lady Bluebottle?" I said, sighing. "I'm expected, the name's Miller, fetch someone who knows what they're doing!"

It took only five minutes, and an escort arrived.

Tam greeted me in a side room, looking tired, for

whilst she always smiled there was an anxiety about her, a weariness that was occasionally apparent. The fact that she betrayed her calm exterior was in itself unusual.

"It's wonderful to see you, Miller: Grimnir's given few clues as to your activities, he keeps your affairs rightly private."

Looking at her, wanting to read her thoughts, but sensing nothing, I revealed the whole of my experiences, but offered to come back at a better time. "You look exhausted, is there anything I can do?" I worried that I encroached upon her peace.

She smiled and closed her eyes. "Secure ten miles around the town, rally an army, defend the castle, defeat all the kingdom's enemies," and pausing for a few moments, "perhaps later you might!"

"Give me forty men, and I can secure the land, though you will have to ignore some complaints."

Tam, opening her eyes, looked at me. "We may not have forty men, for every spare man is being summoned northwards; Culanur will fall, and then petty kingdoms will emerge, people will be used as pawns, and times more difficult will be upon us."

I was surprised, for although I knew Culanur's north-eastern border was threatened by fierce barbarian tribes I had heard no rumour, neither had Grimnir revealed any hint of these troubles.

"Grimnir gave me no clue, he revealed nothing, neither did I see any preparation for war," although I added, "not that he ought to tell me anything."

"What would you do, Miller? Defy the King, or

defend a lost cause?"

And I understood. "I would do as Grimnir does," adding very mischievously, "more lives will be saved in Cragtor."

Tam spoke with a cynical expression on her face. "Now you understand, but this is not to be discussed, for matters may take months to unfold."

"Who do you think I would be discussing it with? Even when drunk I'm avoided."

Tam was going to contradict, but ultimately changed the subject.

"Let's go down into the basement, I'm fascinated by your association with this entity in your mind." And an eagerness entered my thoughts as she said those words.

"How do you feel about using your scroll? You could have tried before." Tam, sitting down in her delicate chair had just whispered for Sandy.

"I'm excited by the prospect of an intelligence that might want to associate with me, be my ally, for I'm certain I would have been in mortal danger had the warning, the disquiet, not sounded in my mind," and looking slightly away from her, head half turned, "I doubt my hope."

Smiling once more, given a cheerful task, Tam said, "Sandy will be with us shortly, he's a minute away."

And I sensed him approaching, as moments later he rose above the ground.

Touching him as he emerged, the synergy slightly less strong, I could feel his warmth and companionship with Tam.

"I spend hours listening to them, but in Hedgetown I could not reach deep enough." I meant the small spirit creatures, but they understood.

Sandy looked at me expressionless, I could faintly sense his goodwill, and after a minute of private conversation between Tam and Sandy, she said they were ready.

"I'll go first as before." And as she knelt upon the ground Sandy sank away, and I was alone, worried, braced for disappointment.

Placing my hand on the ground, meditating, controlling my breathing, trying to thrust anxieties aside, I fell.

The ocean of altered perceptions sped below, colours flashing across my mind, the earth song growing louder, the trumpets sounding, a chorus of instruments, tumultuous colours merging with the senses, tasting the music, all senses combining and enhancing, complimenting one another.

Falling deeper, the connective energies of the earth whipping past me, too fast to gather, I fell faster, Sandy and Tam beside me, and something sped ahead as we were drawn deep down.

Sandy buoyed me, slowing my descent, and something else wanted to come close.

Slowing, the connective forces of the earth gently floated past. We approached the purple haze, a mist where the small entities began, and communicating that I should be able to hold myself, Sandy released me.

With great concentration I succeeded in steadying my position, and then I felt an affinity to one small spirit; he entered my mind, reinforcing my concentration, and I was elated.

Dwelling, absorbed by my friend's goodwill, I lost my connection with Tam and Sandy, or rather I was wholly distracted, like a child forgetting their manners, in receipt of a fabulous gift.

Unaware of time, enjoying the emotion and experience of my new association, he spoke, like water washing over rocks, to and fro. We communicated, until finally he said we were being summoned back, and 'he was willing'.

As Sandy bore me aloft, the spirit creature stayed bound to my consciousness, and coming out of meditation, sitting on the ground, I probed my thoughts, sending a question to myself, for I could no longer hear him, but an affirmation, a gentle hidden emotion testified to his continued presence.

Tam sat quietly, allowing the time to pass, allowing my thoughts to become reconciled to my experience, and after twenty minutes said, "Dream allies are rare, you'll never see your ally above ground, nor in physical form."

"Does it matter?" I asked, knowing that I wanted the union.

"No, probably not, but you just needed to know."

I reached in my backpack, seeking the scroll that Tam had given me. An arcane rune etched on the front described the contents therein, and breaking the seal, noticing the tiny writing, knowing that Tam herself had made this for me, I looked at the words, waypoints of an incantation, the energy magically stored within the parchment.

"I'll leave you now, Miller." And Tam, rising from her chair, Sandy sinking into the ground, closed the door behind her as she departed. I was alone, yet not so.

This was a most personal moment, uttering words beautifully written, my hand shaking, quietly summoning the power contained therein. Gently at first but increasing in intensity the dweomer spread throughout the room, circling in the air like gossamer mist blown gently on a light breeze, swirling through and around my body, engulfing my entirety, the energy passing through, unimpeded by my physical form, and although Tam had said it wasn't a marriage, it felt like one.

The clarity and enhancement of mental acuity, an affirmation of union combined with trust, my mind delighting in the sole association, a sharing of destiny.

I could hear my tiny entity willing me on, exalting, eager to accept the bond of a lifetime, wrapped in harmony. Images of the earth's music played across my mind, and each knew that life would be different.

Normally when craft is actioned there is a dissipation of the force gleaned from the earth, yet on this occasion, there was no such diminution, the energies remained absorbed within, a fortification against decay.

I knew the thoughts of my ally and he played beautiful pictures across my mind, showing hidden places deep within the earth, giving me his name, unpronounceable, almost as a story, the name I knew, yet others could never know. Unique, personal, a secret known only to myself.

He spoke across my waking thoughts, describing his abilities, and in turn fascinated by my application of craft, my prowess with weapons, seeing through my eyes a world wholly new, delighting in the bond.

Journeying in the earth song, clutching the ground, deep in meditation, racing through the connective energies, he guided my gathering of the strands, buoyed up, not as Sandy or Tam might do, but through the strengthening and reinforcing of my own concentration, so I no longer feared the lack of natural resistance.

Under his guidance with fabulously enhanced awareness I harvested complex connective forces, my expanded comprehension allowing the fabrication of all my spells, many, which until recently were only within my potential.

Time and space became irrelevant, and hours passed, until he advised someone was knocking gently on the door, and I had nothing to fear for it was only Tam. He didn't disparage Tam, but simply knew there was no danger.

Speeding across the ocean of altered perceptions, I emerged into consciousness. 'Wisp', for I had thought the name appropriate, remained with me and I could hear his thoughts.

It was after midnight, and two guards walked with me through the town, I, oblivious to their company, but reaching 'The Hen', and knocking on the door, a shutter opened, and the landlord escorted me to my room.

I fell asleep, but my dreams were marvellous, superb, my heart celebrating, triumphant in the magnificence of this new association.

*

It was three days later that I awoke, mid morning, and I was totally disorientated. Not until the landlord greeted and handed me a message, written in elvish, did I start to realise how long I had lain undisturbed.

Tam had paid for the week, but should I wish to talk, I would be most welcome to visit. She had vouched for my continuing use of the room, though having no idea how long I would be staying, I still needed to settle any extra costs.

Git, my hound, was overjoyed to see me, and bounding forwards expressed his enthusiasm, imagining himself abandoned.

I spent time wandering through town. Wisp could sense the thoughts of people when they stared at me, and if I asked he would visit them at night, reading their dreams and reporting the next day.

He made me laugh, because to Wisp these experiences were new; he was constantly asking the meaning of human dreams. Many of those he visited had prurient minds, and he like myself was naive.

We were both young and there was so much he and I learned together. Our bond and understanding grew daily, yet it would take a year for the maximum symbiotic harmony to be reached.

During the days ahead, I would harvest the energies required for the application of craft, and port myself and hound some four miles out of town, the new enhanced limit of my ability.

However, the first time I transported myself, my connection with Wisp was broken, or rather absent is perhaps a better word.

I was distraught, thinking I had permanently severed the bond, wroth with myself, momentarily despairing, comprehending the devastation a parent feels when a child is lost to misadventure or disease.

But twenty seconds later Wisp reconnected and I spent half an hour checking and querying the meaning. Why couldn't I transport Wisp? I worried that I risked tragedy.

In the end, that first time, Git and I walked back into town, fearful to risk too much, anxious to ask Tam, who later reassured me that portal travelling only applied to physical presence, as with the case of Sandy, but not pure intellect, such as Wisp's, for I had disclosed his name to her.

I sat in front of her, waves of relief washing over me, almost tearful, yet I can assure you, the reader, no wetness protruded from my eyes, anathema. I don't cry, but in the telling of this story you need to understand just how relieved I was.

I added an addendum, a scribe being recalled, for reading that which they wrote, I thought I had told my scribes to delete this passage. Perhaps I hadn't. Such was the emotion, rekindled when events are recalled to mind.

EPILOGUE

For the next three months, whilst waiting for the arrival of early spring, I spent some time in Tam's company, and yes, I allowed her to tutor me in some aspects of craft, the fashioning of spells of greater order. She showed me how to magnify applications of transport, such that the four miles I could accomplish without accurate knowledge of my destination, could be enhanced ten or possibly twenty fold, but only with a detailed recollection of where my destination was, a precise knowledge, for there were risks in travelling too far.

She explained why only Sandy could transport us to the driest part of the earth, for Sandy being an earth elemental had already visited the area, and it was his accurate knowledge that allowed the enhancement of Tam's craft.

As we sat, so many times in her deep room, the bowels of her castle, she taught me the ability to sense other practitioners of craft, how whilst dwelling deep in mediation and allowing my mind to reach out through the timeless rhapsody, listening to the music, you could feel the ripples of energy filling voids, giving an idea where others harvested the strands of power, for just like water flowing into a hole, you could guess the direction of currents, and according to the depth of your meditation, it was possible to glean a very rough idea of the power being gathered, and thus the strength and skill of a distant sorcerer, or rather the ability of the practitioner.

We journeyed together, Tam, Sandy, Wisp and I, learning how to enquire of other spirit creatures, learning the events that unfolded deep within, and upon the earth, though in this Wisp was mostly ignored, for his order in hierarchy was small, and whilst the little energies were fascinated with his association of Sandy, he held no authority except amongst his peers, who for the most part gave him a modicum of deferential treatment.

The weeks marched on, and I was waiting for the coming of spring. I needed to escape the confines of Culanun, wanting no report of future activities to tar my relationship with Tam and Grimnir.

It seems an oversight now, but I hadn't considered that Tam would have a library, a scroll room, and waking one morning, Git and I walking around the castle boundaries, it dawned on me with certainty that Tam would have maps and knowledge far beyond the scant recollections of clerics, their limit stories of lands far away.

So with access unrestricted, yet seeking Tam's permission, I pored over maps, copying charts and learning about towns and kingdoms far away, seeking a destination where I could cause mayhem. Little kingdoms with petty rulers, the edge of wildlands, barbarian chiefs, and especially those lands inhabited by my brethren orcs, lawless places on the perimeter of the known world.

With winter turning to spring I had one serious matter to attend to, the matter of Krun. So long had I been dilatory, for he was obnoxious; even here, so far from Gledrill, did he cause distress.

There were rumours of his thievery and bullying, of his brutality to women, and he wasn't popular even amongst the town's militia.

Yet I had purposefully restrained any action against him, aware that Tam would automatically suspect me. She being cleverer than I, she could almost read my mind.

With the passage of time, winter turning to spring, I could wait no longer, and bidding Tam farewell, I booked a room at the Haggard Hen, a cheap room for three weeks, instructing the landlord not to trespass inside, for I wanted the furniture to be exactly arranged as my mind's eye could visualise it.

As for Krun I knew when he would reappear, for he frequented the whore houses and watching him, I pointed him out to Wisp, so he knew his mind and could visit him at night, deep in his dark dreams. For I was leaving and I needed to know how to find Krun when I was ready.

I bought rations and general provisions, including

tarpaulin and a horse, though I rode the animal for a few hours making sure the creature was suitable. Having been caught out with Grimnir's spare animal, I had no intension of being sold crap.

Satisfied the horse was sound and gathering all my silver together, I converted half into small gems and gold coins, for whilst gold is heavy, nonetheless compared to the volume of silver it replaced, it amounted to a few less pounds in weight. Thus prepared I set off into the wilderness, Git running alongside, my powers significantly enhanced, lethal as Grimnir predicted.

As I rode or walked, heading initially for the great rolling hills and moorlands, I crossed north east passing farms, the decaying lines of the Grey Mountains forming the distant horizon, and pondered my missed opportunity with Miriam, and my lack of experience with girls. Yet I hoped these matters would be resolved in time. Git enjoyed his freedom, running free, a liberty I could understand.

Wisp would forewarn who was ahead, for like Sandy, he could enter the earth song and instinctively know of all life that dwelt nearby.

Initially we passed alongside farms and were watched by many people, including the odd patrol, and counting and speaking to men we met, I knew Tam's recruitment drive was underway.

Farm lads made their way inwards, mothers hugging their sons, fathers offering up old swords, heirlooms passed down through the generations, hung above fireplaces, antiques in many cases, yet serviceable. Parents and siblings anxiously wishing their sons and brothers their love, worrying if they would see them whole again, yet proud, not revealing their own fears, lest it undermined courage.

I was fourteen years old and had shaved my beard as it was an embarrassment, now a slight stubble formed around my chin. The scar upon my face itched slightly, yet I looked older than my years and felt comforted with my travelling companions, an orc with his hound as it seemed to others, yet Wisp added so much more.

As I travelled away from Cragtor and Tam, I wondered if I should have stayed and fought alongside her, but her defence did not depend upon my presence, rather the number of men she could muster, and encroachment upon her lands was many months away. I could help if need be, I would know through the earth what befell.

The images Wisp had shown me of the great caves deep in the ground, the fabulous vistas that Sandy had described, allayed some of my fears for Tam, for the cost of running a large town such as Cragtor could easily be covered by the wealth Sandy could procure.

At first, my travel had been hindered by the avoidance of crops, not that I would have bothered riding through a corn field, but this was still Tam's land and I had circumvented fields, avoiding antagonising outlying farmers, yet as the fields gave way to rough fenland I found my progress no better enhanced, the old east road fallen into disrepair, large stretches absent.

I was hailed by one of the last farmers who questioned my motives, yet was polite as his manners and upbringing allowed.

"Now then, sir!" He was collecting potatoes; two labourers worked alongside. He was the poorest of farmers I had seen, dressed in rags, so that it was hard to discern who was master and who was paid employee.

"Are you joining the band of turds who live without paying?" he said, although I had no idea of what he spoke, but it was clear he was being infracted upon.

"Master farmer," I answered for my hound was weary and it wasn't so far till I pitched cramp, indeed I was not instinctively an enemy of this man for he had greeted me fairly and was poor, the rags reminding me of my miserable existence barely a year before.

"I'm leaving Cragtor, heading towards the mountains," and I was happy to reveal my identity. I, similar to Tam, wanted to be seen to depart.

"What turds do you speak of?" For I was curious; there was little amongst the day to stimulate the mind. My affinity to Wisp was wonderful but it did not preclude all other interaction.

He didn't enunciate his thoughts and heading towards him, I had sympathy, a trait that was rare, but the man worked hard and he hadn't shied away because of my mixed blood.

The farmer, thinking better of the association, was at once reluctant to explain and yet conflicted.

Wisp imparted his thoughts to me.

Scared, yet tired and exhausted, for men stole his

sheep, he was poor and bereft of friendship, his wife had died in childbirth, and these his sons were eager to escape their obligation, seeking out the town and an easier life.

"Who infracts upon you?" I said, and thinking that when I created a kingdom, there would be justice for all, yet ruled with an iron fist, blood and retribution swift.

"Turds in the wild, who the fuck knows? But the guards are meant to patrol, and I've complained enough. What's the point?"

This was all a lesson to me. I knew that every copper piece counted, especially when you were poor and that you never gain anything by taxing a man who had nothing; this was Tam's land.

"Now then, master, you give me food and shelter tonight and I'll shit on your enemies?" Of course there were other discussions, he asked how, and what I intended to do, cursing profusely and bending my ear with incidental drivel, but my countenance arrested too many question, and in the end he offered me a bed and stabling for my horse, though the animal was better off being left alone.

I sat outside his hovel, a collection of buildings made from mud brick and thatched with straw, and whilst I ate fairly well I regretted stopping, for there was no way I wanted to sleep on his mattress, sharing a room with his sons.

As the night drew in I sat next to my host aside a fire that smoked profusely, part filling the room with fumes for his chimney needed cleaning and the flames were not drawn properly.

Wisp had entered the ground and was scanning the area, aware of life within a few miles, but importantly capable of distinguishing between sheep or wolves and men close to this humble farmer's land.

So it was that. I knew who approached and lying under my tarpaulin tent, Wisp entered my dreams, waking me two hours past midnight. People were moving from a neighbouring farm, heading this way.

What was I doing? Why did I bother? There was no advantage to me, yet it was a tenuous service to Tam, and this farmer was poor.

Clouds passed overhead. The half-moon, occasionally breaking through, cast grey shadows over the land, and a light mist clung close to the ground.

I knocked on the hovel door and waited as his two hounds barked, also announcing my movement, and after a moment a latch was drawn back and opening the door the farmer stood there, a dagger in his hand, looking nervously at me.

"Master Willum, had I wanted to kill you I wouldn't have knocked." But I understood his concern, and told him men approached and that they were his neighbours.

"Bastards, I thought it might be Shanks and his lads. Which direction do they come from?"

And enquiring of Wisp, I pointed. "They're avoiding your house, circling round, three of them."

He called for his sons and a lantern, but I held up my hand, and asked what he was planning to do. Despite his cursing, he hadn't really any idea, hoping matters would develop as he confronted his neighbours, yet not sure.

"I'll kill them or cripple them if you like?" I said. "Or I can drag them bound so you can hand them to the militia, you decide." And he looked uncertain. "But you stay here for it is my debt to you, you fed me, that was the deal."

"I want to see their faces, but it means trouble either way for they have extended families. I'll not have those bastards stealing from me, I'll just fight for what's mine, sod the consequences." The farmer seemed wretchedly conflicted knowing there was nothing else to do, and trouble lay in any course of action he took.

And understanding his determination, and approving of his courage, I suggested I would scare them away, and save him the trouble of a feud.

"Now then, Farmer Willum, I will reveal a secret that will scare you half to death and if it scares you it will terrify your enemies." For I was inventing an idea in my head, a way to scare his enemies into never returning. "You do not know me, do you?"

Willum looked suspicious, and said he didn't but that I was obviously a warrior, a man with mixed ancestry.

"I'm a servant of the Abyss, slave to Akrraatsy, goddess of the hidden pits, and what you see now is not my normal appearance."

I flicked my fingers and told Git to stay on guard.

"I will repay my debt, and after tonight you will have no more trespass on your lands, but you need to see what they will see, for when I leave, you will never see me again."

Willum had no idea what I meant, but watched as I sat on the floor meditating for ten minutes, whilst he packed my tent away and saddled my horse.

Git sat next to me, and Wisp travelled whilst I furnished my craft, two simple spells – one to enlarge and the other an illusion spell, Wisp reassuring me that Wallum was presenting no danger.

Waking from my meditation, I smiled, and said I had sought permission from Akrraatsy to reveal myself, and that she approved of his courage.

"But only if you say to your neighbours that you summoned me to protect your farm. Repeat it…"

"I am to tell my neighbours that I summoned you to protect my lands?"

I led the horse and Git some two hundred yards away, loosely tethering the animal to a fence post, and walked back towards the open door. Wallum, having picked up a cloak was considering his options.

"Walk with me, Wallum, with a lantern, but just you, not your sons."

And Wallum thinking it a trap, complied, knowing that if I had wished to kill or maim I could have done it by now, for he had no idea what I was talking about, servant of the Abyss, slave to Akrraatsy?

"What you will see will make you shit your pants, but I have no quarrel with you, repeat what I said."

"You have no quarrel with me." He looked confused and worried.

Walking towards a corner field some quarter of a

mile from Wallum's hovel, I turned and said that his neighbours were hiding behind those bushes, at the far side.

"They can see your lantern. Stay, and watch, do not move, and neither run away," I said, for he was desperate to confront the thieves.

And walking into the middle of the field now invisibly to both Wallum and his hidden enemy, I cast my craft, enlarging myself, no sound emanating from my mouth, and I grew, clothes, boots, sword and all. I towered over the potato field like a giant, fifteen feet tall, yet I wasn't finished.

Bellowing at the top of my deeper rumbling voice, I cried in agony, imploring Akrraatsy to smite farmer Wallum's enemies, beseeching Akrraatsy to send me two of her hounds, swearing to protect these lands from all trespass, my position unknown to all that listened but close enough for the men hiding to fear the night.

I completed my second application of craft, the forming of two giant hounds, wreathed in flames, loosed from the gates of hell, consumed in fire; they appeared at my side baying in the night air, their light coming from their illusionary flames, yet silhouetting my outline so that I looked like a demon from the very depths of the underworld.

All total bollocks, an illusion, but what they saw and heard terrified them, and walking towards where they hid, they fled, scared for their mortal souls. I could smell piss on the wind; they would never be back, though that partly depended upon Wallum carrying on the pretence.

I strode to the bushes, the hounds rending the silence of the night, and I cried death to any that returned. They heard. Looking back, I noticed that Wallum was running away, he had dropped his lantern, yet I could see him clearly in greyscale.

Approaching the house and dismissing the illusion, the hounds flickering before they extinguished, I waited a few minutes longer for the enlargement spell to dissipate, and I returned to normal size.

Walking past the closed door of Wallum's hovel, I collected my horse and hound, both nervous and skittish. Git cowered in long grass for he had heard sounds not wholly of this world, yet far enough away that neither he nor the horse had bolted.

Wallum would have no more trouble, and that was my last service to Tam, at least for a while, and leading my horse and hound, I passed into local legend.

Two weeks walking, and reaching the foothills of the Grey Mountains, some seventy miles north of the dwarven mines I came upon a cave, about twenty-four feet deep, yet dry near the entrance, and surprisingly free of occupancy. There were bears and wolves in these parts, and I had managed to avoid the camps of wildmen, due to Wisp's abilities.

Yet my three weeks were nearly spent, and my lodgings at the Haggard Hen would cease in a few days' time. I needed to visit Krun, but was perplexed about the horse, for whilst I could transport Git into my lodging room, I could hardly do the same with such a large beast.

There was no chance of leaving the horse unattended for wild animals would attack unprotected creatures. Strange animal abounded, creatures Wisp didn't know how to describe, all within a mile of anywhere I stopped, and this cave was no exception.

The horse had cost me sixty silver pieces, and I was wroth to abandon the animal, yet passing through the mountains I would need to use craft and the animal was becoming a burden.

In the end I decide to approach one of the wildmen's camps, and see if I could barter the animal's sale, so removing most of my provisions I headed off to where I had seen smoke rising the previous day, leaving equipment but not my silver or scrolls in the backpack stored in the cave.

To say they were wildmen, was perhaps a misnomer, yet they were certainly free of any laws, save the ones they made themselves, and their camp was better described as a small burh; little fortresses, earth embankments with wooden palisades, or ditches surrounding small piled stone walls, yet these defences sufficed at keeping animals at bay, and offered difficult terrain for any would-be attacker to overcome.

During the day the women and men would hunt deer, fell trees, collect wild plants for food, and they would keep sheep, initially stolen, or goats, geese with clipped wings, and wild pigs, now semi-domesticated.

Approaching just such a place, I walked along a path cleared in the trees, and stopped at the inner treeline, looking across basic smallholdings and allotments, cleared land, for anyone approaching would been seen crossing the clearing, thus giving time for any enemy to be countered. Indeed I had already been spotted, for someone followed me, just out of sight, hiding behind trees.

I rode a further thirty yards forward, and called out, announcing my presence and asking if I might approach. I wore my chainmail, sword hung at my side, axe over one shoulder, and Git at my side. I had long since given up cleaning my mail, yet the light oil sheen had kept most of the rust at bay.

"What do you want, stranger?" Two men stood on a small plank bridge that spanned an earthen ditch.

"I want to sell my horse, for I'm crossing the mountains, and I'll have trouble in the high passes," and instantly regretted saying it, for it would weaken my bargaining position.

"A horse, eh?" And he walked forwards, at the same time as three men, a child and two women exited the wood to my left.

"Is it the animal you are riding now?"

"The same, and the saddle and tack is included." And dismounting, I allowed the nearest man to inspect the horse.

"Why don't I just take it from you?" he said, spitting out something he had been chewing.

"If you're not interested I ride on, but if you think there are enough of you, you could try and take it." I wondered if I should have remained seated in the saddle.

"Just a joke, no offence, how much do you want?"

And it was a bad joke, and I needed to take control of the situation, for this was just one man talking, and others might be interested.

"I'll let it go for sixty silver, which is less than I bought it for, and the tack and saddle are thrown in for free, a bloody fine bargain in these parts."

"Sixty silver? Where do you think I'll get that from?"

"I'll take gems, anything small, I'm not fussed." I stepped back as he lifted a leg, checking the shoes, and examining the fetlock, before moving down the side and rubbing his hand along the shoulder, checking the bone structure on the horse's chest.

"Looks a little unloved, how about twenty?" He didn't look at me, but just worked his way around the animal, pulling on the saddle strap and checking the leather work.

"Sixty is a fair price, perhaps your fellows have a better offer." I didn't like the number of men approaching, this was getting potentially dangerous, yet I relaxed as a woman called her husband over, and said she could do with acquiring the animal if the price could be negotiated.

"Careful!" I said as a dirty bearded man started circling me, looking at my weapons and armour.

"Check the animal if you want," and staring at him, my hand resting on my dagger, "but don't walk behind my back."

After twenty minutes, the woman came back with six pieces of amber, and two small gold coins. "Tis worth your sixty," she said, trying to place the items in my hand.

It wasn't anywhere near sixty silver in value for the gold had been clipped excessively and the amber pieces were small. I hadn't a clue what amber was worth yet reckoned she offered me close to forty silver pieces, and we agreed on the sale, although I asked for four eggs as well.

I had no intension of departing the way I had arrived, for whilst she went to fetch the eggs I had seen men disappearing before the deal was finalised, heading into the wood, no doubt intending to ambush me, and reclaim the amber and gold.

Crouching down, storing my eggs, I held Git by the scruff of his neck and muttered words quietly, transporting myself and hound four miles towards the cave, some three miles short of the distance needed.

I ate the eggs raw, whilst Git leaped ahead running through the undergrowth, startling grouse, who clucked rapidly and noisily as they bore themselves aloft, warning all other creatures of my presence.

*

With the fire established at the entrance, and Wisp warning that there were no men within five miles of the cave, I fell asleep, Wisp leaving my dreams and checking the location of Krun.

The following day, having meditated and prepared my camp, and placing a ward at the entrance, I studied the cave in great detail, picturing each crevice in my mind, so that I could visualise the location and thus return by craft.

The Grey Mountains were less majestic at this location, but looking south I could see they grew in height and splendour and I had a plan in mind for Krun, but fist I needed to capture him.

Git didn't like being grasped by the scruff of his neck, for he knew what was coming, so he whined a little as I spoke the words, visualising the room at the Haggard Hen, and moments later feeling slightly disorientated I sat down on a three-legged stool waiting for Wisp to catch up.

It would be too easy to simply kill Krun; a dart fashioned by craft might stun him, and then a knife in the neck, but I had a cruelty especially prepared that was more worthy.

Wisp took about three minutes to flit across my consciousness, and he told me that Krun was recovering from beer, resting on the floor of a whore house. Wisp didn't understand the concept of drunkenness, but knew the state a drunken mind felt like when he visited the dreams of people inebriated.

And allowing Wisp to guide my travels I appeared in the rear room of a brothel. Separated from the corridor by a curtain, not quite closed, Krun lay face down on a pile of straw oblivious to my presence.

As I stood over him, I could hear the raucous laughter of men and women in different cubicles and wondered if I would ever humiliate myself by paying for sex, and looking at this dirty bastard of a bully, I smiled, for he would be begging for my mercy, yet my revenge would be slow, and he would cry before he died.

Drawing my sword, and reversing the blade, I swang the haft with violent ferocity, clubbing him unconscious with one stroke.

Now bound and gagged, Krun had been transported back to the Haggard Hen. He lay staring at me, wriggling on the ground, for clubbing him violently I had worried that I struck too hard, thinking that the blow may have been fatal, yet there he was alive and wondering what his fate was.

"On guard." I clicked my fingers so Git knew he was to protect, and making sure Krun had absolutely no chance of escape, nor of alerting the landlord, I fell down into meditation, for my powers were nigh exhausted.

Wisp raced ahead pointing out and finding the strands of energy I needed for my craft and whilst there was the usual exalted feeling of wonderment, this time we both knew I could not tarry and racing back across the sea of altered perceptions I awoke, not certain how long I had been absent, yet Wisp confirmed that little time had elapsed.

It was still morning, and the inn would not be full and I so wanted to wash and eat but that would have defeated the whole point of my subterfuge. No one was to see me, so crouching down, one hand grabbing Git by the neck, and the other touching Krun's leg, just above the heel, I closed my eyes and carefully visualised the cave, recalling to mind the fissures, the fire, my backpack and the dirt on the ground, the water dripping down the sides at the far end, gaining an accurate image. Muttering words, convoluted and strange, the words of my craft, and moments later, scarcely a blink of an eye, we returned to the foothills of the Grey Mountains, yet I didn't release my grip on the hound, commanding Git to sit, stay.

I could sense the dweomer across the entrance, we had been undisturbed, and waving a stick across the invisible lines of the ward, I discharged the magic protection. A slight bang, a minor flash of discharge, and I could smell the energy dissipating, it smelt like air during a thunderstorm, yet Git was now free to roam, and I sent him out.

Krun could see, yet the gag prevented him from speaking, and I searched his clothes, looking for silver, and finding none, I started tormenting him, removing the gag, watching and listening to his curses.

I drew my dagger and threatened to blind him, but I needed him to see, for that was part of my torture yet to come. Not knowing any of this he revealed where he had concealed four silver pieces and a small gem. The gem was stolen, and not worth very much, but he wouldn't be needing it.

Krun's feet were loosed, yet his hands were tied behind his back, and I was confident he could if left to his own devices and given an hour or so, manage to untie himself, yet my plan only required a few minutes and Krun to his credit didn't beg, I was marginally impressed.

He would beg shortly, he would cry, but I was not going to kill him, he would kill himself.

With my sword drawn, point thrust lightly into his back, we walked to the bottom of a towering sheer cliff, rising some five hundred feet, and scrambling over rocks that lay strewn at the base, I smiled and told Krun to kneel.

"You stinking bastard!" said Krun, certain that I was about to kill him.

"I'll not kill you, I'll release you if you like?"

Turning his head he called me a liar, but I looked

at him with sincerity, and reinforced my comment, that I would release him.

Placing a blindfold over his eyes, I looked up, and taking hold of Krun's arm, muttering words that he had heard before, yet each action of craft is subtly different, and I stood upon a ledge six feet wide and eight feet long, Krun kneeling before me, I told him to lie face down so I could cut his bonds. He complied, swearing retribution.

"You shouldn't release me, you orc turd. Kill me for I'll get my revenge." He snarled worse obscenities at me. Yet I kept my word, and his arms became free, and as he reached to remove his blindfold, I uttered words, my last application of craft, and he was alone. Three hundred feet on a ledge, a precipice, and he screamed in terror.

Sitting one hundred feet away from the bottom of the cliff face, I watched Krun shaking. He pled, cried, cursed and looked desperately for a way he might climb down, or up, for he considered both options of escape. There were none, he was buggered, for my view was better than his, and I watched enjoying the spectacle, relishing Krun's misery.

My revenge was seldom this enjoyable, and the more Krun begged the nastier my delight, but as midday approached I decided to return to the cave and stoke the fire. Git needed feeding, and I would meditate, spend a few hours enjoying the earth song, and later I would hunt for wild boar, or whatever Wisp said was nearby.

I didn't want to tarry too long, wishing to set out across the low mountains and reach the other side as quickly as possible, but I felt Krun might yet entertain me a little longer, and whilst I could use craft to transport my hound and I, the terrain was difficult and not knowing my destination, I was severely restricted in where I could transport myself magically, a limit of four miles at a time, not enough; the mountains were at least twelve miles across, possibly more.

As night fell, the light of the waxing moon cast shadows across the cliff face, for I had wandered back, wondering if Krun had fallen, but he was still there, and I tormented him some more.

"It's getting cold, your hands won't hold if you try to climb down now, I suggest you try tomorrow, for I'm heading off across the mountains."

"Help me get down, don't leave me here!" he cried, weeping tears.

"Sorry, I'm far too busy, but your best option is to climb down on your right-hand side... Pass on my regards to Cragtor?"

There was no advantage to his right side, but it appeared there were hand grips that could be useful, I just knew they petered out, a futile option.

During the night Wisp enhanced my dreams, and I recalled the lessons Tam had taught me, yet I awoke in the early hours before dawn. Git was growling at something outside. The flames from the fire impaired my night vision, yet I could faintly make out a shape moving beyond the edge of fire light, and Wisp told me it was a bear and that Krun was still on the ledge, so I fell back to sleep.

Krun fell to his death just before midday. I hadn't been present, but he died cursing, for trying the right-hand option, he had become stuck, neither able to ascend nor descend, and shaking like a leaf, his strength finally failing, he fell. His ruined body lay broken, dashed on rocks, to be eaten by carrion and other creatures.

The mountains were lower in height the farther north, yet still formed a difficult barrier, and I had stored three portals and an exploding flame spell, and setting off, headed into the mountains. I was confident that there was an old drovers' trail, a mountain pathway used many years before by cattle herders and merchants. But finding the path would be difficult and once found, staying on it would likewise not be easy.

Gathering my cloak tight around me, I walked onwards, concerned by how cold it was becoming, for the wind blew down from snow-capped slopes, and it had begun raining, not sleet, yet still bitterly cold.

"Bloody hell! This isn't fun." Yet my cloak was waxed and I guessed the mountain range wasn't too wide.

All the paraphernalia that was so easily slung across the horse was now piled on my shoulders, and I stank of smoke and cooked boar, for slaughtering a wild boar the night before, Git and I had fed well, yet the excess cooked meat was storing inside my folded tarpaulin. My tent would stink for weeks to come.

It would be a miserable night tonight, for there were few trees, and as we walked on, these sparse sources of firewood disappeared altogether – no fire to keep me warm – and as I thought these thoughts, a boulder came tumbling down a mountainside, rolling and crashing into other rocks so that as I looked for the source I could see a line of wolves traversing the side of the mountain, some half a mile away to my right, no doubt following me. Bugger! A sleepless night ahead.

I used two portal spells to transport Git and I some six miles, less than I hoped as the mountains were precipitous, and there was no advantage in arriving halfway up a slope, unable to see ahead. So preserving the last application of craft in case of emergency, we walked two or three miles on foot, hoping we would only need to spend one night in the freezing cold.

As the light failed I came upon the ruins of a drover's hut, falling down, lichen growing in between dry stone walls, yet I eschewed this option, for there was little protection from wild animals who could sneak up unannounced. The tiny building was in such a dilapidated state it offered little in the way of security, so taking stones from the decaying walls, I pitched my tarpaulin on a rocky outcrop, some fifteen feet wide and about the same in length, yet accessible only from the scree-covered mountainside.

It took me an hour to construct sides, for the rocks were piled about three feet high, the tarpaulin stretched across. No room to stand, yet enough to lie down, perfect for Git, or a wolf for that matter.

I fed the hound, encouraging it to eat as much as possible, and likewise myself. The smell of day-old roasted boar would attract every wolf within miles, perhaps I shouldn't have stopped, or better still not have brought the meat.

*

Git was a coward, and he lay at the back of the tent whilst I sat freezing cold, slicing and cutting at every wolf in all creation, the starved and emaciated animals circling below whilst occasionally a bolder wolf would seek to attack, trying to access across the scree.

These wretched creatures, malnourished, riddled with worms, hunted across the unforgiving mountain, normally sought grouse or lapwing, goats and rabbit. Attacking me was their worst option, but they seemed oblivious to the fact and I was doing my best to educate them; several lay dead or dying.

"Sod off and attack a goat or something!" I bellowed aloud, their threat not desperate, but I wanted to sleep, and it wasn't going to happen. "Oh look, it's bloody snowing, can't you just fuck off?"

And whilst I was dry for my cloak protected me from the sleet, the wind was fierce, sliding down the mountainside, gaining access to every fold of my cloak, as though having a map to the warmth of my body.

Sod this! It was too cold, and after slaughtering ten wolves, I was wondering how I could drive them away, convince them of their error.

I loosed an explosive flame, and the light of the blast lit the surrounding area, my vision impaired, and whilst I couldn't be certain, I think three wolves died, and the animals fled, yet thinking myself free of their malicious attacks they returned half an hour later, less bold but still persistent.

This was becoming a potential problem, for whilst I didn't worry for my safety there was a chance that attrition could wear me down, the cold and sleet were certainly a factor.

I couldn't rest, I had but one act of craft left, and no means to learn more. My ignorance of travelling across wilderness and mountain ranges was so profound, I'd made too many mistakes. I thought my time on Joe's farm mill had taught me about animals and living a hard life, that I could sleep in hedgerows, gleaning an existence from the land, but no, my lack of experience had led me to this rocky outcrop, in the middle of a mountain range. I'd be damned if these wolves would gain my hound.

If I pressed on it was looking increasingly likely, for they would pick Git off, whilst they flanked me. Sodding hell! I spoke to Wisp and asked that he check the cave we had left near Krun's cliff, just my luck if a bear had taken up residence.

Wisp was gone for five minutes which in the dead of night seemed an eternity. Here I was alone, stood in the light snow surrounded by more than one pack of wolves, who driven by hunger weren't getting the message that their efforts were futile, my hound cowering at the back of the shelter. At least I could see through the snow, which was turning into a blizzard.

Do wolves like blizzards? And looking across the hills I could see more animals arriving. No wonder the drovers' trail had been abandoned, it's a death trap. Bear or no, we were heading back and I knew that a fire placed at the entrance of the cave would ward against most creatures.

Wisp returning told me there were two bears within four hundred yards of the cave mouth, yet none inside, though he couldn't guarantee the situation in ten minutes.

What the hell were bears doing walking around at night? But I was ignorant, for many bears are nocturnal.

Every time Wisp was with me, my mind had heightened perception, greater mental acuity, and as I swiped at a wolf that was edging around the slope, emboldened by his numerous peers, I darted into the tent, scrambling on all fours, grabbing my backpack and clutching a near frozen hound by the neck, none too gently, for there was no coming back. I uttered my craft, conjuring the waypoints inscribed in my mind, visualising the ashen remnants of a fire, fissures deep within walls, the outline of the cave mouth, and forming the best representation of where I wanted to be. I hoped that in my haste I hadn't missed any pertinent detail.

Transporting myself by craft could be done relatively safely up to my limit of four miles, but as Tam had taught previously, provided I knew the location and could visualise it in my mind accurately the distances could be magnified many times over. Yet the risk was immense for an inaccurate mental image could cause the effects to go tragically wrong, ported in the wrong direction, arriving in peril at a location that wasn't safe. You couldn't look at an oil painting of a scenic landscape and rely on accuracy, you needed to be very familiar with the destination.

Blinking out from the rocky outcrop, and appearing some ten feet within the cave, no taller than Git, my backside sticking up in the air, I arrived as I started, on all fours.

Wisp was absent, all normal, but I drew my sword, and bellowed into the night air, hoping to scare any bear away, for most were cowedly and would seek to avoid confrontation. But only Wisp could confirm their location, and that took a whole forty seconds before his arrival and a further three minutes whilst he checked the area.

"One hundred and fifty yards away and moving off," thus he spoke across my thoughts. Too bloody close, I needed a fire, and there was scant wood available; a few half burnt snapped branches but not enough for the night. I made do. Wisp would advise when the animals were farther away, but after ten minutes of occasionally shouting into the night air, I had succeeded in mustering a measly flame, and whilst it wasn't snowing, there was still rain and I needed better warmth.

To the reader, I always knew I had Tam's rusty nail, a nondescript object that could bring me into her castle bedchamber, although thinking of it, I had no idea whether Git could come with me. Nonetheless it was a succour, a bisque, a letting off in times of distress, an advantage to be played when the situation was dire, for my powers of craft would not avail when distances were too great. This cave was a waypoint perhaps. I would build up a repertoire of these known locations, landmarks that were immutable and I could leapfrog between.

The night, what remained of it, was nigh near over, yet I foraged for wood, for I would spend the next week both allowing Git to recover and plotting my passage across the mountains, plus if truth were known, I was glad of the warmth. The cave gave shelter whilst the passage through the mountains could be forgotten.

On the second day I transported myself alone to the rocky outcrop, and discovered with some dismay my shredded tarpaulin, yet over the next four days I found landmarks that I could port to, and before the end of the week, I had furnished enough information to avoid the drovers' pass completely.

So it was that with better preparation and allowing the passage of time, Git and I arrived at a cairn of rocks some three miles beyond the far side of the Grey Mountains. It was a fine spring day, and we had travelled directly by craft avoiding the mountain pass, a distance of approximately fifteen miles, and sitting down I waited for Wisp to arrive whilst I unpacked my lodestone and map, the map copied from Tam's library, and although Wisp told me there were men similar to me yet different within half a mile, I still chose to remove my mail and orientate my position.

Lodestones, a form of compass, naturally magnetic rock would when hung by a thread, indicate north, and after twenty minutes, I marked my position, looking at the sun, triangulating the approximation of where I was, for I knew the drovers' trail on Tam's map, and I was simply approximating for added accuracy.

This land east of the Grey Mountains was about one hundred and thirty miles long, wider in the south yet narrowing the farther north, bordered by the Eastern Sea, and full of petty kingdom states who for the most part were in constant turmoil. Tam had warned there was one significant practitioner of craft, by the name of Edric, and he had built and supported an empire of barbarians originating in the far distant east, far the other side of the Eastern Sea, yet there were others still, less powerful, three his lieutenants, most scarcely sorcerers, but there were perhaps eight in total.

There was smoke away to my south south east, almost southerly, and I needed to find shelter or acquire it one way or another; it was six hours before midday, and I walked cautiously towards a clump of trees, towards the humanoids Wisp had described as similar to me, but Wisps understanding of people was still very limited. One of the first lessons I had furnished him was the approximation of distance, a philosophy wholly alien to a spirit entity, yet he had picked up the concept quite well, so when he described one hundred yards or two miles he was with practice fairly accurate.

Redressed in mail, my backpack lighter, devoid of tarpaulin, yet still I was ladened down, I walked forwards. I was free of Culanun, but like the coming of age, it seemed no great difference and hesitating, hand on the pommel of my sword, I asked Wisp for guidance.

Shit! Wisp shot back into my conscientiousness, knocking my thoughts aside.

"Three twenty feet to your left." And looking, I couldn't see anyone, which meant trouble. "Like you but different." I wondered if Wisp meant orcs.

"Get your stinking hides out here!" Pointing to where I knew they lay hidden, stepping back a few feet, I looked at Git. "Stupid useless hound, couldn't smell a cesspit at twenty feet?" And I kicked Git back, for I wanted to kick him forward, but he would die.

What was wrong with the hound?

There was a pause for nothing happened and I repeated my words in orcish, thinking to do the same in elven, yet everyone spoke the common tongue, it wasn't necessary.

The application of craft is a combination of your potential to fashion spells and the ability of an intelligent mind to store and recall the energy stored in the body, plus the means of gaining the connective forces deep in meditation. Tam had counselled against vanity, saying depth of mediation wasn't the same as power.

There were magnitudes of craft; a practitioner could cast many weak spells or only a few powerful applications and I, having known I would only be transporting myself once, plus an allowance for escape, had several options available to me, all weak in effect, only one useful for this situation.

So drawing my sword, I bellowed that they were turds, and that I would slaughter them all if they hadn't been spawned in a puddle.

Twenty feet wasn't so far, and so walking slowly forwards, brandishing my sword, seven orcs stepped towards me, some rising from thickets, others advancing out of trees.

I already knew what I wanted, this would be my first test. I needed to dominate and kill their leader, so I watched, looking for authority, judging who if any had control, and I would probably fail in dominating for no one succeeds at their first attempt and I was very young.

They snarled, spoke with little varied vocabulary,

not many words greater than five letters, as a child might speak, and with crass, banal stupidity.

Looking at them I was hopeful to find some redeeming qualities, a sense of humour, intellectual comprehension, anything! Yet their filthy rags were riddled with lice and ticks and their manners betrayed their witlessness. I had found myself a band of feral, ignorant orc peasants, not a great start.

Standing before them dressed in mail the contrast was stark; my sword was probably worth more than the whole of their possessions, and looking them in the eye, one after another, they shuffled nervously and I was despondent.

There is a futility in ignorance, never mind how much I could try to teach these individuals they would always be a liability.

Eventually one spoke then followed by another, demanding that I drop my weapons and submit. The seven orcs wielded clubs and daggers and one had a pitted sword.

"You'll live if you give us your copper and silver," thus spoke two at the same time, a well rehearsed challenge, for the two spoke identical words.

"Such ambition!" I said, and staring at them I wondered how they had managed to survive for they couldn't rely on intelligence and their leadership was of dubious quality.

"May I keep my gold then? Thirty pieces, if all you want is copper and silver?" I watched. I didn't actually have that much gold but this was mildly entertaining.

All my future years I would make sure my

followers were intelligent, and I was off to a bad start.

I drew my sword and told them to lie on the ground or die and surprisingly one complied whilst the others rushed at me, screaming and cursing in orcish. They died, although it was slightly harder than I imagined for fighting is at least one task ignorant orc peasants can manage.

So I had my first follower, the only one of the seven who had the wits to know they would lose.

It was a beginning, barely. His name was Berrek and he lay at my feet, a supplicant for he had witnessed my sorcery and was glad to be alive.

"Get up, and clean my armour with sand and cloth." He knew how.

Printed in Great Britain
by Amazon